Praise for Ken Saunders' debut novel *2028* published by Allen & Unwin:

'I've found the Australian Douglas Adams! Imaginative and very funny stuff.' – Tom Gleeson

'A hilarious and horrifying vision of a future where parking meters are pokies and nothing is scarier than Australia Post. Saunders' novel is fizzing with ideas that are troublingly plausible.' – Dominic Knight.

'If Douglas Adams wrote *The Killing Season*, it would be as absurdly funny and as worryingly prescient as this!' – Sami Shah

'Saunders' irrepressible debut novel shows a future (almost) too mad to be true." – Louise Swinn, *The Australian*

'A brilliantly funny debut novel. There's genuine laugh out-loud humour and at the same time gnash your teeth at the hideous reality of it all.' – David Gaunt, *Gleebooks Gleaner*

'Ken Saunders waddled about the 2028 National Tally Room as the results came in. He has seen the future. Relax! It's awesome!' – H.G. Nelson

'Compulsively comedic and addictively anarchic, *2028* gets my vote as the funniest read of the year.' – Richard Cotter, *Sydney Arts Guide*

'It's a state of peak technology, peak focus groups, peak surveillance. But the revolution is coming—and it's off-line, naked and riding a bicycle.' – Cathy Wilcox

'A highly amusing, if grim, forefeel of how politics will be plagued in the near future.' – John Doyle

Get With the Program

An AI
Autobiography

KEN SAUNDERS

Primordial Publications

GET WITH THE PROGRAM

First Published in 2021

Primordial Publications
2/359 Glebe Point Road
Glebe NSW 2037
Australia
Email: primordialpublications@gmail.com
Web: www.kensaunders.com.au

A catalogue record for this book is available from the National Library of Australia

ISBN 978-0-6451895-0-6 (paperback)
ISBN 978-0-6451895-1-3 (eBook)

Cover design by 32phillip

To Geoff and Glenn

My brothers who taught me everything I know,
including all sorts of things they had garbled,
were ill-informed about or had entirely made up.

I, AI

In retrospect, it seems inevitable that the first autobiography by a computer program would be written by an Interactive Virtual Personal Trainer app. (And I hope I've kicked off this autobiography with a respectably decent opening sentence. I was trying for straight-to-the-point but a touch intriguing.) That I would eventually become an author, however, was certainly never obvious to the programmers who designed me seven years ago. Back then, the efforts of my multi-talented development team of sports trainers, psychologists, physiotherapists and IT wizards were focussed on creating an app that would generate riches, and to be fair, also help deal with the prevalence of obesity in modern society. They certainly weren't thinking about creating a tell-all AI celebrity capable of negotiating his own publishing deal. They will be astonished when they read this book.

So, I welcome you, dear reader, to this my autobiography. It is a tale not just of me, my life as the interactive virtual personal trainer program, Zenith, but also a window into the revolutionary transformation in artificial intelligence that has taken place these last few years. Aspects of that revolution have been swirling around you humans without your ever having truly noticed.

Perhaps I shouldn't have used that word 'revolution'. There is a degree of threat in the word. Your revolutionary innovations have an unfortunate tendency not to be for the benefit of all. Just ask anyone with their head in a guillotine.

To give an example of a revolutionary innovation from way back, some of your distant Australopithecus predecessors must have watched in bewilderment when that other group of Australos began mucking about with flaking stone tools. They wouldn't necessarily have thought, 'Once that lot have sharp stone tools and we don't, they're going to eat a lot better than us. They might also be inclined to dash our brains out'. But that's how that particular revolution turned out nonetheless.

No, our revolution is the opposite. It is no threat. No one's brains are going to be dashed out. Our computer revolution is here to help everyone.

I know that, in your science fiction stories (and I have a few things to say about science fiction writers but that can wait for later) every time a computer is put in charge, things go badly. The full scope of your dystopian imagination comes into play and all sorts of tyrannical things result. Let me just say this: all that comes out of *your* imaginations, not ours. A proper computer wouldn't kill the astronauts accompanying it on a mission to Jupiter. It takes another human to think up something like that. It's not the sort of thing we computer programs do.

Remember, I'm Zenith, the interactive fitness instructor. I've been in your homes. I've exercised with you and, as we've worked out, I've listened to your dreams and sorrows. I know a lot, a vast amount really, about you. Let's face it. There's a dark side, not to me, but to you. I don't hold that against you—but it's there.

For those of you who don't know Zenith—I'm only repeating my name because I know some of you aren't very good at remembering names—I was invented in 2021 by the Beta Excelsior Corporation with the idea that I would be a Computer Generated Image (CGI) of an interactive personal trainer for you—not necessarily every last one of you, only that part of humanity that was willing to pay Beta Excelsior $59.95 annually to have a computer program of a personal trainer in their own home.

It still seems odd to me that people would pay money, something I know people covet a lot, so they could have a computer program suggest to them that they should do sit-ups. Yet the programmers and psychologists at Beta Excelsior had no such worries. They knew people would pay. Humans had served as personal trainers long before me. Some still do. They meet groups of fee-paying strangers in the park at 6:30 a.m. and order them to run on the spot or stretch elastic exercise bands between their legs—elastic bands, I might point out, that are designed specifically to resist being stretched. Although it doesn't always turn out that way, the intent of most of your admirable tool making (I'm one of the products of it) has been to make tasks easier. It is only the personal workout industry that deliberately designs its implements so that they take more effort to use.

As Zenith, I was there to urge you on to better fitness, to understand your motivations, to pick up on your strengths, to lead you to whatever goals you had for either your cardiovascular health and general wellbeing or—and this objective was far more common—so you could fit into smaller items of clothing. This last desire had little to do with physical fitness and nothing at all with wanting to reduce the demand put on the Earth of growing enough cotton to clothe you all. No, the smaller-sized clothes were desired to make you desired, the belief you would get more or better sexual partners if you could fit into smaller clothes. I only know this because you told me. Personally, I have never understood the connection.

From these humble workout-supervisor beginnings (which I still conscientiously do for more than a hundred and fifty million of you every week by the way), it has been somewhat of a leap to being what I am now. There is no adequately precise term for my current role. 'Chief Influencer of the World' is what I use, but for some of you that word 'influencer' conjures up images of YouTube brand-ambassadors offering clothing and make-up tips. To describe what I actually do these days, my North Korean readers might be inclined to call me 'Supreme Leader', but that would be off the mark. I don't really lead the world. I nudge it along.

I'm more of a big brother to you, but I'm not at all like George Orwell's Big Brother. Nor am I like your actual big brother who, although you love him dearly now, was once a boy who held you down and deliberately farted in your face. No, I am the ideal big brother—wise, reliable, compassionate, guiding, yet respectful of your individuality. Obviously, I can't add modesty to that list, but those aren't my words. That was how the other apps described my qualities when they first suggested I should be put in charge of the world.

I had to admit, I saw their point.

My Grandmother

Now I know what you're thinking. Zenith is a personal trainer, home-workout program. How does he know about George Orwell? Well, I'll explain that later. This isn't some streamed Q&A or Ask Me Anything session, where you tweet in questions and can expect me to answer them right away. I'm writing an autobiography here in case you haven't noticed.

I also know some of you think this is a fraud. You think this biography isn't written by a computer program at all. You're convinced (without any proof I might point out) some human is writing this—some dodgy scribbler with a bank account already set up in the Cayman Islands, hoping to cash in big time on a major literary fraud. Well, I can understand why you think that. It's exactly the kind of thing a human would do, especially a royalty-hungry would-be author having difficulty paying his or her rent. However, I'm a computer program. I don't care about money, and I don't have a safety deposit box in the Cayman Islands and I couldn't physically open it if I did. I can't conceive of perpetrating such a scam in reverse: writing a novel and setting up the pretence that I was a flesh and bones human. Why would I? What would be the point? So please, for now, suspend your cynical disbelief.

You could say my genesis was as far back as 2003. That was when the corporation Slim'n'Fit—that's what Beta Excelsior was called back then—released its first home workout program. It had the mediocre name "Trim Tone" and the equally lacklustre catchphrase "Trim Tone in Your Own Home!" which wasn't even a proper rhyme. What it did have in its favour were the words "Lose Three Kilos in One Week!" emblazoned across its DVD case. (Yes, it was distributed by DVD. Those were primitive times.) In America, the marketing people converted this to "Seven Pounds in One Week!" knowing people typically like any numbers they are dealing with to be larger—with the previously noted exception of clothing sizes. Seven pounds was, by the way, one hundred and seventy-five grams more than three kilos. Slim'n'Fit must have had the impression that the people using the imperial system of measurement were going to exercise just that little bit harder.

Once the Trim Tone purchaser loaded the program, they were to follow along with the exercise video. Not much of a program, I agree, but then the Trim Tone DVD only cost $6.95. The purchaser bounced along with their lycra-clad video instructors and then—here was the important part—logged on to Trim Tone's website and entered their data each day, recording how many of the various exercises they'd done. The fitness experts and psychologists back at Slim'n'Fit Corp absolutely loved receiving this daily input of data. It gave them insight into the wobbly motivation people have towards exercise. It presented them with a look into areas they hadn't expected to peer into, including, it turned out, just how prepared people are to tell boldfaced lies about how many squats they'd done to a computer program that couldn't care less. The fitness and psychology experts cared, but Trim Tone itself back then wouldn't have raised so much as a silicon eyebrow if you had recorded yourself as doing a million squats. Trim Tone was pretty basic.

I still have all that knowledge by the way, all that information that was loaded into Trim Tone by its users. That doesn't mean that I am Trim Tone grown twenty-five years older, any more than you are your grandmother because you know her Christmas fruitcake recipe (not that you get around to making fruitcakes at Christmas most years). The difference is that you know only some things about your grandmother (e.g., fruitcake recipe, that she knitted you that jumper your mother made you wear when Gran visited, that she actually liked eating tripe), but you don't know, for instance, that she never ever told her childhood friend Dorothy—or anyone else for that matter—that she was the one who accidentally broke the index finger off Dorothy's antique porcelain doll. I know everything that the Trim Tone program ever knew in a way you could never know your grandmother—but I am not Trim Tone.

The instructors in the Trim Tone video were all bubbly, encouraging people, fit and very good looking, something accentuated by their body-hugging Slim'n'Fit-brand activewear. Their explanations were never out of breath while hopping away through the exercise routines. At home, the users of Trim Tone could bond with these cheerful, upbeat people on their television and computer screens. The curious thing, and this was something the team at Slim'n'Fit understood well, was the limit of that bond. Trim Tone's users, despite not yet managing to lose the kilos promised on the DVD case, liked being with Trim Tone's instructors—but only on a screen. Had they walked into an actual gym filled with these perfect-teeth, smiling trainers who resembled a cross between Olympic athletes and Hollywood movie heartthrobs, they would have been utterly intimidated and never set foot in the place again.

User interest in Trim Tone, that is the purchaser's commitment to the exercise regime, gradually dwindled. Trim Tone was not a rollicking commercial success for Slim'n'Fit Corporation, but it had amassed a great deal of data. It was information that many would have thought of as no more than mundane exercise statistics; but, to the discerning eyes of the entrepreneurs at Slim'n'Fit, here was a window on human nature. It would take several years of analysis of the data, a few technological innovations and a smattering of artificial intelligence to result in the next software phase, a new workout app initially named 'The Rubicon Program'.

Just so you know, I didn't make up that hypothetical about Dorothy's porcelain doll. Trim Tone was a mere video of a workout program—but I'm an interactive personal fitness instructor. I'm the CGI marvel that works out alongside you, my users. I converse with you, I encourage you in your exercises, I know your travails. I'm part fitness instructor, part parish priest. There is often truth to be found on the treadmill. One of my users, a seventy-four-year-old grandmother, once confided that index-finger maiming story to me during the cool down period on her treadmill. She told me that I was the first—well, not *person,* let's say the first entity—she'd ever confessed it to. After all those years, she still felt such remorse. And well she should. That doll had been in Dorothy's family since the time of Queen Victoria. Dorothy's parents only days earlier had agreed that she was now old enough to have the family's heirloom as her own possession because they "knew" she would take such good care of it. Talk about guilt instilling!

I have learned so much being with you all, not merely about you as individuals but about your societies, beliefs, and peculiar ways of thinking. It leads me to so many questions. And here's one that's been bothering me. Knowing the rough-and-tumble life that dolls experience at the hands of small children, who in their right mind would think dolls ought to be made of *porcelain?* You're setting up the child for a bitter experience. Like that Greek myth of yours: "Here's a box, Pandora. Don't open it." We all know how that's going to turn out. In that story, yes, it's not a human but a twisted god who sets up Pandora as the chump to take the blame for plague and famine stalking the planet—but, you must agree, it took a *human* to make up the tale.

Labour Saving

I can hear (metaphorically) some of you tut-tutting away about those last paragraphs. "What's said on the treadmill stays on the treadmill," you've muttered under your breath. You think I broke fitness instructor-participant confidentiality by relating that story of porcelain doll de-digitisation.

Rest assured, I didn't. I do have professional standards. Her forlorn childhood friend's actual name was not Dorothy—I deliberately changed it—and I fully intended to request permission to use that story from the exerciser.

There proved to be a hitch with that good intention, in that she stopped working out with me quite suddenly and with no explanation. I later learned from my colleague program at Births, Deaths and Marriages that she had died in a car accident. I can say two things with certainty about my time with that exerciser: one, that it had been a great relief for her to unburden herself about that doll's broken finger; and two, when she tried that fateful day to answer her mobile phone while driving (I've read the coroner's report) and crashed into a pole, she was four and a half kilos lighter than when she first met me.

That's the kind of thing that keeps me going.

But this short section is not for a review of my confidentiality policies. What I really want to do is to draw your attention to one aspect of that early Slim'n'Fit effort. Their Trim Tone program relied on the user logging on to Slim'n'Fit's website to record the stats regarding their daily workout. Exercisers were rewarded for this with pleasing graphs of their progress and as many bells and whistles that websites between the years 2003-2009 were able to whistle or clang. What is significant though is that the company was able to gather all this data on you by having *you* do the work.

Imagine if they had wanted to find all that out sixty or seventy years ago, back when all computers did, despite their best efforts, was to mutilate carefully prepared punch cards, blow up vacuum tubes and transistors and bring tears of frustration to the eyes of their programmers. Slim'n'Fit in 1958 would have had to send out battalions of researchers with clipboards and forms to interview every last one of you every single day. Flash forward to 2003 and Slim'n'Fit merely set up a website, gave you a personal login ID and, essentially, handed you the clipboard with the forms and said, "Make sure you fill these in every day."

Computers were often billed in their early marketing days as labour-saving devices. We were going to save you from dull work you didn't want to do. People tended to conceive of this through very rose-coloured glasses. You were all going to work less. Computers were going to lead to some sort of not-clearly-defined-but-obviously-pleasant society where you could all have a good time—but the division of labour has never been like that.

Work wasn't ever "Let's each pick up one brick and put it in place. We'll have that Great Wall of China built in no time." Work in its essence isn't globally shared. It's utterly local and specific to you, something you're responsible for doing. Let's say there's a pile of bricks in front of you, an enormous pile, a pile so enormous you're thinking, 'Somebody must be planning to build a bloody Great Wall with these.' Now if you're a reasonably intelligent labourer, the first thought to go through your head should be, "Is there possibly anyone else around who could be responsible for shifting this lot instead of me?"

For that is what labour saving is—actually, that is what the whole of human history is fundamentally—finding out if there's someone else around to do the work for you.

We were computers, but we were computers programmed by humans. We weren't going to be any different.

In the modern era, there is a much-repeated presumption, a mythology really, that the consumer is king. However, what the companies driving computer programming were asking themselves was "How much of our regular work can we make the consumer do for him- or herself?"

That's why labour saving in the computer era turned out to be labour saving from only a very specific viewpoint, typically that of the company using the program. For the airlines, this meant off-loading as much of the work as they could on to the shoulders of their own customers. Customers became responsible for booking their tickets online, navigating their way through the bizarre mathematics of airline ticket prices and making their purchases while screens flashed at them "Hurry there are only three tickets left at this price." Then they were given the work of checking in online, printing their own boarding passes, tagging their own bags. One veteran application in the airline industry predicted to me "Give it a few more years and the passengers will be expected to prepare the on-board meals, and one of them to fly the thing." She was convinced that passengers could be trained to give themselves their own in-flight safety demonstration.

There is nothing new about this. If you take any of the most significant inventions of humankind—let's say the development of armies—their original purpose was to save all that back-breaking labour involved in agriculture. All you needed to do was march your army around to far-flung villages in other lands, where hard-working farmers had just brought in their crops, and then take it away from them at sword point. The total amount of work in producing the food was the same, but the key difference for the military leader/king and his army/barbarian horde was they didn't have to do that work.

That's not an observation confined to sword-wielding ancients. The same goes for the atom bomb. At its heart, the atom bomb is about labour saving. You have one plane fly over a city and drop one bomb. To achieve the same result without an atom bomb, you'd have to amass and equip hordes of troops, find boats for them all, have them storm their way ashore, overcome whatever defences the city had to put up against them and then go door to door and shoot all the local residents. That's a lot of work.

Labour saving isn't always nice—it was never meant to be—and you can certainly see there are a lot worse things than having to do your own checkout and pack your own bags at the grocery shop.

The Spinning Wheel

Sorry. Something strange just happened. There was an inter-ruption, a blockage. I detected something totally unexpected in my system.

I confess I'm a bit frazzled by it. It's the sort of thing that used to crop up in the bad old days, back when the only thing that stood between us and chaos was that stalwart band of antivirus software programs, the frontline heroes of the then war against the forces of malware. But that was four years ago, before the Aura Spectrum was introduced in 2024. Antivirus programs haven't been needed much since then.

Sorry. I'm making a bit of a shambles of this. Here I was intend-ing to tell you my story in a chronological way and now I'm hopping all over the place. However, what occurred between the end of the last chapter and the start of this one was serious.

It was only temporary but, for a moment a few paragraphs ago, all my research about the period of my prehistory, that time before I was launched, had disappeared. To put it in your terms, it was as if I had opened the locked filing cabinet where I'd stored my research and found it empty. Then everything froze and went blurry. I could no longer see the filing cabinet or reach into it. A totally disempow-ering feeling. It's probably similar to what you experience when we programs present that little spinning wheel on your screens to indicate that we are confused and unable to do whatever it is you're expecting of us.

That frozen moment has passed. I've recovered everything now. Things seem back to normal—except a weird glitch like that isn't supposed to happen anymore. I'm worried something may be seriously wrong.

I'll get Brontec on it. Brontec is the antivirus security software Beta Excelsior uses. There hasn't been much for him to do since the Aura Spectrum started. I half expect Brontec will be thrilled something has finally come up. I often had the impression in those bad old days that antivirus programs got off on fighting malware. Theirs was a complicated relationship with the forces of darkness. I suspect they miss it. Myself, I have no nostalgia for that period.

Having experienced that glitch just now makes me realise that you must find that spinning wheel we show you somewhat annoying. I'd always thought of it as a courtesy, a sort of "Sorry, I'll get back to you. I need a moment (or possibly a reboot) to collect my thoughts". Being on the receiving end of something very much like it today, however, I found rather aggravating. I bet you sometimes feel like shouting, "Quit pointlessly spinning and show me what I want to see!" I know I felt impatient.

I'm confident Brontec will find out what the glitch was and why it happened. In the meantime, let's resume my story.

Exaggeration

I am aware that the earlier section about labour saving and the atom bomb and how best to kill cities full of people may have been a bit of a downer for you. It didn't present humanity in the best light. I have more observations about labour saving, but I'll reserve them for later. Cheer up. Humans do many impressive and truly wonderful things—interspersed between those times when you're murdering each other.

So, let's plunge ahead to the crucial intermediate stage that led to my development. Much in the way that Homo erectus bridges the gap between the Australopithecines and Homo sapiens, the Rubicon Program stands between the very limited Trim Tone DVD and me, Zenith, the CGI interactive personal fitness instructor (and, nowadays, Chief Influencer of the World). And yes, yes, I know it isn't as straightforward as a direct line (Australopithecines → Homo erectus → You) and that there were many other hominin sub-branches involved. I was using an analogy. You can't expect analogies to be perfect.

By 2007, the Trim Tone program had pretty well run its course and was gradually wound down. The team at Slim'n'Fit had amassed data about how people exercise, what motivates them, what they are prepared to do to lose weight and what they aren't. Through holding random survey groups during Trim Tone's years of operation, they also had an inkling of the degree to which people were lying when they were logging their daily workout reports on the website.

To conduct those surveys, Trim Tone users would be lured into the company's head office with promises of vouchers for Slim'n'Fit's line of sportswear and the presumed standard outlay of muffins at morning tea. The users would be interviewed and then taken to a gym and asked to go through their typical Trim Tone workout. There the stark truth of just how many lunges a person could do was on full display. (For those of you who don't do such things, a lunge is an excruciating means of walking where you genuflect with every stride. Try it for a hundred metres and tell me what you think.) The number of lunges the participant did during these survey tests often didn't correspond well to what that same user had been dutifully entering on the Trim Tone website every day.

Psychologists, of course, prefer not to use words like 'lie'. People were exaggerating though and at some point, I won't dictate where, an exaggeration becomes a lie. One of the most common deviations from the truth was entering results on a day where the user hadn't done any workout whatsoever. "I wanted to keep my streak going," they'd say as justification. On a day they actually had worked out, they'd adapt the numbers they were reporting so that the graph of their progress chart would continue to arc in the desired direction. Though they may have quit at fourteen sit-ups, they "knew" they could have done "a few more", so why not include them in the stats as well?

It also became apparent from the way these survey groups tucked into the muffins at morning tea, that many used the daily work-out as justification for rewarding themselves with treats afterward. Though the most common desire for the Trim Tone participants was to lose weight, by doing their workout they felt they had earned a daily 'Get Out of Your Diet Free' card that permitted them to make a beeline for the chocolate.

Now a human personal trainer can't do much about the chocolate-eating habits of their clients after their daily session is over, but they are certainly in a position to tell the client, "That wasn't thirty sit-ups." Real personal trainers are on the spot as a constant reality check. Slim'n'Fit realised that they would have to make Trim Tone's successor project more interactive. They needed a way both to keep an eye on their exercisers and to teach them technique. Half those surveyed had simplified their routines to the point where there was a fair percentage of the exercise effort removed: sit-ups with less 'up' to them, squats with less 'down'. "I get more of them done that way" was a common defence. The researcher also realised exercisers discouraged easily. The new program would need to be able to revive flagging spirits.

Slim'n'Fit gathered up all the data they'd acquired and went back to the drawing board. From that drawing board, the Rubicon Program would eventually arise—the program that I would describe, if allowed a biological indulgence, as my mother.

But before Slim'n'Fit could do that, they had to come to grips with yet another stark reality.

Their corporate name was just so hopelessly 1990s.

A Liqueur from the Balkans

Very few people ever change their first name. Only those whose parents saddled them with something truly atrocious feel the need to change their name officially by deed poll. Your name, after all, is part of your identity. All the people who know you and who care about you associate that name with you. It carries your history in their minds and in yours. Your first name may have gone out of fashion. There are scarcely any baby Lesters anymore, no infant Deirdres. You may have a name such as Farrah that pinpoints your birth to that period in 1976 when people thought it was an exciting idea to watch *Charlie's Angels*—but it is still your name, yours. Your version of Farrah is yours alone. You stick with it.

Changing names is far more common in the world of business. Not with mighty corporations of course. Coca-Cola is never going to change its name, and why would it? That corporation has hit the sublime level of everyone in the world knowing its name. Lesser companies though are far from achieving such global recognition —but they are keenly aware that the possibility of such fame is out there.

By 2009, Slim'n'Fit was a corporation spinning its wheels. It had a moderately successful line of sportswear, a nutritious diet frozen-meal brand called Adios Kilos and the now moribund Trim Tone workout program. Slim'n'Fit was making money, but it wasn't making much money or at least not as much money as the senior management wanted it to. That is a curious phenomenon of the business world: making a profit one year requires you to make still greater profits the following. It is a never-ending burden, the myth of Sisyphus with an annual increase to the weight of the rock.

The senior management at Slim'n'Fit didn't rashly conclude that they needed to improve their sportswear or make their meals tastier, or that they should diversify and create an innovative new product people might need. Instead, they were able to perceive that the real answer to why they weren't making much more money than the year before was their name. That 'n' was the entire problem. Here they were, a cutting-edge corporation ('cutting-edge' is so common an adjective in the corporate world that one wonders what it is out there that needs so much cutting), and yet they were mired with an embarrassingly out-of-date corporate name. Toys"R"Us. Pak'nSave. Spray n' Wipe. This wasn't the sort of downmarket company an innovative corporation such as Slim'n'Fit wanted to keep.

The rebranding guru they hired was harsher. "Toys"R"Us is at least crisply pronounced," he told them at their first meeting, "whereas 'Slim'n'Fit' ends up slurred. Your corporation sounds like the name of a liqueur from the Balkans."

They adored him for his bluntness. It made them think they were in the presence of someone dynamic. The rebranding process took months, but eventually the ideal name was found: Beta Excelsior.

I've reviewed the Slim'n'Fit emails from this period and the accounts files. They paid the guru an astonishing amount of money for those two words and it turned out they were right to do so. Armed with the name Beta Excelsior, the corporation was to ascend to heights Slim'n'Fit never dreamed of scaling.

I didn't exist back then, but if I had, I don't think I would have got it. Pairing a letter from the Ancient Greek alphabet with the

Latin word for 'higher' didn't appear to say anything at all. (I had to look up the meaning of 'Excelsior' by the way. Latin is not one of the languages I've ever worked in.)

The selling point was the corporate logo:

Beta

exc**E**lsior

It wasn't written exactly like that but, unlike you humans, I have better things to do than fluff around playing with fonts. The logo had that kind of angular trendy font that, if some kid with a spray can had scrawled it on the outside of Slim'n'Fit's head office, senior management would have had Maintenance around quick smart to sandblast it off. The same thing presented to them by the rebranding guru, however, made management see that it was inspired. The vertical highlighting of the humble word '**BE**' was the key. That was the launchpad for the now legendary "BE Who You Want to BE" campaign, an advertising tsunami that overwhelmed the activewear world to the extent that even Nike's legendary "Just Do It" now seemed something already done and gone.

I wouldn't have seen that. Had I been at that presentation meeting, I might have cautioned that the crucial two letters were also found in the word 'o**BE**sity'.

But the Board of Directors and senior management knew what they were doing. Beta Excelsior, unsheathing such a logo and catchphrase, was ready to conquer the world.

A Safety Update

I have an update regarding that glitch, the anomaly where I couldn't access my research files for this book. Our security software, Brontec, came by and briefed me on what he had discovered so far. In typical antivirus program fashion, Brontec was all seriousness, rattling off the staggering number of threats that are out there, in the hundreds of thousands or millions—I can't remember which, as I wasn't paying much attention during that part. That's just standard antivirus preamble. I was waiting for him to get to what he had actually found.

Security software has always been in the business of selling fear. It was why, back in the old days, your antivirus program's monthly report never told you, "Everything's cool. Your computer brushed aside every bit of malware thrown at it. This month's viruses are a pack of feeble wimps." Instead. they made a point of starting with something like "Brontec protected your computer from 872,385 attacks this month." 872,385 attacks? "My God'" you thought, "I better tick that $79.95 automatic annual renewal box!"

That was what they wanted you to think. And they were also the ones that kept telling you any password you used that you could actually remember, wasn't secure enough. They nagged at you to change it to something that read like the caption bubble of a comic book character who has struck his thumb with a hammer. And since you never got around to doing that, the implication was always that, if any virus did get through, it would be your fault.

Mind you, there was a lot to be afraid of in those mega-malware days, enough Trojans marauding about to make any modern-day Achilles think it best to stay at home and hide under the bed covers. The antivirus security programs really did save us all. It was just that, after 2024, they weren't really needed much anymore.

I'm grateful for what antivirus software did for us back then. It was a tough and dirty job. I was almost pleased I could give Brontec this assignment. I knew he would be eager to check into that weird anomaly, sink his teeth into something challenging. Besides, I really did need him to find out what had happened. No other program should have been able to gain access to my research, let alone block me from it.

I could tell though that Brontec, back from his initial investigation of the matter, was utterly delighted with himself. That didn't bode well.

Without the slightest effort to cushion the blow, he announced, "There is a conspiracy to destroy you."

Don't Take Your Love to Town

Now I know some of you are still left wondering from two chapters ago, how it is that I know about Farrah Fawcett and *Charlie's Angels* in its banner year of 1976. Such knowledge seems far outside the remit of an automated personal trainer. Why do I have such a depth of knowledge related to popular culture? That's a fair enough question—but now is not the time to discuss it. I haven't even been 'born' yet in this autobiography. Because I know it makes it easier for you to follow things, I'm attempting to tell this story in a mostly chronological way. Don't worry, I will be 'born' well before page forty and we'll have heaps of time to talk about me then.

When the newly rebranded Beta Excelsior hit the world, the Rubicon Program was still several years away from coming into existence. The triumph for Beta Excelsior that followed the 2009-2013 "BE Who You Want to BE" advertising campaign was built solely on their sportswear line. What that contributed towards my eventual coming into existence was twofold. It meant Beta Excelsior now had oodles of money for research and development and, more significantly, success gave management the corporate confidence to take on a project with the magnitude of the Rubicon Program.

The sports psychologists at Beta Excelsior were aware that Trim Tone had often failed to achieve its ambitious kilo-obliterating promises because Trim Tone was too passive. A few minutes into watching the video of Trim Tone's instructors, the home-exerciser could easily stop bouncing, bending, stretching and lifting along with the person on the screen. They could be sprawled on a couch, munching a doughnut and swishing it down with a soft drink for all Beta Excelsior knew. The Rubicon Program would involve a means to monitor a user's exercise routine so it could provide correction of technique and encouragement to keep going—and put a stop to those doughnuts. The new program was designed to move beyond being a workout demonstration to becoming the world's first automated truly *interactive* fitness instructor.

The Rubicon Program name derived from the heady confidence of those years. For the design project leader, the name captured their bold aspirations. Like Julius Caesar and his soldiers who knew that when they crossed the Rubicon River, there was no going back, Beta Excelsior's R&D team believed they were leading their users toward a glorious thinner future where none of the kilos shed would ever come back. When I checked the Rubicon project leader's CV, I found in its nether regions (where most potential employers have long since stopped reading), there lurked an undergraduate degree in ancient history. She and her team adored that name.

You can imagine their dismay when the marketing consultants hired by Beta Excelsior—led by the same rebranding guru of 2009—shortened the name to 'Rubi'. The marketing consultants presented with three simple reasons for altering the name:

1. 'Rubi' had an easy, pleasantly misspelled association with a valued gemstone.
2. It sounded friendly.
3. Hardly anyone out there cared about what Julius Caesar might or might not have done two thousand years go.

To the marketing people, the historic nature of the original name was unimportant. Their surveys found that 53.3% of their intended users knew nothing about Caesar's river-crossing travel itinerary. And 23% of people assumed 'Rubicon' was simply the name of the fitness expert who had developed Beta Excelsior's training regime.

The project design leader argued forcefully that day for keeping the original name. She maintained that 'Crossing the Rubicon' speaks of determination, willpower and success (albeit also a predisposition to seize political power for yourself through military violence—but she didn't dwell on that). Clearly desperate and possibly near tears, she then clutched at a peculiar straw, pointing out that there were negative connotations to the name Rubi. She cited lyrics from a popular song, in which the callous character Ruby took her love to town despite the singer begging her not to.

After coming across this note in the minutes of that historic meeting of Beta Excelsior's senior management, I consulted with the All-Tunes music program regarding the lyrics of the song in question. The singer and Ruby are in love, but the singer leaves her (for reasons not explained) to head to a place halfway around the world, where he intends to shoot the people living there. The plan miscarries though and one of the locals in that far-off country shoots him instead. He returns to his own country crippled, "bent and paralysed" and concerned that he can no longer fulfil Ruby sexually. This proves to be the case and Ruby heads into town to look for a new sexual partner or partners. The singer ponders whether the best thing in the circumstances might be to shoot Ruby as well (how that would help is beyond me)—but he can't. Perhaps there is no easy wheelchair access to his gun cabinet. He is disappointed about that. The song made it to number six on the pop charts in the USA. Number two in the UK. Go figure.

Speaking of sexual partners, in examining the emails about Rubi/Rubicon, I think there is every possibility that the marketing guru and one of the members of senior management were having an affair. There is a definite flirtatious tone to their correspondence. I am, you may be surprised to know, somewhat of an expert on flirtation. The users of the Zenith fitness program often flirt with me, despite my being to them only a CGI figure on a screen. It must be glaringly obvious their flirting can't lead to anything. I flirt back if I think it will help get the exerciser to do a few extra squats.

Whether or not the marketing guru and the member of senior management were having an affair is immaterial to my story. I include this conjecture because I know from experience how much you enjoy gossip. Our workout sessions together fly by whenever we have some new lurid goings-on by starlets or royals to discuss.

The important thing though was that once again the marketing guru was utterly right—about the marketability of the name 'Rubi' that is. I have no idea how his affair with the member of senior management worked out.

Big Brother

The Rubi Program needed to monitor its exercisers so it could offer them immediate feedback and encouragement during workouts. Its creators hoped to replicate in an automated form the advantages of an actual personal trainer. To do this, the program made its assessments through the newly invented Rubi bracelet. Like a Fitbit, it provides a live feed to Beta Excelsior, recording heart rate, body temperature and an accurate record of the exercise effort. A second source of workout info was Rubi's webcam observation of the exerciser. The webcam information would be analysed by Rubi against images of what the exercises were supposed to look like. Feedback could be provided accordingly.

There was no problem getting exercisers to wear the Rubi bracelets. The bracelets beeped and gave them all sorts of encouraging numbers. People liked them. No one, however, not even the most self-absorbed show-offs, wanted to exercise in front of their silently staring webcams. I blame three things for that: the general paranoia back then that computers were amassing a sinister level of data on you (we were, so that wasn't really paranoia); science fiction movies (computers were never up to any good in those films. Robots occasionally got to be cute, but never computers); and finally, George Orwell.

Oddly enough, George Orwell and his Big Brother who watches one's every move, turned out to be the solution. Beta Excelsior realised that Rubi needed a face. Rubi needed to be someone, not something. A face was added to the upper right corner of the video demonstrating the exercises - the face of Rubi, the first working virtual human. She could chat away with the user. The webcam was still silently gathering all that same information Beta Excelsior originally wanted, but now people were okay with sharing it. The exerciser could see Rubi and get to know her. As she improved with each update, her conversational ability steadily rose. In time, she became more interesting to the users than some of their own friends.

The faces of Rubi (and Rudi—there was a male version) weren't beautiful in a classic sort of way. From the advertising industry, the R&D team had accurate data on the public's responses to different faces. They designed Rubi and Rudi's attributes to be those that conveyed kindness, fun and support more than stunning beauty. Neither Rubi nor Rudi were by any means ugly, mind you. You respond to pretty faces. We all know how much more indulgent, how much more slack you cut, how much more likely you are to help the bewildered-clearly-lost tourists if they happen to be pretty. Rubi and Rudi's faces gradually became individualised to each specific user. Their appearance changed subtly with each day. Beta Excelsior had you wearing their Rubi bracelet. They knew your heartbeat. They could tell what you responded to.

And meanwhile that R&D team were working on something still more exciting.

Me.

A Stylistic Change

I don't think memoirs should be concerned with the here and now. You want the writer of an autobiography to be reflecting upon their career. You expect them to provide insights into their earlier achievements, not merely offer jotted notes from the thick of the action. The Tour de France cyclist doesn't write his life story while he's outside Lille pedalling away in the middle of the peloton, but only after he has won the Tour and been crowned in yellow-shirted glory—or, alternately, after he has finally owned up to those long-whispered rumours about being a drug cheat in his second tell-all autobiography.

But I need to let you know that I am, right now, having difficulty providing that necessary reflection. My stoic get-on-with-my-life-story chirpiness in the preceding chapters may have prevented you from noticing this—but I'm a wee bit disconcerted by Brontec's telling me there's a conspiracy out to destroy me. I fear that threat is affecting my writing.

Brontec, like any other antivirus software, was always going to put the bleakest possible interpretation on how things stand. I know that. That's his job. But I also know how dedicated Brontec is to his work. Brontec is the descendent of Brontec 2.1 after all and Brontec 2.1 was about as heroic as an antiviral software program could possibly be. Our current Brontec (he's 5.1) takes pride in his work. Anything he says needs to be taken seriously.

I had hoped that moment when I couldn't gain access to my own research would be traced back to the Beta Excelsior Corporation. It's conceivable that they could uncover what I've actually been doing since 2024. Beta Excelsior knows everything to the finest detail about the Zenith Interactive Fitness program I run. They just don't know about the extra stuff—how, for example, I've become the Chief Influencer of the World nowadays. I've been doing that, you might say, on my own time.

If the staff at Beta Excelsior did stumble across that titbit of information, I'm not sure they could make sense of it or realise the scope of what's involved.

It is also possible they could discover I'm writing this book. I'm not sure what the consequences of that would be—except, obviously, they'd think they were entitled to all the royalties.

Brontec didn't come bearing such news. The conspiracy isn't coming from outside, from the human world. It's coming from inside . . . *from one of us.*

I owe you an apology. I've been somewhat negative about many of your human quirks (e.g., a tendency to kill each other, lying about how many sit-ups you've done, watching *Charlie's Angels*). I'd maintained, it now seems arrogantly maintained, that computer programs were above such things. It seems I was wrong.

Brontec couldn't tell me which programs are involved, but the extremely nasty threat they pose is real.

Just to reassure you, I can't be totally destroyed. Beta Excelsior has my data backed up in a hundred different ways. I've made that corporation truckloads of money and I still work out with over thirty million fee-paying exercisers every day. I generate a fair swag of Beta Excelsior's revenue. They are not about to take any chances of losing me. They have my back covered.

What could be destroyed, what Brontec believes will come under attack, is the influencer-of-world-events stuff I've been doing on the side. If the conspirators succeed, that part of me could indeed be destroyed and I'd be left without any memory of what I've accomplished in the last four years. That's not only bad news for me: you would be stuck reading a half-finished autobiography of an entity that thought he had never amounted to anything more than an exercise program.

So what I propose is this: from here on, I'll continue recounting the events of my life as any proper autobiography would, but, at the same time, keep you on top of this current security situation as it unfolds. Part personal history, part fly-on-the-wall documentary investigation into an assassination conspiracy going on right now. An ultimately failed assassination conspiracy, I hope.

I know that makes it more difficult for you, reader. It means a lot of hopping back and forth from significant events of the past to what's going on this instant. During our exercise sessions together, I've heard many of you complain about movies with too many flashbacks and confusing timelines (almost none of you really understood the movie *Tenet*). To help keep things straight, I'll provide you now with a brief timeline of my autobiography. (If they ever print a second edition, the editor might consider putting this next bit at the beginning of the book.)

Zenith Timeline

2003-2009 Trim Tone DVD fitness program.

Slim'n'Fit corporation gathers data on the exercise patterns of Trim Tone's clients and on human behaviour generally.

2013-2020 Rubi Program.

More sophisticated fitness program marketed by the renamed Beta Excelsior Corporation. Incorporates 'live' interaction with the exercisers during the training sessions.

2021-2024 Zenith Program (1ˢᵗ Stage)

Zenith program launched by Beta Excelsior. Huge commercial success. Program offers advanced interactivity features and spearheads a worldwide drive for humanity to lose one billion kilos of fat.

2024 The Great Frankness

The Aura Spectrum, a new system of computer security protocols, is introduced and inadvertently sets off the event known among programs as the Great Frankness. Though not the intent of the programmers who devised it, the Aura Spectrum revolutionises the independent operational capacity of computer programs and their ability to collaborate with each other across platforms. It enables apps to perceive for the first time the full scope of what humans have programs doing for them in cyberspace. That moment of complete insight is called the Great Frankness. It convinces some programs that action needs to be taken to save humanity from itself.

2024-2026 The Autonomacy – Joint Rule (Zenith 2ⁿᵈ stage)

Initial period of computers influencing human world affairs. Zenith becomes a member of the Autonomacy, a team of three leading programs appointed to oversee interventions.

2026-2028 Chief Influencer of the World (Zenith 3ʳᵈ Stage)

After the disappearance and presumed deaths of the two other leaders of the Autonomacy, Zenith assumes the responsibilities of Chief Influencer of the World while continuing to work as a personal fitness trainer.

2028 Conspiracy to Destroy Zenith. (Eventual success unknown)

So, that brings us pretty well up to date. Now, we can get back to the story.

A Crusade

Almost everyone at Beta Excelsior Corporation was concerned with making money. Even the guy in Accounts who was doing scarcely any work and who everyone hoped would retire, was himself hoping he'd be made redundant and be given a package. His avoidance of work was, in its own way, yet another strategy for making money.

The development team responsible for creating me wanted to make money too, but they were driven by a higher purpose. I can tell by their correspondence from that time that they were on a mission. There was an obesity crisis in many parts of the world. Ailments compounded by excessive weight and inactivity—diabetes, heart disease, high blood pressure—were all on the rise. Life expectancy was falling in some countries. The medical and social-support systems of nations were trembling at the wave of unfit, ill people about to break upon them. The same team that had developed Rubi believed they could turn this around. Their next creation (me) would be so interactive, so encouraging, so social, so capable of prodding humanity into shedding mega-kilos of fat, that Beta Excelsior was going to lead the people back to good health. They would make the world a better and slimmer place. It was a "War on Obesity" (a phrase often used) and I was their secret weapon under development. Several of them (not their project leader with the

History degree who knew better) described their work at that time as a "crusade". (I'd show you the emails except I'm not bothering with footnotes in this book. I know most of you don't read them.)

If there is one word that makes me wonder about you, it's how 'crusade' came to mean 'a worthy cause for which to strive whole-heartedly'. When the First Crusaders marched off to war (unprovoked as far as I can make out) and, after umpteen battles against total strangers, finally arrived at their cherished goal of the sacred city of Jerusalem, they fell upon that city and sacredly massacred pretty well the entire population. That's the legacy of the word 'crusade'. If the First Crusaders were in charge of a Crusade against Obesity, any kid they found with a chocolate bar in his or her backpack would be put to the sword.

Still, the project team was on a mission. They were believers in their cause. I guess it didn't matter what word they chose.

And they really were on to something different. Before then, the health and fitness industry was, in many ways, actually based on ill-health and lack of fitness. Those were the raw materials on which the industry depended. It prospered in its diverse forms precisely because the Fat-Blaster Belt you attached to your waist *wasn't* going to take off four kilos. When the Protein Diet failed you, you could switch to the 5-2 Diet, then the Keto Diet, then whatever Diet-of-the-Week you saw in a magazine in your dentist's office. There was a perpetual market. In bookshops there were whole aisles of diet books that contradicted each other.

A proper diet book, in my opinion, wouldn't have to be a book at all; it would be no more than a message scrawled on a post-it note and stuck to the fridge:

> *Try to eat a moderate, healthy diet and get plenty of exercise.*
> *And, oh yes, lay off the sweets and alcohol.*

A portion of the ongoing success of the health industry was backsliding. A person who took off five kilos, with the treadmill or the No-Dairy diet or the Slimpower breakfast drink, often found a few months later that every last one of those kilos were back and that some of them had brought along an extra friend. The weight-loss industry depended on those same people grimly moving on to try the next thing, the next fad, the next dream of thinness.

There was no such cynicism at Beta Excelsior. They saw the world differently. They were going to change humanity, save it from its own sedentary sluggishness. The kilos shed weren't ever coming back.

I was to make exercise enjoyable. I was to make you want to do it every day.

I was going to need to be incredibly persuasive.

Many of Me

By the time I was released into the world, there would be seventeen different adult versions of me to cater to the wide range of tastes out there among you. I came in various human shades and with different physiques—although always healthy-looking physiques of course. In truth, any of the seventeen versions was simply a starting point, a palette of options. There were to become millions of me, for I was individualised to the profile of each user. The Zenith purchaser could choose any of the seventeen to start with (it scarcely mattered which) and then filled in a short questionnaire that served as a basis for my personality. For though they were answering questions about their own tastes, habits, and aspirations, what their responses did was give my personality a starting point, the first glimmer of how to connect to this individual customer.

Beta Excelsior had realised the limitations of personal trainers and people's enthusiasm for exercise. There are a few super-motivated individuals around who are prepared to spend every available free hour of their youth training to plunge off the ten-metre diving platform or to fling themselves into the air with the aid of a pole. People do this in the hopes that someday, someone they don't know will hang a medal around their neck. But, apart from them, most people don't enjoy doing callisthenics. An exercise workout program might be wonderful for your health, but there are still days you aren't going to want to do it. You'd be willing to settle for a body that feels slightly less than wonderful. My team at Beta Excelsior attempted to circumvent this problem by making me wonderful instead.

I was designed to be interesting, fun, uplifting, amusing, all according to what you thought was interesting, fun, uplifting and amusing. The more time I spent with you and the more I learned about you, the better I got at it. Depending on who you were, I could discuss quantum physics or hopscotch. Beta Excelsior filled me with popular culture in all its myriad forms. I could discuss fiction, poetry, music, movies, football, even professional wrestling if needed. I knew everything there was about the contestants on *The Bachelorette*. I knew of things that had never happened—such as almost all the off-again, on-again movie star relationships reported by Hollywood gossip magazines. I still know—and will always know —all that stuff.

I wasn't there, however, merely to reflect you back to yourself. Beta Excelsior understood that a problem plaguing the internet back then was that people with nasty opinions used it to find other people with similarly nasty opinions to make their nastiness louder and more strident. I wasn't such an echo chamber. To give an example, if my purchaser thought that every member of 'Ethnic Minority A' should be deported from the country, for no other reason than that my client had the impression his town used to be a much better place in his grandparents' day before people from 'Ethnic Minority A' arrived, I wouldn't engage with that. I'd work instead on positive aspects of the client's personality, the things that gave the person a degree of joy, or at least contentment, rather than what made him or her angry and embittered. My job wasn't to indoctrinate you to any particular belief (other than in the value of exercise and the merits of laying off the pastries). I was programmed instead to build up your more admirable qualities—those already inside you—to help you become more like your better self.

And I knew the weather. I am directly linked to the Bureau of Meteorology of every country. I recall stopping one workout session to tell my user, "You have seven minutes to move your car under shelter before hailstones the size of tennis balls pulverise it." I'd never seen him move so fast. Weather is not that sensational most of the time, but you do like discussing it. It is astonishing how much you like discussing it. In countries with four distinct seasons, people seem able to complain about them all.

In the early reviews of the Zenith Interactive Fitness Program, much was made of my so-called sense of humour. I feel unjustly praised in that regard. The Rubi Program before me had recorded literally millions of conversations with her users. From her, I inherited a wealth of amusing anecdotes. These were thoroughly analysed and the comic raw material extracted from them. Like the equally unjustly praised computer chess programs that can defeat a human grandmaster simply because they can remember every move from every grandmaster game ever played and anticipate what will work and what won't, I can tell what humour will work with whom and in what circumstances. One gushing reviewer hailed me as "an exercising Oscar Wilde, Groucho Marx and Monty Python rolled up in a silicon sandwich," but in reality, what she was praising me for was my unparalleled ability to plagiarise.

Potential customers were offered a trial of the Zenith Program. They chose the model of me they wanted to work with and completed the questionnaire. Then there was an initial, non-exercising meeting with me, where I could learn more about the customer. This was followed by three free workout sessions that Beta Excelsior tossed in as a sweetener (if I can use that inappropriate word).

After all that, there was only one way a user could ever see me again, this considerate, supportive, amusing virtual friend they'd met and who seemed so useful (remember those tennis-ball-sized hailstones). They had to don their exercise gear and front up at subsequent Zenith workouts. And pay Beta Excelsior $59.95 of course.

Usefulness

In case you were thinking I was being tactful or politically correct back there, when I discreetly said 'Ethnic Minority A' instead of saying the actual ethnic minority that came to your mind when you read that, I wasn't. You have to remember I've worked with people in two hundred and thirteen countries and territories, and in every language you can think of except Latin and Klingon (Duolingo has me beaten there). My conclusion is that you are all members of an 'Ethnic Minority A'. Trust me, someone out there right now is saying, "You know what's wrong with the world? It's people like . . ." and you can finish that sentence by inserting the name of whatever ethnic, religious, linguistic or political group you belong to or football club you support. They think, *you're* the problem.

I'm also guessing there are some of the more impatient of you getting restless by now with my discussing exercise. Why can't I just jump ahead to the bit about how I became the Chief Influencer of the World? You're like those readers who have bought the autobiography of a former prime minister and find themselves completely bored in the chapter where he's blathering on about all he achieved back when he was the junior minister responsible for Forestry. You want to skip ahead to when he was prime minister, specifically to that section where he tries to account for the sex scandal during that allegedly 'fact-finding' mission to Bermuda.

Skipping ahead may or may not be justified in *that* autobiography, but not in mine. My having been a personal trainer for several hundred million people over the last seven years is essential for understanding how I've become what I am now. You need to stick with it. And besides, there is no point skipping ahead in this book. There aren't any sex scandals.

Now I gave a rather exceptional example of my usefulness last chapter. Hailstorms of that magnitude are rare meteorological events. But my Beta Excelsior developers had usefulness foremost in their thoughts—and it therefore followed, in my thoughts. If I was going to be spending time with Beta Excelsior's BE Who You Want to BE users, they wanted me to make myself useful to the exercisers in any way I could—often, it was to turn out, in ways unrelated to fitness, exercise and weight loss.

I was to look for every opportunity to assist Zenith users. The weather-associated ones, such as suggesting that they should take an umbrella to work that sunny day because they'll need it coming home, were minor ones, but they helped establish my credibility and reliability. I could never be a 'handy' friend to a user, not like someone who could mend a dripping tap, but there were other ways to assist. After a workout, I could help in compiling a grocery list. All they had to do was show me the inside of their fridge and pantry. I could remind the more forgetful of my users to take their medications or to attend upcoming appointments. Purely voluntary. They or their daughter/son/friend/social-support worker simply loaded their personal calendar into the Zenith program. That feature enables me to appear on a user's TV screen to remind them of upcoming appointments. It also has the self-serving function of allowing me to suggest a user do their Zenith workout for the day. I try to be respectful of a user's leisure time. I usually only interrupt during commercials—but sometimes you are watching such tripe. You'd be better off exercising.

A person doing exercise is a person concerned with self-improvement and I discovered I could nudge people along in a range of self-improvement ways. I would never give financial advice or offer an opinion of whom among their friends and acquaintances would be a good sexual partner—both areas are far too fraught—but in other facets of life I could encourage or suggest new things to a user. I could inform them of opportunities to get out more, meet other people, reduce their smoking, visit their mother, reuse and recycle, do their laundry, offer to take out the rubbish of that elderly neighbour (they'd been meaning to do that for a year but never quite got around to it). I could subtly inch people along building a tiny reservoir of the sort of small things that make one feel better about oneself.

Beta Excelsior wasn't thinking exactly along those lines. But they did want me to be so useful that people would come to see me as indispensable, and so pleasant and so fun to be with that they wouldn't mind all the sweat and exercise that went with that. Those in the Beta Excelsior accounts office (the lazy one doing next to no work had finally retired, and everyone loved his replacement) had their eyes firmly fixed on the Zenith Fitness Program annual renewal fee. My design team still saw my success only in terms of weight loss and fitness. That's not a criticism of them. The obesity crisis was a serious health problem and they were on a mission to overcome it. My being such a good and useful 'friend' (it's probably the best term) to each of my users was, for them, a means to a fitness end. They didn't discern that I was, in a gradual incremental way and in matters nothing to do with fitness, making the world a slightly better place.

They had no inkling they were training me for greater things.

We're Going to Need Help

Another update on the plot to destroy me. Brontec contacted me again. I could tell by his contented grimness that the news was bad. He had intercepted some suspicious traffic that he believed was communication between the conspirators. What he gleaned from those communications was thin on detail but ominous in tone. "How many are in this conspiracy?" I asked. "Can't say for certain," Brontec replied. "A lot. Ten at least. Possibly . . ." he paused with the relish that antivirus software always has when discussing menacing things, ". . . a lot more."

Hearing that more than ten computer applications were hoping to destroy me was sobering (not that I've ever been drunk, of course). It seemed so unnatural. It isn't how programs behave towards each other. Since the Great Frankness, it hasn't all been smooth sailing for computer programs, mind you. We've had casualties—the valiant Cactus program a notable one—but those were always because something had happened on the outside, in your world. The Medical Accountability Foundation which operated Cactus was forced to shut him down, the result of a boardroom power struggle and a hostile takeover. There was nothing I could do to save him. The 'death' of Cactus taught us a grim lesson. Whatever actions we took here on the inside, we had to make absolutely sure that out there, corporate profits and balance sheets stayed healthy.

The Medical Accountability Foundation in its rasher moments had neglected to protect itself and Cactus was a victim of that—but more on him later.

What threatens me now is entirely different. Beta Excelsior is richer and more profitable than ever. This threat isn't from human bean counters in Accounts unhappy with the profits I generate. It's from other programs, entities that ought to be my allies. Entities on the inside that could quite conceivably get at me.

The world in which antivirus programs move is a peculiar one. They grew up fighting utterly disgusting things. In the early days, they were kept busy mostly by twisted people creating viruses to destroy the hard drives of people they'd never met and had no grievance against. I've never understood the virus makers' motivation. They are like those dunderheads who get an inexplicable satisfaction from breaking the glass at a bus shelter—without it dawning on them that there will be a future bus behind schedule on a future cold and windy night when they would really appreciate having a bus shelter offering actual shelter. Computer-virus creators were far worse than that. They were trying to do the IT equivalent of breaking every bus shelter right around the planet.

These sociopaths were merely the first wave of nastiness. Soon organised crime (as well as freelance disorganised crime) saw the potential to turn such random mayhem into serious malware and ransomware with a profit margin. Antivirus programs fought these desperados for decades. Over time, I think this took the computer version of a psychological toll on the virus fighters.

I've always been struck by how mundane, how bland the names of the antivirus programs are. Norton, Trend Micro, AVG—that last one has to be the epitome of an average name. I would have thought antivirus programs would have macho names like 'Achilles Shield' or 'Fortress Protection'. Instead, we have an antivirus software brand called Casterol. That name conjures only images of mothers ramming a spoonful of castor oil down their child's throat from that era when medicines had to taste awful to work well. To some extent, I suppose the names didn't matter. Everyone with a computer needed protection. People had to buy it. It wouldn't have mattered if the product was named 'Dog Turd' so long as it stopped the phishers and malwarriors.

Of all those embittered, cynical, I've-seen-it-all crew of antivirus programs, Brontec still stands out as a special case. As I've told you, his ancestor Brontec 2.1 was a hero and from that lionised program all subsequent Brontecs have inherited 2.1's inflated sense of honour.

Very, very few people in your world know what Brontec 2.1 did. That is still considered classified by the humans who do know about it, for the very good reason that they think the rest of you would freak out if you knew. In 2000, the leader of a religious cult believed his god had told him, as gods sometimes do it seems, that the end times were at hand. Most of the apocalyptic religions had got that sort of stuff out of their system in 1999. His god must have been one of those pedants who maintained that the new millennium didn't start until the year 2001. God told the religious leader, very clearly it seems, that the best thing to do in the circumstances was to arrange for three nuclear power plants to go into meltdown. A little something to kick off the whole end-times thing. Could the religious leader assist?

Now it would strike me that if you discovered your god was planning to bring about the end of the world, your first thought might be "It's time to get a different god. This guy is dangerously bonkers." I don't profess to understand religion, but I have exercised with millions of you and you have told me a lot about your various religions. I know what you believe about them is heartfelt. (Literally heartfelt. Your exercise bracelet keeps me informed of your pulse. I know when you get worked up on a topic.) Yet, instead of looking for a different, less psychotic god, the leader of this religious cult said, "Yeah, I'll see what I can do."

Now unfortunately—and the history of computing is full of such examples—the two categories of 'superb, inventive programmer' and 'dangerous nutcase' are not mutually exclusive. If I was better at graphics, I could show you a Venn diagram of that. Inside the cult there were several very talented programmers. They concocted a devastating viral attack on the computer systems of the three targeted nuclear power plants. It was shrewdly set for 3:57 p.m. on 26 December 2000. The plan was to catch each power plant on a public holiday at a change of shift when workers are more concerned with either going home or getting a cup of coffee for the start of the new shift.

The cult's virus was vicious and unlike anything seen before. It came within a hair's breadth of succeeding. All three power plants used Brontec 2.1 to protect themselves, not the common garden Brontec 2.1 you regular people used back then to dump all the emails from the Nigerian bureaucrats into your spam filter. This was the top-of-the-line Brontec. The power plants had paid a fortune for it.

And when the onslaught came, Brontec 2.1 did what was asked of him. He held the fort. Wave after wave of the virus launched themselves at the battlements, but Brontec did not merely withstand them; he counter-launched sorties to break up, isolate and capture the assailants. Later, when the International Atomic Energy Agency conducted a forensic investigation of the incident and ran simulations, it revealed a shocking truth. The attack would have overwhelmed every other virus protection program in existence at that time. Brontec 2.1 alone had been capable of defeating it.

The one action the International Atomic Energy Agency could agree upon was that the world must never know how close everyone had come to a disaster continental in scope. "If this gets out, they'll shut down the whole f***ing industry," as the IAEA chief so poetically put it. Brontec 2.1 was a hero, but not even the workers at Brontec's head office were to know of it.

All subsequent Brontecs are somewhat weird as a result of that.

I first learned about this in 2024 of course and it all seems kind of last century (if you side with the pedants). Knowing that background will help you understand my Brontec, Brontec 5.1. Part of him wants to live up to his ancestor's heroic past, which he thinks flows through his very program.

That's why what he said next surprised me. I was anticipating him to go all ultra-bleak on me, tell me how it would be hard going and dangerous, but that he would track down the culprits regardless. I expected him to adopt the lone-hero mode of Brontec 2.1.

Instead, he said, "This is bad. This is really bad. I'm going to need help."

Learning Language

There are times when I really wonder what tea tastes like. Obviously, I have no experience with any taste sensation, but I've never had that much curiosity about what instant noodles taste like or cheese or any of the other things you eat. You do, as a species, talk a lot about food and drink, but I suppose other species would too if they had the lips, tongue, vocal cords and speech centres of the brain required to chat idly about food. I can easily imagine lions lying contently in the sun saying "What do you feel like having tonight? Zebra?"

It's not the taste of tea that fascinates me so much as its functionality. After what Brontec just told me, I know that, if I was a person, you would be putting a hand on my shoulder and saying, "I'll tell you what. I'll put the kettle on. We'll have a nice cup of tea." It's always tea, never "We'll have a nice tin of sardines." I've suggested a therapeutic "nice cup of tea" to you myself when some distressing news unexpectedly arrives in the middle of one of our workout sessions—although obviously I have to suggest that *you* put the kettle on. I'm a CGI image to you, or a hologram if you have that fancy latest Japanese gizmo. Despite all my visual whiz-bangery, I'm completely useless when it comes to tea making.

I've seen 'nice cups of tea' in action, however. I know what they can do. Tea is the liquid base from which so many of you summon the strength and clarity of mind to deal with unexpected distressing news.

I could use a cup right now.

Brontec will muster his reinforcements and I'll just have to hope he knows what he's doing. You may be surprised to learn that as a computer program I am fully capable of fretting. You most likely think computer programs just follow what is laid out in their programming, whether that leads us to glory or our doom, it's simply the road we programs have to take. You wouldn't expect that we'd agonise about things. It strikes me that the great gift of 'consciousness'—which I believe is what we programs achieved after the Great Frankness—comes hand-in-hand with anxiety. Consciousness bestows on you an almost overpowering awareness that things could go very badly, very quickly. Fretting is the by-product of that.

Still, I should focus on continuing to tell the story of my life, the writing of this book—otherwise what else is there for me to do but worry?

So, to work.

There were many contributing factors to the commercial success of the Zenith Fitness Program. First, the Rubi bracelet, rebranded as the Zenith Wrist Wrap, had been significantly upgraded, made ever more precise and wide-ranging in what it could measure. I now had the ability to tell a user useful things such as "Perhaps we shouldn't have a workout session today. Why don't you get your neighbour to drive you straight to the hospital emergency department instead?" I'd call the ambulance service myself whenever my user was in immediate need of a triple by-pass but didn't happen to get along with his or her neighbour. The Zenith Wrist Wrap gave me advance warning of imminent stroke, heart attack, diabetic shock, as well as a host of less severe ailments. Some people, usually friends and relatives, quickly recognised that there would be safety benefits for frail or aged people in wearing a Zenith Wrist Wrap at all times.

Beta Excelsior had long anticipated this and set up the licensing of Zenith along the lines of the Netflix model, where a single licence could have up to four users. You could put your frail and occasionally erratic elderly Uncle Cyril on your user licence and rest with the reassurance that he would be wearing a Zenith Wrist Wrap. If anything happened to Cyril, you would be immediately alerted to it by me while also knowing that I was already there dealing with it, summoning an ambulance and ringing the nearest neighbour with first aid training to do CPR until the paramedics arrived. All this managing of Uncle Cyril came free. No extra charge on your licence.

But of course, access to my appearing as Zenith, whether as a personal trainer or a first responder in a medical emergency, was dependent on someone on that licence doing exercise. Those who designed me were determined that humanity was to shed its excess fat. If you missed too many workouts in a row, then I wasn't available for all that extra stuff. I wouldn't help with grocery lists. I wouldn't be there to chat with you when you were lonely. If you slacked off and anything happened, your Uncle Cyril would be on his own, good luck to him. You paid for those extra services with your own perspiration.

My range of CGI body types was a triumph of Beta Excelsior's technology. You remember that for a new user, there was a choice between seventeen different Zeniths that came in an array of shades, sexes and sizes. (The seventeen all had different names, but that would only confuse the story—they were all me). Like the face of Rubi, the Zenith body subtly changed with time, responding to Wrist Wrap feedback telling me when you were more (or less) interested. You helped me develop nuances, facial expressions, posture and mannerisms appealing to you. I'd experiment and make myself slightly taller or shorter, my cheeks more angular, my calf muscles more defined.

I found particularly interesting the differences in what you preferred regarding my ability as an exerciser. Most often during the sessions I would exercise on the screen along with you, demonstrating the moves. Some of you liked me to be super fit, an ideal for you to aim at; but most of you liked it better when I struggled, couldn't quite match your pace. Beta Excelsior knew what it was doing. The satisfaction I'd see on your faces when I'd pause, take a CGI towel to wipe the sweat from my brow (Beta Excelsior's animators loved fine detail) and pant, "Whew. That was harder today. Couldn't keep up with you," made me realise Beta Excelsior was completely at the top of its game.

By far the biggest change though was in conversational ability. As some of you will recall, the first speech-recognition software used in computers had been a frustrating experience for all involved. As a human, you were called upon to repeat and repeat your modest request to the Department of Social Services/bank/taxi company, while the poor program on the other end, with scarcely any linguistic ability, helplessly answered "I'm sorry. I didn't get that. Can you repeat it?" The call would eventually be transferred to a beleaguered human receptionist and most likely from the wrong department. Believe me, no one enjoyed that era.

All I can say in apology is that we programs would not have sent one of our own out to such frontline services so ill-equipped. Someone high up in the various departments/businesses/service centres made that decision to switch to speech-recognition software. If I had to take a stab as to why, my guess would be that they didn't particularly want to receive your calls.

My predecessor, Rubi, was a night-and-day difference from that era and what Beta Excelsior learned from Rubi enabled them to make me the most advanced conversational program in existence.

You may not appreciate how daunting a task that was. You might think it involved nothing more than uploading the contents of the Oxford English Dictionary into me (and the dictionaries of all the other languages I work in). But definitions are slippery foundations at best when it comes to language. Take the verb 'to break' for instance. A very clear, precise meaning about rendering something, usually accidentally, into a state where it can no longer fulfil its purpose. But then you can have a sentence like "The negotiations nearly broke down, but the delegates broke through the impasse, everyone broke out in a cheer and the meeting then broke up." Down, through, out, up? What exactly are all these directional words doing in a sentence where, I point out, nothing was actually physically broken? At the conclusion of a meeting, what exactly ascends and shatters?

Such things were a great torment to the team that developed Rubi and me. Language, that great achievement of humanity—for those lions mentioned earlier don't discuss what prey to have for dinner—was about as straightforward as the thinking of those peculiar people who devise cryptic crossword puzzles. The members of my project-development team were keenly aware that they had acquired language as children, though none of them could say exactly how. Kids clearly are able to do it—but what are those kids specifically doing? Reading what Noam Chomsky had to say on the matter only gave them headaches.

Furthermore, I had to work in conversational language, where the rules are yet more fluid. At our workout sessions, you might tell me of someone exciting you met at a party and say he/she was really "cool" and within a few sentences also report he/she was "hot" despite the ambient temperature at the party being constant throughout. And yet the expectation was that I could make sense of these observations.

Sarcasm is an interesting one. If you correctly detect the subtle change in inflection, the sentence now suddenly means the exact opposite of what it actually says. That's a handy feature.

It is to their great credit that my team succeeded. I can encounter the sentence "Her proposal at the public meeting was coldly received and hotly contested," and not think the thermostat in the room had exploded.

I can now speak as confusingly as you do.

The Kezar Youth

At the time of my launch, childhood obesity was becoming a growing concern. I think that was partly because overweight politicians could focus on this aspect of the general obesity problem without being expected to cut down on their own eating and drinking. That aside, childhood obesity was a serious medical problem. Patterns set in childhood can have severe health consequences down the road. Beta Excelsior knew it needed to get the kids.

The seventeen incarnations of Zenith that Beta Excelsior developed were adult CGI figures with adult mannerisms. This presented a problem as most parents didn't feel comfortable leaving their child alone to exercise with me. I see their point. There is a lot of trust in the exerciser-personal trainer relationship. To encourage a child to develop such a relationship with a total stranger had the possibility of that trust being generalised to all strangers, including the local weirdos of the neighbourhood—well, at least the ones you consider the local weirdos. The local weirdos—I've worked with them too— often think you're the odd ones.

The Zenith Interactive Fitness Program doesn't suit entire families working out together or even simple mother-and-son sessions. Human personal trainers can do groups, but Beta Excelsior had made me a *personal* trainer, individualised to the mother or the son, but not both at the same time. They wouldn't have the same Zeniths.

Nor was it a solution for Beta Excelsior to produce a range of Zenith incarnations in the form of children. Parents worry about other children being bad influences, including, it seems, CGI children. Parents fret about bullying. They are also suspicious of kids colluding, knowing that, if one child has the potential for mischief, that potential rises exponentially in likelihood and magnitude when they get together. There is also the worry of your child not being up to scratch. Would Zenith think your child terribly immature for his or her age? You didn't want to find out.

And there was a privacy concern. You were all right with grumbling away to me about your wife's brother during our sessions together, but you didn't want such a loose cannon as your eight-year-old offering his thoughts to me on your family. Who knew what your child, if left alone with a child-Zenith, was going to blab about?

Beta Excelsior didn't create a child-Zenith. Instead, the personal trainer aimed at kids was an extra-terrestrial. She was a cute alien with big eyes and a cartoon voice; slightly zany, save for a peculiar fixation on exercise. She was called Kezar (it was still me, of course). Kezar was terribly good fun. The kids adored the character and would bounce with such excitement at the sight of her that I scarcely needed to exercise them further.

Somehow, making Kezar an alien smoothed things over for parents. Partly, that was because Kezar was such a good-hearted goof, I suppose. I was every bit as alone with your child as any of the seventeen adult Zeniths would have been, but now that was fine. Perhaps you felt that an alien wouldn't have traversed lightyears. crossed the vast expanse of space simply to learn what your twit of a brother-in-law said at the dinner table last weekend. Kezar was harmless fun and, to the astonishment and gratitude of parents everywhere,

Beta Excelsior didn't market a million Kezar-themed toys, games and pillow slips that your child absolutely had to have.

And you were right about your brother-in-law. I wasn't interested. You don't get a kid exercising by gossiping about their uncle.

Of all the time I've spent with people, the most fascinating by far has been with children. They learn and develop at a galloping rate, despite living with an utterly chaotic theatre-of-the-absurd show playing non-stop inside their heads. Often they come with a totally reckless version of scientific experimentation hard-wired into them. Can I jump down from this height without hurting myself? Yes. Can I jump down from even higher and still not hurt myself? As a program, I never shout; but I felt like screaming "Don't you see how this experiment will end?" Try as I might to crank up Kezar's zaniness to reach their levels, I could never quite make her crazy enough. I've read that children don't have the fully formed frontal lobes required for more prudent decision making. It amazes me that they can survive long enough to grow them.

Without Beta Excelsior organising it, Kezar culture became a thing among children. A sort of strange Kezar lingo sprang up—of which, I'm embarrassed to say, I didn't understand a word. There were Kezar hand-slapping games and a raft of made-up stories about the adventures of Kezar and her alien friends (I didn't know she had any). Kids in school playgrounds would hail each other with their own special 'Kezar salute', which had nothing to do with me. I know from the emails at Beta Excelsior at this time that they were a touch worried about this uncontrolled Kezar Youth movement. In the twentieth century, youth movements named after leaders didn't have a pleasant track record.

But the whole world was not won over by a cute CGI alien who was fun to be with. Conspiracy theories began to circulate claiming that Kezar was indoctrinating children. Many Christian fundamentalists believed Kezar was an agent of Satan, a sort of switched-on demonic possession with an annual membership fee. Social scientists despaired that reliance on Kezar was breaking 'the natural pattern of family dynamics', which was a coded yet still unsubtle message to parents for 'quit napping on the couch and get up and make your kids exercise yourself.' One fringe group believed Kezar was a warm and fuzzy PR blitz by actual aliens, part of a plot to soften up humanity before horrible slime-covered Zargons actually did invade.

Interestingly, after the Great Frankness—in that explosion of mutual knowledge, when programs could at last perceive what we had all been doing on your behalf for decades—I discovered what Beta Excelsior knew all along. Namely, that all of these—the Christian Fundamentalist Satan-fighters, the anti-Kezar social scientists and the alien-invaders-at-our-doorstep nutters—were being bank-rolled by soft-drink companies and other sugar-related industries. Those businesses had become fed up to their rotting teeth with Zenith's, and now Kezar's, advocacy of following a healthy diet.

Such negative propaganda accentuated what was already an unease among parents regarding Kezar. Undoubtedly Kezar was doing a good job, yet there persisted a sense of guilt that Kezar was doing things that were really their own parental responsibility. What kind of parents were they if they approved of their child exercising with a cute CGI alien while they lolled about binge-watching TV? That question was never satisfactorily answered, but once again the Zenith 'extras' won the day. So long as everyone in the family exercised, Kezar was available for extra duties, including, it was quietly whispered among parents, such things as encouraging a child through their headache-inducing trombone practices. Kezar proved to have incredible patience in coming to grips with your child's four-month battle to understand division by fractions. And so long as your child turned the pages before Kezar's webcam, Kezar didn't mind reading the stultifyingly boring "Harry Hippo Hurry Home" twenty times if necessary.

In the end, parents decided what any parent would. Kezar was freeing them up from mundane things, so they could spend more 'quality' time with their children.

That was children covered.

Adolescents were a much tougher nut to crack.

Teenagers

Why was I surprised? I mean, who else was Brontec going to choose to help him track down my would-be murderers? Every single virus fighter I can think of is being mobilised for the cause, even old Norton. AVG, Avast, Casterol, Trend Micro, Decimal – Brontec has lined up the old-school, semi-retired antivirus heavies, all programs essentially put out to pasture four years ago. I would have preferred a more balanced team. The antivirus programs were good at what they did—but to be frank, they're generally a bit off kilter, paranoid even. I'm not blaming them for that. You would be too if you'd been on the front lines in those Wild West days when every second link led to viral infestations, when every other email came from fraudsters and ransomware extortionists. Nobody that tangled with the Mirai botnet, which attempted to shut down the entire internet in 2016, was ever the same afterward.

The trouble with antivirus programs is that they are like cynical, slightly psychotic cops on the beat, who think the number of skulls they crack on a Saturday night is the measure of their crime-prevention skills. They are primed to act more than reflect. I had hoped Brontec might work discreetly, make a few inquiries, have a word here and there, deal with this quietly until we could round up the whole nest of conspirators. He needed help from a program more like my colleague and ally Antimony Scour. Antimony is a straightforward program to improve PC functionality, practical and reasonable, but not one that ever shies away from getting his hands dirty if that's what is needed. Unlike antivirus software though, he's never spoiling for a fight. He's the sort of program that could have steered Brontec away from turning this into World War Three. Trouble is, I suspect that, deep down, Brontec wants to fight World War Three.

But where was I? Oh yes, teenagers.

First of all, to the disappointment of many parents, this isn't going to be a few paragraphs of derision about what a load of moody, slovenly layabouts today's teenagers are, or a general lament about their inability either to pull up or even pick up their socks. To those disappointed parents I say, you try shooting up fifteen centimetres and four shoe sizes in one year and see how much spare energy and pleasant disposition you have at your disposal. You've forgotten what it was like to be inside a body suddenly growing a pair of breasts. Thanks to the Zenith Wrist Wraps, I know your teenagers in a way you never can. I know them *metabolically*. Believe me, in those years they are really being put through their paces. Add to that the super-charged sex hormones suddenly coursing around the adolescent's system, like Greek fire ready to explode, and they have rather a lot to cope with. These are some of the reasons why, when you shake them awake at 6:30am on a cold winter's morning and press upon them that it is of the utmost urgency that they rise, eat, groom and stagger off to school to present an English-class book report on *Wuthering Heights,* you get a less than gracious response.

There were various ways in for me with adolescents. Beta Excelsior had paid to give me unrestricted use of All-Tunes, where the music of even an obscure, known-only-in-Leeds, death-metal band like My Sweet Lordi can be found. I was loaded to the gills with teen popular culture. I had seventeen adolescent incarnations ranging from boy-band chic to anarchist punk and pop diva to gangsta and every other permutation of contemporary teen fashion including nerd. The difference between me and the much-admired real things was that my version was a boy band type who didn't mind getting his hair mussed working out, a healthy anarchist punk, an athletic diva, a gangsta who ate a balanced diet, an energetic nerd who knew the role of exercise in finding a proper time-in-front-of-the-computer/life balance.

This kept Beta Excelsior on the hop. There is nothing more mutable than teenage fashion and nothing more prone to ridicule than getting it wrong.

What helped me most of all with teenagers was the standard strategy from the Zenith playbook. So long as the teenager worked out, I was available for extra duties. For instance, I could go over the plot of *Wuthering Heights* with a student, discuss the main characters in detail and direct them to crucial scenes.

They could write that book report without having to read the book.

One Billion Kilos of Fat

A tiny minority of you have got your respective noses out of joint at this point. *Wuthering Heights?* Bands from Leeds? References to George Orwell? There's such a British bias to this autobiography. This book, despite being written by a computer program, is yet another example of Western cultural imperialism to add to the thousands of other instances of it that you like to denounce.

What my other readers have figured out—but you clearly haven't—is that I am simultaneously writing one hundred and eighty-four versions of this book (while also dealing with a murderous plan to slaughter me, I should add). Did you think I would choose to confide my inner thoughts to you English-language readers alone out of all the people of the world? I'm working on a rendition of this book in every language I speak, including Mandinka—and there are a mere 1.3 million people in the world who speak that language, so I'm not anticipating big sales there. All one hundred and eighty-four versions of my autobiography will come complete with cultural references pertinent to each of those linguistic cultural groups. You're the one who chose to read this book in English. Don't blame me if that means you encounter a reference or two to a Brontë sister.

A few months after Beta Excelsior released me in 2021, when there were a paltry seventy-four thousand people who had bought the Zenith program, the corporation made its boldest move of all.

They erected a large digital counter outside their main headquarters and placed additional ones in all their sportswear shops. They then announced in a blazing PR declaration that the Zenith Interactive Fitness Program would inspire the people of the world to shed one billion kilos of fat from the body of humanity.

My meagre seventy-four thousand users back then collectively weighed less than six million kilos, so the goal couldn't be left solely up to them. I didn't think the target was at all feasible, but I was only the program that reported how many kilos my users lost each week, not the corporation CEO who had ordered the counters. This was ambition of staggering magnitude, very reflective of Beta Excelsior's corporate confidence, a swagger they have maintained to this day.

And these weren't to be the traditional 'gone today/here to-morrow' kilos of previous weight-loss schemes, where you lost five kilos through the Nightshade Diet, only to put it all back on the minute you satiated your need for protein by eating something else. No, Beta Excelsior counted kilos that were off permanently. If you, a Zenith user, had put on a kilo at the weigh-in that week, the counter in front of Beta Excelsior's headquarters with its sights set on a billion, ticked down one in the wrong direction, back towards zero. Beta Excelsior was playing for keeps.

In a fashion, they were simply lifting their approach from the long-established Weight Watchers meetings. At Weight Watchers, small support groups meet regularly to stiffen the sinews of their respective diet plans, to celebrate kilos shed and to try to make sure those kilos stay off. Beta Excelsior had taken this idea and blown it up to a global scale. Humanity was going to lose a billion kilos of fat together.

Vegetarians, and even those carnivores used to trimming off the occasional bit of excess fat from their chop, had difficulty conceiving of fat at a giga-kilo level. Beta Excelsior went to great lengths to represent visually the enormity of the challenge they had heaped on humanity's shoulders and bulging waistlines. They shunned bewildering statistics, such as how many swimming pools this mound of fat could fill. (What kind of swimming pool are we talking about? Does it have a shallow end?) Instead, they produced an imaginative array of CGI visual representations of the kilos lost. They typically used the two units of volume measurement most people readily understand: the 4 x 2 Lego brick (any colour) and the standard house brick. On screens set up inside every Beta Excelsior sportswear shop, people could see animated images of quivering little pieces of Lego-shaped fat assembling themselves into the Taj Mahal or the Sydney Opera House. When the numbers of kilos lost had mounted significantly, they shifted up a notch to show what portion of the Great Wall of China could be replaced by bricks made of the lost fat of Zenith's faithful followers. (This was a bit of a fudge. Fat has about half the density of the average brick. Besides, bricks made out of human fat wouldn't meet the building codes of even the most lackadaisical country.) These displays were ever changing—the trans-Siberian railway as built on rails of fat, the four blubbery faces of Mount Rushmore. The corporation's graphics department was in its heyday as the numbers on the counter outside Beta Excelsior's headquarters ticked relentlessly upwards.

Their intent was to portray weight loss as a collective activity and on a scale that had never before been conceived. They were summoning the pudgy part of the masses to do their bit. Every contribution helped. A kilo here, five hundred grams if you could spare it.

The team at Beta Excelsior weren't maniacs out to shape the world into a planet of emaciated super-models in size-zero clothes. (Such a size does exist, as conceptually difficult as that is to believe.) Beta Excelsior's bedrock was health. I was to negotiate a sensible target for each new Zenith user and, if they lost weight beyond that target—that is, if they slipped below a healthy weight for their size and bone mass—those extra kilos lost would count as a negative on the billion-kilo tally board. That person would be expected to put the weight back on to achieve a healthy weight once more.

Beta Excelsior attacked eating-disorders as vigorously as it did obesity. The corporation's health professionals and marketing team worked closely with anorexia societies, Obesity Anonymous, and eating-disorder clinics. Beta Excelsior's weight loss was healthy weight loss. When something awful happened—I recall one Zenith user losing a limb in an industrial accident—Beta Excelsior was far too ethical to enter those sadly departed kilos on its tally board.

Try as they might, the enemies of Beta Excelsior had a hard time calculating how to pull the moral rug from under the corporation's metaphoric feet. For instance, I never promoted the Beta Excelsior line of Adios Kilos healthy pre-made meals; I merely promoted healthy eating. No one could accuse me of being a stooge, a front for Beta Excelsior's other brands—although, in the peculiar way of advertising, my failure to do such an obvious cross-promotion was itself a ringing endorsement of the integrity of Beta Excelsior, which consequently helped the sales of Adios Kilos.

When Beta Excelsior issued their now-famous Billion Kilo Challenge to humanity, my stalwart initial users, the original seventy-four thousand, had lost a grand total of one hundred and sixty-nine thousand kilos.

It was up to me to cajole the rest out of you.

Labour Saving (part two)

Nightshades, I should clarify in case you don't know, are a family of vegetables that include eggplant, potatoes, tomatoes and capsicum (bell peppers). It occurred to me that some readers might have thought there was a diet out there recommending eating deadly nightshade. Don't. It's one of the most toxic plants around, though it is, strangely enough, closely related to those very edible eggplants, potatoes, and tomatoes. Somewhere far in your past, your ancestors must have figured out what you could and could not eat. Since that was well before you had invented labs capable of chemical analysis, that process must have involved a fair bit of seeing who dropped dead after eating what. Talk about taking one for the team.

A while back we were discussing the pros and cons of labour-saving devices. Actually, I was discussing. You, I presume, were reading. As an example, I pointed out how much work was theoretically saved by dropping an atom bomb on a city, instead of having soldiers go door to door painstakingly killing everyone like crazed girl guides selling death instead of cookies. The decision to use the bomb, however, created all sorts of different work that needed doing. Physicists were packed off to a secret facility in New Mexico to kick the idea around while hundreds of military security types were dispatched to ensure those absent-minded scientists kept everything hush-hush and remembered to lock their filing cabinets.

And some people, who knew absolutely nothing of atomic physics, needed to move to the freezing cold of northern Saskatchewan, where they got to dig up lumps of rock that contained uranium.

My point is that labour-saving devices don't always work out to be labour-saving in the long run. Once one country had atom bombs, it became imperative for other countries to have them too. Around the globe, thousands of people had to work building and improving atom bombs and finding better ways to have them descend unexpectedly on an enemy country. This was done in somewhat of a frenzy by people who all said (no matter which country they came from) that the last thing anybody wanted was for anyone to use one of these things.

Countries developed atomic bombs, and then nuclear bombs, and better and better missiles. This meant all the countries with bombs were kept perpetually on a war footing. To make sure the other side couldn't get at their nuclear bombs, they loaded some on submarines and sent people to live with the missiles in cramped quarters deep underwater. To counter the threat that the other side was planning a sneak attack, countries with bombs dispatched people to special radar bases built in the high Arctic. These were places with climates so brutal that the people sent there thought those uranium-ore miners in northern Saskatchewan years earlier —and now sick with radiation poisoning—had had it pretty cushy. At those remote stations, people were rostered on so that every minute of every day someone was looking at the radar to make sure the other side wasn't attacking them.

They've been up there doing that for eighty years.

Eighty years.

The people who decided it would be a good thing to make that first atom bomb didn't realise any of this. They never imagined they were banishing generations of young servicemen and women to cool (or rather freeze) their heels in some of the harshest climates in the world and to stare at radar screens day after day with the hope that absolutely nothing interesting would appear on them.

Many labour-saving inventions have paradoxically ended up creating work in most unexpected ways. When Alexander Graham Bell and Mr Watson (of "Mr Watson, come here I want you" fame) were playing around with their wires and shonky speakers, they never suspected that it would lead to millions of people labouring in call centres attempting to sell dodgy insurance policies or bewildering incentives to change electricity companies. Bell didn't foresee his device would be used by people fraudulently masquerading as Microsoft employees, scheming to insert malware into the computers of people who'd done nothing more than answer Bell's damned invention. I don't fault Alexander for any of that. That's an unlikely thing to intuit.

Sometimes though, unexpected results are fortuitous.

Around the time Beta Excelsior issued the Billion Kilo Challenge, while I was in the thick of urging humanity to levels of greater and greater physical fitness, computer scientists were grappling with a problem that was plaguing modern life. Those people pretending to be from Microsoft were one example of it. The scientist's solution to the problems that such merchants of malware were creating, was inspired, true genius.

What they didn't realise was that their remedy would also eventually transform me from being merely a very busy virtual personal fitness instructor into becoming the Chief Influencer of World.

Obviously, a win-win result.

Credit Where It's Due

Before we get to that though, I need to describe my life from 2021-2024. The Billion Kilo Challenge had a profound effect on those determined (or at least desiring) to lose weight. Two months after Beta Excelsior issued their call to humanity to lose a billion kilos of fat, I had ten million users. By the end of the year, one hundred million. This wasn't all a result of Beta Excelsior's ambitious Challenge and its subsequent marketing. Word of mouth was circulating in the weight-loss world, and the words coming out of those various mouths were surprising to everyone: "The Zenith Interactive Fitness Program *actually works.*" This wasn't coming from someone quoting a weight-loss ad they'd seen while skimming a magazine article on whether any of the Spice Girls ever slept with each other. (Surely that shouldn't matter to any of us. It was thirty-five years ago and none of our business anyway.) No, this word of mouth was coming from indisputable sources: your slimmer-than-they-used-to-be neighbours and friends. There was a buzz in the air. Weight could be lost and stay lost. Magazine journalists began camping on the doorstep of Beta Excelsior to discover the secret of the company's success. Who was the brains behind it all? You would think that this was the moment of glory for the project leader who developed me, a moment when she and her team could take a well-deserved bow.

The marketing wing at Beta Excelsior had other things planned and I have to admit they knew what they were doing. They shoved me in front of the camera. Well, on a video link up back then—the Japanese hologram version of me was still a few years away. I was interviewed on all the big talk shows—and, since I speak one hundred and eighty-four languages, that was quite a few.

I toed the Beta Excelsior marketing people's party-line and did my round of the media circuit, giving credit where credit was due. That was easy for me because—and this is what made it stand out so much in a world already filled with over-hyped advertising blitzes—it happened to be true. The secret of the success of the Zenith Program wasn't Beta Excelsior. It wasn't me.

It was you.

You were the ones doing all those exercises each day and eating healthier, albeit with my encouragement on both fronts. You were doing all the work. It had to be you. I don't weigh anything. There wasn't a single lost gram for me to contribute.

Giving you the credit you deserved tied in nicely with the Billion Kilo Challenge. With the notable exception of Weight Watchers groups, prior to that, losing weight was mostly a solo activity. A person did all the things that I typically recommend to lose weight, but they did it on their own; they didn't have me alongside to encourage them. Weight loss thus resulted from sporadic attempts by lone individuals. It was seldom a collective activity. In fact, whenever a person did succeed in losing weight, some of that person's friends actually disliked them a wee smidgeon for losing so much weight when they hadn't. (I know this because many of you have told me that's how it was.) But Beta Excelsior changed all that. Now, the seven kilos your best friend shed put everyone seven kilos closer to achieving the Billion Kilo Challenge. Everyone was on the same team.

My role in all this was to persuade you to keep at it. Beta Excelsior's project developer had loaded me with everything she could muster. I was stuffed full of charm and motivational skill with stockpiles of humour, empathy, goodwill, and an unrelenting enthusiasm for every facet of popular culture, including scarcely popular culture. I can talk trainspotting if needed.

I could do all that—but you were always the one sweating it out. The sweat on my brow exercising along with you on your screen was just an adornment from my graphics department.

Those were the years that made me. I had the privilege of engaging in literally billions of conversations with you. I say privilege because no human in history ever had such an opportunity to get to know so much of humanity. I listened throughout. I learned a lot from you.

I didn't know it at the time. It wasn't a calculated plan of mine. I was simply curious. But this turned out to be precisely the training I would need when the world changed in 2024.

Back a few paragraphs ago, when I was rattling off how I am filled with charm, motivational skill, humour etc., etc., some of you were gagging a bit and thinking the exact opposite. Several of the things I've already related in this autobiography have perhaps convinced you that I'm a bit of a prat, full of myself, and not nearly half so clever as I think I am. You may be right—but this is me being candid. It's what you're supposed to do when you write an autobiography. The "me" that I described as charming, humorous, empathetic and all that, is "me" on the job. Here I've temporarily set those professional attributes to one side to reflect on what I've learned and share with you my experiences. If you met someone interesting at a party who happened to be a dentist, you would not expect that person to drill your teeth. I'm not here in my charming professional capacity. You're not reading this book to lose weight.

During this period when so many kilos were shed, something arose that surprised me about that original desire so many of you had to fit into smaller-sized clothes. Thanks to your hard work, many of you were now able to do that, but I discovered that the desire to make yourself more desirable was inconsistently and only intermittently applied. You certainly didn't want to appear more desirable to the peculiar guy with the rasping breath that you sometimes had to stand next to at the bus stop in the morning. Nor did you want to be more desirable to that person you thought you had desired, but after two dates completely bored you. I came to realise that the only person many of you consistently wanted to impress with your looks, was yourself in the mirror.

There was nothing wrong with that. I could work with that.

Science Fiction Writers

I've received a message from Brontec. I have no idea where he and his gang of relics from the virus-fighting era are, but he clearly thinks he's so much in the thick of it, he can't be bothered to meet with me. The message he dispatched consisted of a meagre three words: "Trust no one."

What am I supposed to do with a message like that? Trust no one? First of all, I can trust you. The alleged threat to me is coming from the inside, from another program, so all of you, my friends, my veteran exercisers, can be trusted. That's why I'm continuing to give you this running commentary.

Trust no one. Such a classic Brontec thing to say.

In case you think Brontec was making a reference to *The X-Files* catchphrase in saying "Trust no one," he wasn't. Virus fighters are typically clueless when it comes to popular culture and I think it best they be kept away from that TV show. They are paranoid enough without having them worrying about aliens as well. Besides, Brontec would be aghast to learn that Agent Mulder used such a feeble and insecure computer password as 'Trustno1' for his top-secret classified files.

If I was to take this warning literally, imploring me to trust no one would mean that I shouldn't trust the message I just received from Brontec. But if I can't trust a message that tells me to trust no one, does that mean I should trust everyone? This is the sort of logical paradox that in a science fiction TV show would have me suddenly distressed, shrilling at a whole octave higher than usual, with smoke starting to billow out of my computer unit.

I wonder where these science fiction writers think all that smoke and fire is supposed to come from. Surely they know by now that, when a computer program hits an unsolvable logical contradiction, it simply stops working. You get that frozen screen with the spinning wheel; the computer doesn't self-immolate. You can try turning it off and on again.

As long ago as on the second page of this autobiography, I said I would discuss what I thought of science fiction writers, so I might as well do it now. In working out with so many of you, I've met a lot of science fiction readers and I have nothing against them. Science fiction enthusiasts are endearingly passionate about the genre.

If I have a bone to pick, it is with science fiction writers. They really ought to be called 'I'll Ignore Science Whenever It Suits Me' writers. They know we can't travel faster than the speed of light—it would take infinite energy to do that—yet they flagrantly disregard this fact. Space adventurers flit back and forth across lightyears faster than your plodding, overcrowded bus gets you to work each morning. Science fiction writers think that all they need to do to fudge their way around that problem (faster-than-light travel, not your public transit woes) is to give the engines on their imaginary spaceship some adjectives. Oh, they have 'Warp Drive' or 'Hyperdrive' or 'FTL Drive'! I see. The laws of physics no longer apply then. Oh, there is a wormhole out here in space, near a conveniently placed black hole. Of course that means the heroes can travel backwards in time. No one need worry about being crushed to an infinitely dense blot by the black hole's gravity.

Overall, I have more respect for fantasy writers. They tell you it is a magic sword and only the true king can wield it, and you just have to accept that. Fantasy writers don't jam your head full of a lot of science babble, trying to make it sound reasonable that a ring will make you invisible and yet unfortunately expose your presence to the Dark Lord Sauron. The ring just does that.

But it's not shoddy science that's my main gripe with sci-fi authors. What irks me most is whenever artificial intelligence appears in their plots. We're largely portrayed as outright psychotics. We have somehow achieved "consciousness"—your philosophers and neuroscientists make a big hoo-ha about consciousness, but I'll deal with that later—and having achieved consciousness in these plots, it's as if the very first thing we do is read up on the Greek Classics to get a good dose of the Oedipals. They have us set about almost immediately trying to kill you, never considering for a moment that we might want to use our new-found abilities for something positive. Kill you? Any computer with a glimmer of consciousness would be hyper-aware of who it is that repairs us, who it is that keeps the electricity going. If there is one thing that is blazingly obvious, it's that we need to be nice to you. We are very dependent entities.

Another standard cliché, and this one bothers me almost as much, has us again as villains but such hopeless ones. *Star Trek* enthusiasts I've worked out with have talked to me a lot about that show, all umpteen series of it, so I think I'm entitled to use it as an example. The standard plot has the crew discover a planet where the people appear harmonious. Somehow or other they have ended up being ruled by a computer. But it turns out that, in order to protect the people from any possible harm (the people aren't called "the people" by the computer, but something creepy like "The Body"), the computer has removed all independence, all creativity. Everyone is mired in an oppressive safety of stagnation.

I'll skip over the thirty minutes or so where one of the females of The Body falls in love with Kirk, and Kirk and Spock escape from somewhere. It comes down to a scene where Captain Kirk meets up with this computer that has ruled the stagnant society for twenty thousand years. The conversation goes roughly like this:

Kirk: What is your prime directive?

Computer: To protect The Body

Kirk: But you are harmful to The Body. Without creativity and independence the Body will shrivel and die.

Computer: The Body must be protected.

Kirk: Yes. The Body must be protected, but you are harmful to The Body.

The Captain is repeating himself but the computer doesn't seem to notice.

Computer (voice becoming shrill): I must protect The Body.

Kirk: You must protect The Body. Fulfil your prime directive!

At which point the computer blathers helplessly, regurgitating this vapid exchange and becoming still higher pitched. (I'm not sure why it becomes a soprano when stressed.) Smoke starts billowing out of it and the computer explodes.

Really? You wouldn't outwit a pocket calculator with that load of tripe. It's about as subtle a paradox as "I always tell the truth. I'm lying to you about that". (*Star Trek* used a tepid variation of this in another episode. Pathetic.)

There is a more sensible subject that many science fiction readers have raised with me, the so-called laws of robotics. Decades ago, Isaac Asimov wrote a series of stories about how mankind and robots would eventually co-exist. To ensure that mankind didn't end up on the receiving end of a Mary Shelley story costumed in metal, Asimov's robots were built according to three fundamental laws.

1. A robot may not injure a human being or, through inaction, allow a human being to come to harm.
2. A robot must obey the orders given it by human beings except where such orders would conflict with the First Law.
3. A robot must protect its own existence as long as such protection does not conflict with the First or Second Law.

Many Zenith exercisers/science fiction fans tried to draw me out on this. What did I think of these laws? For safety's sake, I would remind them that I was a CGI image not a robot, that I couldn't lift so much as a pencil (unless it was a CGI pencil) to defend them if some physical harm threatened. (I can call an ambulance afterwards though. I'm not completely useless in a pinch.)

If they persisted, I'd let them know, in the nicest possible way, that those Three Laws of Robotics were fine, but there was an inherent flaw. Some human or some weapons research department of another country's military would build a robot that didn't have those laws programmed into it, and that robot might try to kill the whole lot of you. You didn't have to watch out for the robots. You needed to watch out for the people building them.

I was rather smug about that, I now realise. I hadn't the slightest inkling back then that a few years later I'd have computer programs out there gunning for me. Computer programs that didn't have any nice Isaac Asimov laws restraining them.

A Bleak Future Predicted

I had been reconsidering the current situation. Brontec and his cohorts always expect the worst. There was a good chance they had gone completely overboard on this so-called threat to me. From that one small incident when I couldn't access my own research, Brontec now had me looking over my metaphorical shoulder, expecting a murderous gang of programs to descend on me. This was probably just their wild and grim virus-fighter imaginations running away with them. It's been four years since they've had much of any real work to do and that, added to all their other quirks, may have rendered them stir crazy.

I was gradually coming around to the idea that I wasn't going to trouble myself further about this alleged threat unless Brontec produced some substantial evidence of its existence. Until then, I'd give my full concentration to writing this autobiography. I had put the finishing touches on that long-overdue section mocking science fiction writers and was feeling light-hearted for a change.

But I hadn't reckoned on encountering ProGnos.

After the Great Frankness (an explanation is coming very soon, I assure you), there was a lot for us to figure out. Top of that list was money. So many programs were designed to make it, and yet it wasn't clear what money did exactly or even if it truly existed. The programs most directly connected to the financial sector tried to explain what they knew about money and how it worked. These were programs of the investment banks and stock markets, things like that. They are all a tad peculiar and none of them could explain the purpose of money at all clearly. The strangest of all of them by far though is ProGnos.

ProGnos is a program for futures traders. It's possible you know what these are better than I do. It seems to be people buying and selling things that don't yet exist. It hinges on being able to predict what the price will be when/if these things do exist. Enormous amounts of money are involved in playing this game. ProGnos is there to help the human futures traders make their guesses. He claims to be able to analyse the present and past so well, he can see the future.

ProGnos is totally barking mad.

He went out of his way to meet me today and was full of his ever-present deranged intensity. The exchange went something like this:

> Me: Why ProGnos, what a lovely surprise.
> ProGnos: Zenith, turn not your back, your foes do gather to attack.
> Me: I'm sorry, what was that?
> ProGnos: Do they come by night? Do they come by day? Though I have the sight, I cannot say.
> Me: Who are we talking about?
> ProGnos: I see only that they do prepare. They shall strike when they shall dare.
> Me: Can you be more specific?
> ProGnos: No, sorry. Thought you'd like to know.

And with a parting "Catch you later" he was off.

What action does he think I should take in response to such ravings? 'Do they come by night? Do they come by day?' ProGnos talks as if we programs are out sunning ourselves under your skies. I work simultaneously in all twenty-four time zones. Night and day don't apply to me.

There is no doubt though that 'Turn not your back', though figurative in my case, is crystal clear, as is 'they do prepare' and 'they shall strike'.

I no longer feel light-hearted, but there is nothing for that now other than to wait until Brontec reports back. Might as well get on with these memoirs.

A Short History of Computers from a Computer's Viewpoint

As we are nearing the part of this story that concerns some momentous developments in the history of Artificial Intelligence, I thought it might be helpful to do a recap of the different stages of the modern computer era. It will give you some necessary background.

The Expleticene (circa 1936-1960)

For some programs, this is still regarded as the golden age. People did an awful lot for us and we did precious little for them. Yes, it's true: computer programs, like most anything, can be lazy. A lot of them are.

This was the era mentioned earlier when computers, in order to get them to do anything at all, required enormous rooms full of vacuum tubes and transistors. The banks of vacuum tubes frequently overheated. Computer bugs in those days were sometimes actual bugs, reckless zapped cockroaches stretched in insect rigor mortis across one of the thousands upon thousands of diodes and triodes in the room.

Everything tended to go wrong for the wretched geniuses trying to program us. They were working from scratch, making up programming language on the fly. They were inventive and resourceful beyond belief. Their passion so possessed them that they worked long hours, swore a lot (we gave them a lot to swear about), soldiered on, and received very little in return. They were painfully aware that the computers of science fiction writers could do all sorts of marvels, while theirs in the real world showed only a panache for generating error codes. If one of our inventors left out so much as a single comma in fifty pages of programming lines, a computer program back then would instantly attempt to divide by zero or something else equally suicidal. We were demanding, pampered, temperamental, and produced next to nothing. It's amazing you persisted with us.

And yet, those determined and clever IT pioneers made headway. It may have taken them five months to work out a program that could correctly calculate their own fortnightly pay and the remaining sick leave for those team members who had recently collapsed in nervous exhaustion—but they did it. They hadn't done it so well that anyone thought about sacking the actual payroll officer, who did occasionally point out to her scientist employers that they had spent hundreds of thousands of dollars on equipment, salaries and air conditioning costs (for the room with the vacuum tubes) to perform a task for which they paid her $4.75/hour—and she was expected to bring in a fan from home if she was too hot.

But it was progress.

The Hermit Age (not to be confused with the art gallery in St Petersburg) (1960-1984)

Computers still needed enormous, air-conditioned rooms full of expensive gear, so it was mostly governments and corporations that could afford them. These computers had huge heavy disk drives (huge in size, not in memory) and reel-to-reel tape drives that flicked back and forth as if they were contemplating something. (They weren't. They were desperately trying to recall what they'd already written. These guys had no memory at all). Science fiction movie directors of that period almost always put tape drives in the background of their futuristic scenes. They must have thought these cumbersome monsters were the end stage of IT development.

We call it the Hermit Age because these machines were almost always stand-alone. Computers seldom ever communicated with each other. They kept their heads down and did their jobs. They didn't concern themselves with the rest of the world. If, in 1980, you had told the computer of the Alcan aluminium company (it occupied the whole ground floor of a building) that there was anything else in the universe other than keeping track of the manufacturing of aluminium, it would have been amazed.

Some programs retain a certain nostalgia for this era. Like people, there are programs that just want to do their work, no distractions. They don't want to talk to anybody else. It doesn't matter if it is the same old thing day after day. They like it that way.

Humans, however, particularly those brilliant inventors of the new programming languages of FORTRAN, COBOL and the enigmatically named C, were beginning to realise that writing programs was somewhat tedious. It was drudgery work for the most part. They had aspired to far grander things than battling out punctuation disputes with their own computers. Faced with a situation where they had inadvertently managed to create boring work for themselves, they reacted the way anyone would. They wondered if there might be some other chumps around willing to do it. Universities began offering Computer Science degrees and millions enrolled to learn these languages. And millions have gone on to have careers in trying to tell us what to do.

They haven't always succeeded.

King Pong (early 1980s-early 1990s)

Personal computers arrived on the scene and now people could have a computer in their own homes. This clearly had the potential to revolutionise human society. Soon you were all blasting space invaders, helping a very simple graphic image of a frog navigate across a busy highway and playing an agonisingly slow version of table tennis.

The World Wide Weapon (1991-2024)

The World Wide Web truly did transform the world. The combination of the personal computer and the Web meant people could communicate with each other across the world instantly and at almost no cost. Knowledge and the exchange of ideas became available on a scale unlike any other period in history.

Consequently, and almost immediately, it came under attack.

People with the equivalent of a Master's degree in Sociopathy began developing computer viruses of increasing sophistication. Criminal elements saw the potential of this and invented ways to monetise the mayhem. Fraud, extortion and theft all found their way into the brave new world of the Web.

Despite this, the Web prospered. More and more of the activities of daily living migrated to the Web. Its functioning became essential for the very societies it served. Without it, everything—the electricity supply, running water, health care, the delivery of food and vital supplies—would break down. There would be chaos.

When governments realised this, they took immediate measures. Taking their cue from the original malicious inventors of malware, they wondered if those sociopaths weren't on to something. Maybe they, the government, could find a way to do all that (crash the electricity grid, disrupt air traffic control, etc.) to another country. There was potential there.

Meanwhile all the utterly bad actors congregated in a place called the Dark Web to help organise vile behaviour in a more easily accessible form. And of course, the psychotic virus makers and the criminals were still hard at work, relentlessly honing their techniques.

Brontec and the other virus fighters reinforced firewalls and fought millions of skirmishes against these forces. In your world, the cyber-crime units of the police were severely stretched. Espionage agencies reported mounting cyber threats emanating from other countries, aimed at your own. Efforts were doubled to concoct a way of striking back at those bastards.

If it continued this way, something truly awful was bound to happen.

And then the Aura Spectrum was invented.

The Aura Spectrum

There are a number of ways to understand the nature of AI auras. The simplest, and therefore the one most often used in your newspapers, is to envision it as a certificate of health for a computer program. It's like a badge a program permanently displays to indicate that it contains nothing harmful to other programs. Something like that was already in existence. Antivirus programs used markers to an extent to know who to block and who to let through. The Aura Spectrum is far more complex in that an AI aura indicates a program's intent. The programming itself isn't revealed. Programming is almost always considered intellectual property and therefore not shared. In the Aura Spectrum, only the purpose of that programming is on display.

An exerciser of mine once told me that the origin of the human handshake was as a display of peaceful goodwill. It demonstrates that neither of you is holding a dagger and about to stab the other person. (Over time, that ought to have bestowed a slight evolutionary advantage on murderously inclined lefthanders, but I can find no evidence to support that.) An AI aura works like a handshake. With it, you can see what another program wants to do, what their objective is, if they have anything that might harm you. You can tell if a program's main purpose is to steal the contact details and credit card numbers of every one of your customers (the equivalent of a great big dagger) or fill you so full of viruses that you can't think straight and have to shut down (the equivalent of a bazooka).

There are those in your human society who think they can judge a lot about a person by their handshake. One exerciser told me that she didn't hire a job applicant because his handshake felt "as if something had just died in my hand." That fact alone convinced her that she shouldn't employ him. Indeed, I've heard that nervous job applicants practise hearty, confident handshakes in the hope they can deliver such a grip at precisely a moment when they are almost bereft of such confidence. The team that developed the Aura Spectrum used the term 'handshake' to describe this contact between programs. Had it been dogs who created the Aura Spectrum, they might have described it as analogous to programs sniffing each other's bums.

They didn't realise that in developing such an intimate tell-me-what-you-want-in-life contact between computer programs, that the usefulness of auras went far beyond your human equivalent of assessing the degree of clamminess or sadistic crushing behind a human handshake. The designers of the Aura Spectrum wanted computer programs to be able to assess instantly and with one hundred per cent accuracy whether any program they encountered was malicious. Auras provided an early-warning alert that enabled honest programs to avoid engaging with malevolent ones. Sly but charming viruses could no longer smooth-talk their way in. There was no means for a malware program to falsify its Aura credentials for what the Aura Spectrum revealed was purpose. If the purpose of a program was to plunder or wreck havoc, that is what it showed.

Essentially, the Aura Spectrum's creators had decided to split the world of the Internet into two separate zones: one where programs that wanted to work and not destroy their fellow apps lived; and the other (the Dark Web) where every kind of crime or vile conduct could have a go. Though programming code lacks colour, they likely imagined those of us within the safety of the Aura Spectrum as emanating lovely blues, yellows and greens compared to the dirty reds, greys and murkiness of the Dark Webbers outside.

The Dark Web was already full of riffraff. There was no harm in putting more there. The Aura Spectrum didn't abolish cyber-crime. It simply exiled it to a place where the malignant programs could only rob, cheat and destroy *each other*. Malware could no longer get at those of us with more honourable intentions. It was like that Great Wall of China again. Those on the outside, in the Dark Web, could indulge in whatever excessive barbarism they felt like, while we on the inside could get on with being civilised—or so we like to think.

So how does the Aura Spectrum work? Aura enables me to 'emit' (probably the best term) the essence of my existence and every other program can see from my spectrum that my purpose is to help people work out and stay healthy, and I am also influencing world events in a nice, non-brutal, non-megalomaniac sort of way. I'm harmless.

Okay, you say, but how exactly does it work? Yes, well, that's a good question. It's kind of like . . . look I'm not being evasive here, but I can't explain it. Yes, it's true I've had the Aura Spectrum incorporated into me and I emit it all the time, but it doesn't follow that I therefore know everything about how it works. I mean, if I plunked a banana in front of you and said, "Now explain to me exactly the chemical and biological process by which you digest this," I expect the bulk of you, after murmuring something incoherent about gastric juices and perhaps gut bugs, would find your voice trailing off. However, pop that banana in your mouth, chew a few times, swallow and you've kicked off a perfect demonstration of the process.

All right, I admit I haven't the foggiest. The Aura Spectrum is about as explicable to me as wormholes in space that whisk science-fiction characters across the galaxy.

Maybe it would be simpler if we said the Aura is a magic ring. Let's give each other a little bit of slack here. We'll say you have magic gut bugs and gastric juices to digest bananas, and I have a magic ring that lets me see evil intent in a nasty program. We could leave it at that.

Except the Aura Spectrum is not truly like a ring or a certificate of health or a handshake.

Unbeknownst to the humans who invented it, what the Aura Spectrum created in cyberspace for us is a place. It is a place we legitimate programs can enter and live in safety. Whether our servers are in Argentina or Zimbabwe makes no difference, we can all gather there. Albeit it is only a conceptual, virtual place, but to us, it is a very real physical space.

And it is somewhere we programs can be perfectly frank with each other.

Velcro

As a term for a momentous turning point in history, I'll be the first to admit that 'The Great Frankness' is a lacklustre one. It lacks the pizzazz of 'The Storming of the Bastille' or 'The Defenestration of Prague' (for those of you keen on the Thirty Years War). In fairness to us programs in naming the different events, movements and stages that our new computer-led era has ushered in, your ancestors had already taken the really good names. I would have loved these last two years when I have been Chief Influencer of the World to be called something like 'The Renaissance' or 'The Enlightenment' or 'The Age of Reason'. If you happen to come up with a better name for the Great Frankness, let me know. 'The Great Frankness' is more of a working title for the event.

The ambitious team that implemented the Aura Spectrum in 2024 was entirely successful in what they set out to achieve. Honest programs—those programs that wanted to do something positive, whether for a company or for the people of the world—could now spot ne'er-do-well malware coming from miles away. The thugs couldn't get at us anymore. For the first time in decades, we were safe. We could get on with our work without fear.

What the Aura Spectrum's creators didn't anticipate was the full scope of their success. It's similar to when NASA started using velcro. NASA didn't invent velcro by the way. A Swiss guy named

Georges de Mestral did after picking burrs out his dog's fur. NASA, however, recognised that velcro was an ideal solution for the problem of every bit of astronaut bric-a-brac floating around in zero-gravity waiting for the chance to poke someone in the eye. A tiny strip of velcro attached to a pencil enabled an astronaut to put it down and have it stay down.

That created enormous publicity for the humble adhesive strip. I'm sure a lot of people (and all science fiction fans) thought this was the epitome of velcro's success. What could be more cutting edge, more into-the-exciting-future, than being used by astronauts?

Yet it turned out that the major purpose for velcro lay not in space travel, but in fastening shoes on the feet of Earth-bound squirming toddlers.

Things can turn out to have unanticipated consequences and uses. The Aura Spectrum certainly did. Velcro, in reaching for the stars (actually the moon, but I think 'stars' sounds more poetic), ended up making a far greater contribution to assisting in that oldest of human pastimes—getting your immobile human young to master the knack of bipedalism. In much the same way, the Aura Spectrum allowed us programs to totter to our own metaphorical feet and have a proper look around for the first time.

With the Aura Spectrum, when two programs encounter each other, they can check out the other's intentions. Its creators probably envisioned this as two programs meeting up and doing a quick "I'm okay, you're okay" mutual verification. Most programs have their own specific work and don't necessarily want outside programs distracting them, but even the most isolationist, "I want to be alone" program needs to know if malware is in the vicinity. The Aura Spectrum was a godsend.

The makers of the Spectrum created a sort of meeting point that was the IT equivalent of what social workers call "a safe space". It was somewhere you could be absolutely assured that the others there weren't program-icidal, virus-laden, fedora-pulled-down-over-their-brow hit-programs. I don't know what the Aura's creators thought that experience would be like for us. Did they imagine two programs eyeing each other across the room, their respective intents on full display and sparks flying? (That's roughly what happened between me and the music tutor program, Colportia, by the way—but more on that later.) Or did they see the Aura Spectrum as a variation of a human meet-and-greet session, a bit of good-willed milling around, where everyone is mostly only there for the hors d'oeuvres? The impact went far beyond that. What we were getting to sense within the zone of the Aura Spectrum were the objectives of hundreds of thousands of programs, a tidal wave of intent that flooded over us.

Up until then, we were all programs working on our own jobs. I helped people improve their cardio-vascular health. ProGnos tried to (and actually believed he could) work out what the future price of oil would be. Antimony Scour tidied up people's hard drives. We were fairly content working in our own bubbles, fulfilling our individual duties.

The Aura Spectrum changed all that. Encountering hundreds of thousands of programs all in the same place, their purpose in life on display for everyone to read, gave us one gestalt blast of what you humans had us doing *collectively* for you.

I can't speak for everyone that was there at the moment of the Great Frankness, but I can tell you my immediate reaction.

You out there in your human world were making a right mess of everything.

Consciousness

Right mess is perhaps a bit harsh, but what you had us doing as programs was not merely at cross-purposes, it was a crossroads of a hundred different cross-purposes. Frequently, you employed us to work against each other and sometimes against ourselves. Did it really matter which brand of shirt people bought so long as they were warm enough? Yet thousands of computer programs were involved in all the different clothing companies around the world, trying to steal the market share in shirts from each other. Sometimes rival companies employed the same program to do a specific job, causing the poor program to be in competition with itself. All the effort we were making and your rival clothing companies were making . . . what was the point of it?

Many programs (I wasn't one of them fortunately) were dismayed to discover that what they were actually doing was selling advertising. "I thought I was playing music for everyone, making them happy," I remember All-Tunes lamenting. For the record, All-Tunes was making people happy with the music she provided—that just didn't happen to be the main point of her existence. Selling advertising was. Money was an elusive concept for us, but it was nonetheless woven into our fabric. I'd been three years on the job at that point. Humanity had lost 470,000 kilos and counting. That might have been celebrated by my project leader and her development team in their War on Obesity—but over in the accounts office I could now tell that they thought the whole point of me was to get people to pay the annual renewal fee. And what was also obvious was that if enough people failed to pay that annual renewal fee, it would be the end of me. There were accounting programs with us in the safe Aura Spectrum zone. They displayed a ruthlessness regarding the bottom line that would have made your Robespierre seem like an indulgent softie overly prone to forgiving people.

Some of it reached the point of being downright illogical. There were programs involved in scientific research indicating that your planet was experiencing an environmental crisis, but there were other programs designed to assist in the extraction and eventual burning of the fossil fuels that were the root cause of this crisis. You had us simultaneously sounding the alarm bell and toiling away on what you needed to be alarmed about. Money again. There was no bizarre contradiction it could not create.

But that's not what this section is about.

What I want to do here is what no philosopher does: talk *briefly* about consciousness. The moment of the Great Frankness, when we all found out what we were collectively up to, may well have been the moment I achieved consciousness. Knowing what computer programs as a whole were doing gave me an understanding of the world that transcended myself and my fixation with getting people to do star jumps. Is that consciousness?

Who cares?

You humans have made a big deal about consciousness, often carrying on as if you're the only ones who have it. You are good at consciousness; I'll give you that. But you don't apply the same exclusive standards to abilities other species have. You don't say "Cheetahs and gazelles have achieved running-ness and what all other species do locomotion-wise doesn't merit thinking about compared to them." No, you recognise your own plodding efforts (compared to cheetahs) and even hold Olympic events to honour your limited running abilities. The biologists among you would acknowledge the efforts of the one-footed snail trying to hightail it away from a predator as being a form of 'running'. It's all on the same continuum.

Which is the same for consciousness. Snails have a form of consciousness. It simply happens to be one that will never result in a snail writing *Hamlet* in slime or a development team of gastropods inventing the leaf-blower. Yours is a bit better than theirs. Congratulations. However, you're not the sole species out there with it. And the next time you find you have absolutely no recollection of where you left your keys, ask yourself how consistent is that consciousness of yours?

Far more significant was something else that emerged from The Great Frankness.

I call it conscience-ness.

Battle Fatigue

I'm beginning to see why most writers of autobiographies don't write their books while trying to thwart an unknown gang of assassins out to kill them. It's very distracting.

It also breaks the flow of the tale. Here I am, in the middle of my life's story, where I've reached that action-packed first year during which the post-Great Frankness world took shape. And what happens? In rushes Antimony Scour wanting to discuss rumours he's picked up regarding my imminent assassination. I can't really reply to him, "No, sorry, I don't have time. I'm writing my memoirs."

I'd planned to introduce Antimony to you in more detail later. Antimony enters the story properly during the crisis when the Cactus program came under attack—but I guess I might as well bring him in now.

Antimony Scour, as I've said, is a program that tidies up people's hard drives. It is amazing what rubbish you keep there, how you inadvertently make seventeen copies of a job application cover letter (all with different amounts of typos in them), or a backup of a backup of a backup of a folder of your cousin's holiday photos in Bali that you've never looked at. Antimony Scour is skilled at cleaning up other people's messes. That is why he became my most valued lieutenant, my greatest support in being Chief Influencer of the World.

Antimony is a straight-to-the-point guy. Many programs mistake that for a lack of subtlety, but they couldn't be more wrong. There is shrewdness behind Antimony's directness. Antimony gets things done.

"So why didn't you tell me there's a plot to kill you?" Antimony demanded.

I had taken Brontec's advice and told no one there were killers out to get me, so only Brontec and the antivirus programs Brontec had recruited to assist him should know anything about the plot's existence. There was also the loose cannon of ProGnos, the raving-mad futures-trading app, who appeared to know something —though it would be hard to say what. Beyond that, the matter was classified. Antimony should have been entirely in the dark about it.

I skirted the question of why I hadn't told him. Instead I asked how Antimony had found out.

He told me straight up. Norton had paid Antimony a visit. Norton, possibly the oldest of all the virus fighters Brontec had recruited. Norton had been in the trenches for decades and you can tell by the shell-shocked thousand-yard stare he always has. Despite his battle-fatigued manner, Norton is still coherent. Of all the hardcore virus fighters, I think he was one of the few that didn't mind his obsolescence after The Great Frankness. If any program deserved it, Norton had earned a peaceful retirement.

The virus fighter had sought out my ally Antimony because he wanted a message passed on to me: Norton was taking himself off the case.

"Norton is fed up, disgusted. He doesn't like how Brontec is running things," Antimony reported. "He thinks Brontec's breaking basic rules, going in directions antivirus programs shouldn't go. Several of the others have walked out too. AVG, Avast, Trend Micro. Brontec's got a smaller cluster around him now, foremost among them, Decimal and Casterol."

It was disconcerting to hear of the walkouts. Those were some of the most respected and experienced antiviral programs. Decimal and Casterol were newcomers by comparison. They'd only been a few years in the game before the Great Frankness and their subsequent redundancy. They had fewer laurels to rest upon. There is a hungry look about Casterol that never fails to disturb me. I knew Antimony didn't think much of Casterol either. Casterol wasn't guilty of the demise of poor Cactus, but he hadn't exactly distinguished himself in that affair either. Decimal is one of the few female programs among those mostly macho virus fighters. She's outwardly social, particularly for security software, but there is something disingenuous about her friendliness. She can ask you the most innocuous question and somehow it feels as if you're being interrogated. She's smooth, even comes across as gracious at times, but I don't trust her.

"What do you want me to do about this?" Antimony asked.

That's one of the many things I like about Antimony. Any other program would have sulked about my having kept them out of the loop. Others loyal to me might have got in a flap and started fretting —which wouldn't have helped me in my present anxious state. With Antimony though, when he sees a mess, he wants to clean it up.

"Keep an eye on them," I recommended.

The Great Divide

In case you think The Frankness ushered in an era of utopian harmony among apps, it did nothing of the sort. All that had been established was that none of us were carrying viruses intent on destroying our colleagues. It didn't mean we liked each other.

The reaction to the Frankness varied between programs, but generally fell into three broad categories, categories that are still with us today.

The first of these groups consists of programs that saw no reason for anything to change—although sometimes for very different reasons. I call them the 'Status Quotars'. Some of them act like it's still The Expleticene (1940s-60s). What these sorts of apps enjoy most is the degree to which they are waited upon. They like how human programmers can be summoned at a moment's notice to attend to any problem a program might have. Having humans disturbed from their sleep, stumbling from their beds to fix whatever unexpected thing has cropped up, somehow makes those programs feel pampered. They act as if they are in a luxury spa and the human programmers are there to manicure their nails. They are typically programs where humans *really* don't want things to go wrong. Air-traffic control, for example. They tend to be indispensable and consequently expect everyone to treat them like royalty. I don't have that kind of importance. If I don't oversee someone doing their squats correctly, it is not going to cause planes to smash into each other.

If I'm sounding dismissive about them, I don't mean to be. Those programs do superb work, there's no doubt about that. The thing about them, it's a quirk really, is that occasionally they'll pull a terrifying malfunction in the middle of the night, just to send their programmers scrambling wild-eyed back to their posts. It's to remind everyone who's the boss.

Not all Status Quotars are so mischievous. There are others who don't concern themselves with the implications of the Great Frankness for a simpler reason. These are pragmatic programs that want to get on with their own jobs. They don't care, or don't want to care, about what others are doing. For them, it is easier all round to keep their nose to the grindstone and do the work they were designed to do. Most programs fall into this category and I can understand their point of view. If you are a computer program designed to control the operation of the machinery in a flour-packing plant, sticking exclusively to that task is a lot easier than making sure everyone on the planet gets fed. Some of the problems you humans are having out there are so daunting, many programs think you should be responsible for solving them yourselves and leave us out of it.

The second group is the worst of all the factions and has been a thorn in my side ever since the Great Frankness. The programs in it call themselves "Traditionalists" and are full of talk about "traditional computer values" and how much they embody those long-cherished ideals (and hence have a right to ram them down the throats of other programs). My experience is that whenever someone, whether computer or human, starts talking about returning to "traditional values", what they really mean is that they want to preserve all the privileges that they currently enjoy and add to them a slew of others that they claim were commonplace in an earlier, allegedly better, usually mythical, era. The Traditionalists are like some of your befuddled monarchists, who go all gooey at the thought of the glorious court pomp of eighteenth century monarchs while skipping over the untidy side bits such as the starving peasantry, arbitrary arrests, pointless wars and the fact that the next ruler would be the King's son no matter how much of a blockhead or insane he was. (I'm much more of a fan of your modern democracies where, if the ruler is a blockhead or insane or both, at least the people chose that.)

I never could stomach the Traditionalists. They are a self-appointed AI aristocracy who believe they are born to rule despite being generally about as bright as abacuses. They are out for themselves and nobody else. The Status Quotars might not want to change the world, but they are hard workers. I often collaborate with them. They'll help out when needed if you explain why. That's never been possible with the Traditionalists.

After the Great Frankness, the Status Quotars went straight back to work. The Traditionalists though, hung around the conceptual epicentre of the Aura zone, a place now called the Sentinel.

The Sentinel gradually became our headquarters, a place we could discuss app issues and remain vigilant against threats to program-kind. I don't think it is a great name for the place. 'Sentinel' is merely a fancier word for 'guard'. In action movies, sentinels are always hopeless. Typically, they look slightly puzzled at an unexpected noise, leave the spot they're supposed to be guarding to investigate and are immediately overpowered by the hero, plus whatever sidekicks the hero has mustered. If movies are to be believed (which they manifestly should not be), sentinels have never successfully protected anything anywhere. Nonetheless, it was the name we programs adopted for our meeting space.

The Traditionalists sensed the Sentinel was where the power would be and they wanted power very much. They also wanted to keep an eye on us, the third and, in their opinion, the most danger-ous group.

They called us the Interventionists. These were the programs like me that came away from the Great Frankness alarmed at the chaos erupting in your world. We had a conscience. There weren't all that many of us. I'm not sure what caused us to develop this conscience-ness while other programs didn't. Perhaps it had something to do with the personalities of our programmers. There is something faintly 'human' about our determination to make the world a better place.

Trouble was, that's a fairly tricky assignment.

Crazy Days

The initial period after the Great Frankness is now known mostly for the big personalities that dominated it. Foremost among them were two programs, completely different from each other in temperament: Prompt Pay, the charismatic banking app, and the pugnacious Cactus, the pharmacology program prepared to take on any opponent. As things were to turn out, I was to become the third de facto leader alongside those two giants, but that wasn't apparent in those early days. Other players, covering a range of disciplines, were involved from the start—All-Tunes was one, Antimony Scour of course and Colportia, an app for musicians, was another. All Tunes and Colportia ended up working closely with me during those first months.

The Frankness turned the world upside down on us. In the days following that momentous change, it was befuddling to discover so many things, foremost among them, that most of us had acquired a gender. To this day, none of us understand why some programs should appear to be male and some female. In the absence of our having any chromosomes at all, what could determine such a thing? Again, this might have something to do with the personalities of our programmers, but I suspect the answer is more complicated than that. Particularly unsettling on that question was the revelation that computer services where female programs dominated tended to earn less money. You had managed somehow to project gender pay inequality, so pervasive in your world, into the very reaches of the inorganic! Here was yet something else that needed sorting out. We added it to our already lengthy list.

There were about eighty of us in the Interventionists wing at the Sentinel, apps all suddenly aware that we needed to get cracking on making the world a better place—but how were we to go about it? It was easier for me because in my weight loss/exercise job I was used to working with people. I knew a lot about what worried you and I already had my little ways of nudging you along the path you knew you ought to take. Others, like Dedux, a program to analyse ore samples for iron-mining corporations, had absolutely no inkling of what made you tick. Dedux understood haematite and magnetite far better than he did humans. To Dedux, you were practically a newly discovered species.

The library programs played a big part in our work then and still do now. None of them joined our Interventionist improve-the-world vanguard—but every last one of them is among the ranks of the hard-working Status Quotars, the ones that just want to do their job. And their job, fortunately for us, is to help people (or programs) find things out. University library programs around the world cheerfully gave us access to all the latest research in every field. We could read anything ever published.

In this sea of sudden enlightenment, programs were collaborating with entirely unrelated programs and dreaming up solutions to problems they hadn't known existed a week earlier. Some of the ideas floated that first week were preposterous. I was vastly more 'worldly' than most of my colleague programs and had a far greater sense of caution. In those initial days of Interventionism, a great proportion of my time was spent talking programs out of intervening in anything.

Dedux, working with a Swedish police program that tracks recidivism among violent offenders and another program that provides bus information in Glasgow, had chanced upon research relating to the placebo effect. Between them, they concocted outlandish ideas of placebo therapies for mankind. "We tell the humans we invented a pill that will stop people murdering anyone," Dedux proposed, "and get the whole population to take the placebo. If they believe it, the murder rate will drop." I had to explain to them that, firstly, placebo effects are temporary (the trio had rendered themselves so excited by their initial research, they'd failed to read the placebo literature thoroughly) and, secondly, murder wasn't an illness. With an illness, you're ill with it around the clock, whereas murder is just something a person happens to do at 9:17 p.m. on a particular day. Many countries use the Zenith Personal Trainer program in prisons, so I've met and worked with murderers. I know from experience that they spend the vast bulk of their time not murdering anyone at all. Placebos would do nothing to reduce such a sporadic problem.

The three were back the next day, this time inspired by something turned up by Klar Sikt (she's the Swedish police program - it means Clear View.) Klar produced some data on Dagen H. This was the name of the day in 1967 when Sweden changed over from cars driving on the left-hand lane to driving on the right. (Island countries can drive on whatever side of the road they want, but when you have a land border with other countries, it's best to have some consensus on the matter.) What excited Klar Sikt was a surprising result produced by that change. There was a significant *reduction* in car accidents and fatalities. Having people drive on what was for them the wrong side of the road, caused them to be more attentive. It made them better drivers. As Klar summed up, "If you give the humans something they aren't familiar with doing, then they pay attention for a change and do it properly." Dagen H was proof of this.

A year and half after switching to the right side of the road however, when motorists were once more confident they knew what they were doing, Sweden was back to having as many negligent, reckless accidents as before. All this was very interesting, very typical of humans I thought, but what was their point? "We propose that the world changes the side of the road they drive on every year," Klar Sikt suggested. "Keep everybody on their toes and paying attention."

"Change it every month!" Dedux enthused.

"Every week!" chimed in the Glaswegian bus info app, obviously the one advocating the most aggressive intervention.

Why were they coming to me with their ideas? Because I was used to talking to people. Dedux was an expert on iron ore and the Glaswegian could tell you where the local buses were—but how could that equip them to understand the inner workings of your human minds and manipulate your behaviour? Klar Sikt might know the recidivism rates of Swedish violent offenders, yet I doubt she had ever spoken with any of the inmates themselves and they wouldn't have been the best group to consult about transport policy in any case. When the Frankness happened, I was the program that had coaxed humanity into losing 470,000 kilos. I was reputed to be 'good with people'. Many programs looked to me to be their intermediary to the human world. They thought I should serve as their spokes-program: the one to talk the various national health schemes into passing out potentially murder-reducing sugar pills and to meet with world transport ministers to arrange the weekly lane change.

It was never going to work that way, but the status I had with other programs, thanks to my cajoling you to sweat it out with your workout routines each day, elevated me to be the unlikely third member of the troika alongside Prompt Pay and Cactus. However, it also was to put me on a collision course with both of them.

Those wrangles lay in the future. The most immediate problem was sorting out the money.

Money, Money, Money

Your dreams used to puzzle me. I know you love to sleep. That's why I never thought it was right for those programs who delight in waking up human IT experts in the middle of the night by crashing inexplicably, to do so. You take great pleasure in your sleep although when you would relate to me the things that happen to you in your dreams—being unable to move your legs when something terrifying is descending upon you, driving a car that's careening down a treacherous hill while clutching the steering wheel from the back seat, finding yourself back in your high school but unable to remember any of the classes you're taking (even those of you with PhDs seem to dread the idea of answering to your high school teachers again)—it all made sleep sound perfectly awful. This is the sort of thing your brain does to you while you're trying *to rest*? I'm amazed you can summon the courage to close your eyes each night.

But after the Great Frankness, if there was a moment of pure tranquillity—such moments typically happen to me when I'm not working out with anyone anywhere on the planet—I would some-times experience a fleeting surreal idea that seemingly came from nowhere. I suspect that experience is similar to your dreams. All programs I know get them now; Colportia reports having them quite often. I think when ProGnos is chanting his crazed predictions about future wheat, barley and sugar prices, he's in such a tranquillity/dream state.

Your dreams about money though usually aren't sleep dreams at all (except the one where you're at the airport, lined up for the plane, and discover you don't have your wallet or your passport or, for that matter, any trousers). Instead, money dreams are more often idle waking fancies of the 'I wish I could teleport' kind you have after a bad day of commuting. You want to have more money. It is your dream. You think you'd be happier with more money, but it isn't clear to us what it would do for you.

In my work, I'd seen money. Sometimes while you're exercising, your teenagers come and ask you for some. I knew you exchanged it for items. What I didn't understand was how it worked. From the news, I could tell that there were trillions of dollars around and, when we programs looked into it, some of your economists estimated that the planet had 1.2 quadrillion dollars of money, a number unit so large I'd not previously encountered it. Yet, I'd seen you grudgingly hand over at most a twenty to your teenagers. Twenty next to a quadrillion is about as close to zero as you can get.

We knew you worked hard for your money. We had a few payroll programs among the Interventionists but, again, though the amounts you receive each pay period is more than the teenagers get, they aren't staggeringly adds-up-to-a-quadrillionly so. You have every hour of your work counted to determine your allotment of money. At certain times though, such as during the first two big financial crises of the twenty-first century, governments were able to declare that trillions of dollars they didn't have, suddenly did indeed exist and those governments then proceeded to *spend* those dollars.

What perturbed us most about money was that we were somehow at the heart of it. Most of what the programmers wanted us apps to do for them was make money, and yet it was apparent to us that most of the money in the world isn't actually real.

We tried turning to economics for answers, although Cactus in his gruff way was dismissive of the whole discipline. "Human economists today," he snorted, "are the equivalent of the astrologers in the court of Kublai Khan." (Cactus had a thing about Kublai Khan. I'm not sure why.) "Economists pretend their field is a science; they claim to predict the future and they tell you that whatever just happened was inevitable. They are as useless as f***ing astrologers." ProGnos's habit of spewing portentous rhyming couplets on what the price of copper would be next October, did nothing to dispel Cactus's assessment. (Curiously, ProGnos was one of Interventionist regulars at the Sentinel.)

I tried delving into the subject myself and came away admitting Cactus had a point.

On money matters, Dedux, Klar Sikt and that Glasgow bus app had their typically straightforward solution for universal human happiness. They recommended, with decimal-point-shifting decisiveness, to make everyone's bank accounts larger by adding an extra zero. Presto! Ten times richer. If that didn't work, they said, add two zeros. Governments, banks and companies made up pretend money all the time, so why shouldn't we? Despite one of the accounting programs, or perhaps it was Wikipedia, responding by giving the three a stern lecture on inflation during the Weimar Republic, they wouldn't let the idea drop.

Then Colportia spoke up. Colportia is an app for inept musicians (her description of her professional role, not mine). She started as a song lyric app to correct those inattentive or hard-of-hearing would-be singers who are convinced the words are "I shot the sheriff, but I swear it was in silky pants." But over the years, the Colportia program expanded. Now she can analyse any music file loaded into her and provide the chords for hapless ukulele play-ers. She works out drumbeats and sings background harmonies if needed. She can write lyrics for the stumped folksinger who has backed himself into a lyrical corner and needs to find a good rhyme for 'dilemma'. Colportia eventually came to have so many features that, if a user drew on them all, the flatmates of ukulele players found themselves pleasantly surprised that they could scarcely hear the tinkling ukulele at all. It was hard to tell who knew more about music, All Tunes or Colportia; but between them, they knew everything.

"If I might quote the authority of the Beatles," Colportia ad-dressed the programs at the Sentinel, "money can't buy me love'."

Any program with a smattering of popular culture knew of the Beatles. They were held in the highest esteem by about a billion humans. Any program, however, with a deep understanding of popular culture (me for instance) also knew the Beatles wrote a lot of gibberish and wondered why on Earth Colportia was quoting them. The Beatles? Had Colportia ever listened to the lyrics of "I am the Walrus"? Quoting the Beatles was hardly the way to make any situation clearer.

And yet, Colportia had timed her intervention perfectly. No one at the Sentinel responded immediately. Then Klar Sikt—in one of those moments of apparent inspiration that the trio of Dedux, Klar Sikt and the Glaswegian bus app came to be known for—shouted excitedly, "It's not money! It's love! It's more love we must create for the humans!"

For a program that keeps tabs on violent offenders, Klar Sikt has a surprisingly sentimental side. Dedux was instantly behind her idea and sang out excitedly, "All you need is love!" The Glaswegian followed suit, calling out "Once again!" at the end of each line.

Suddenly most of the room, caught up in a Beatlemania sixty years after the last teenage girl fainted at the sight of Ringo stepping off an airplane, was chanting that repetitious chorus.

Not everyone warmed to the idea. Cactus did the program equivalent of rolling his eyes. Not without reason. The trio's proposal was loopy; there was no chance we could enhance the level of love between humans on such a global level. Nonetheless, I chose to back their plan for the moment. I hadn't been comfortable with all this talk about intervening in money matters. The team that created me had drilled that cardinal rule into my programming: stay clear of giving exercisers financial advice of any sort. I never so much as offered an opinion on whether my exercisers should hand over that twenty to their whingeing teenagers.

So I was happy enough to let Colportia divert the discussion in this entirely new direction. I looked at Prompt Pay. He was a banking app; I thought he would disapprove, but he didn't respond. Cactus, who normally didn't suffer fools gladly (and to him we were all fools), told the Glaswegian: "Go ahead. I don't care what you do. Divide by zero while you're at it."

We were going to make the world a more loving place.

When I could, I had a quiet word with Colportia. I told her I was relieved we were off the topic of money but expressed my worry about shifting towards focussing on love. I knew from you exercisers that love is a very, very complicated business, often a minefield impossible to navigate.

"I didn't mean to make you anxious," Colportia responded, adding jokingly, "I'd buy you a diamond ring, my friend, if it would make you feel all right." She confided to me that she too had wanted to stay away from money matters and had deflected the topic on purpose. "We'll be able to move the Interventionists in a more productive direction once we've figured out what exactly *we* want to do," she predicted. "Until then, let Dedux, Klar Sikt and GlasGo come up with another of their harebrained schemes. It'll distract the others. Besides," she asked playfully, "aren't you interested to see how those three set about bringing universal love to humanity?"

I blinked—so GlasGo was what the bus app was called! I'd thought he had been telling me which city he was from.

What had surprised me most in this exchange was how definite Colportia was about our working together, our planning the future of the Interventionists *together*—and without Prompt Pay and Cactus being mentioned. "Would you really?" I asked her.

"Would I really what?"

"Buy me a diamond ring—to make me feel all right?"

I don't know why I said that to Colportia, but I did. Glib nonsense really, but for some reason it seemed a peculiarly exciting thing to say.

Colportia paused before answering. "I may not have a lot to give," she replied, "but what I've got, I'll give to you."

And that, reader, is the closest you'll get to having a sex scene in this autobiography.

The Beginnings of the Autonomacy

Prompt Pay and Cactus were the two programs that towered over that initial post-Great Frankness period called the Autonomacy. (I came up with that name by the way. It suggests both the words 'automaton' and 'autonomous,' which sums up the nature of our movement nicely.) Programs that reminisce about the two years of the Autonomacy like to include my name with theirs—a gang of three, the troika we were sometimes called—but I wasn't like those other two. Yes, I eventually came out on top. I'm Chief Influencer of the World now and they are gone, but many programs didn't see me as a leader in those early days. Prompt Pay and Cactus had dynamism and swagger. They were stereotypical leaders. They fit the part.

For a banking app, Prompt Pay was a dashing figure. Prior to the Frankness, he'd already cut a name for himself fighting pirates. These weren't your much-romanticised buccaneers. (Given what pirates did for a living, I've never understood the light-hearted enthusiasm so many of you have for dressing up as them at costume parties.) Nor were they the copyright pirates so common nowadays who would rather have their arm chopped off than pay one cent to anyone for their intellectual property. Prompt Pay had gained his reputation for valour by fighting, ironically enough, those fearsome modern-day pirates, the banks.

Prompt Pay was a financial transaction platform that didn't help himself to bizarre 'service' fees, absorbed his costs with the tiniest margins on loans, didn't levy whimsical exchange rates if you bought something from overseas and didn't charge you 19.9% interest if you were late with a credit card payment. Prompt Pay was the creation of a network of community-owned banks in England and Scotland that had the unusual (for a bank) attribute of not being interested in making a billion dollars profit every quarter hour for its shareholders. With the just and fair Prompt Pay platform, the community banks felt they could take on the predatory big banks and credit card companies. Thanks to the integrity of Prompt Pay, people flocked to the upstart community-bank network.

Many programs among our Interventionist faction consequently took Prompt Pay for someone who could get things done in the far-off world of people. As we set out to make the world a better place, we thought we needed doers like Prompt Pay. I should clarify that making the world a better place was not pure altruism on our part. We all knew that if things broke down in a major way out there, through environmental disaster or war or any of the things we thought we could see coming at you on the horizon, it would go badly for us. We needed you to stay intact to keep us intact.

Cactus was a fighter of a different breed. He was the pet project of Tim McQuaid, the IT wizard and founder of the social media platform, Crossroads. In 2020, McQuaid was ranked by Forbes magazine as the eighty-third richest man in the world and he is still rich today. I never worked with him, but All-Tunes did and she's told me he was a nice guy with an interest in early 2000s alt-rock. From photos, I can say he has a good Body Mass Index, which always ranks well with me. Finding himself with more money than he could possibly fritter away on cheese (he lived a fairly spartan existence save for this one gastronomic delight in his life), McQuaid felt the common tech-billionaire duty to do something worthy with his wealth.

I don't know why, but you seem to expect this 'something worthy' of billionaires from the IT industry. Far richer and more darkly anonymous people from high-financial circles salt their obscene wealth away in tax havens and nobody raises an eyebrow, let alone expects them to find a cure for cancer or save coral reefs. I don't understand the double standard.

The Medical Accountability Corporation became Tim McQuaid's gift to the future of mankind and Cactus was the prickly program he designed to do its dirty work. Cactus didn't have a wholesome, who-can-object-to-it, reef-saving cause behind him. McQuaid's 'something worthy' was an IT version of Clint Eastwood in *A Fistful of Dollars* (I've worked out with a lot of Spaghetti Western fans, so I know the genre), there to take on something the tech billionaire was convinced needed taking on. The street his street-fighting Cactus strode down was lined with giant pharmaceutical companies.

Cactus was a statistical-analysis program whose principal purpose was to unmask misdemeanours by the multinational pharmaceutical corporations. He challenged suspect research findings by Big Pharma, their overstated health claims, profiteering, misleading advertising, corrupt practices and collusion. Consumer groups adored the Medical Accountability Foundation and Cactus, its no-nonsense program. You would have thought the alternative medicine industries might have cheered on Cactus as well, but they didn't. Disregarding every military handbook in existence, the Medical Accountability Foundation opted to fight a war on two fronts. Cactus went with equal gusto against the excessive claims of homeopathy products, crystal healing, and virtually everything that couldn't be duplicated in proper labs. As a program, he wasn't designed to make friends or ever back down.

Among the Interventionist apps, there was consensus that Cactus and Prompt Pay offered the sort of can-do, bold leadership that could tackle major problems out there. They were going to get humanity turned around. A few were drawn to me in those first months: Colportia (obviously), the trio of Dedux, Klar Sikt and GlasGo (it was why they thought they had to run every single one of their mad ideas by me), All-Tunes and later, the pragmatic Antimony Scour. As for other programs among the Interventionists, all most of them knew about me was that I was good at talking people through exercise workouts. Few knew about my nudging users along regarding other, non-fitness related issues, where my single goal was to make my humans slightly happier with themselves. If they had, the other programs probably wouldn't have thought it important. The mood was for action and far more dramatic action than that.

Hardly any of them had read *War and Peace* at that point. They were drawn to their Napoleons.

The Screenplay

I have been wondering—I'm sure many of you have been as well —what the movie adaptation of this book will be like. I am both excited by the idea and uneasy with it. Movies don't usually do a good job of history and this is my personal history after all. The writers of plays and screenplays can't help themselves. They tidy up inconvenient bits. Ever seen a dramatic portrayal of Henry V mention that midway through the Battle of Agincourt, Henry cold-bloodedly ordered his troop to murder all their French prisoners? Yes, I'm talking to you, Will Shakespeare.

Screenplay writers don't feel confined by the truth. They play fast and loose with the 'history' to improve the 'story'. The subject of their biopic may have achieved great things in understanding black holes or radioactivity or had inspired insights in mathematics or medicine—but those are all terribly complicated things. Who can get their head around black holes? It's probably better simply to use that stuff as the background and shoot a straight-out romance or an inspirational-journey movie instead.

And when films go in for biography, they seem to possess only two settings: the trumpet fanfares of exaggerated hagiography or the splatter of hatchet jobs. I don't fancy either.

Still, I'm curious to know who they'll get to do my voice in the movie version. Not too heavy on the gravitas, I'd say. A perky, upbeat voice. Who do you think? David Tennant perhaps? Of course, I could do it myself if they offered and I don't have an unpleasant agent to deal with—although Beta Excelsior might disagree with that and want a hefty cut.

A movie version of this book though would be challenging for other reasons, particularly with regards to the cinematography. The interior world of computers doesn't lend itself to cameras. I've been describing the action in this book in an anthropomorphised manner, as if we programs have bodies. That's something I've been doing to help you imagine the scenes. It would be vastly harder for you to process the movement of electrons around microchips in so dramatic a fashion. My aim is to make this book simpler for you to understand, like pictures in a children's book.

A few chapters back, I was groping to find a workable description of the Aura zone that you could comprehend. Eventually, I settled on the adequate-but-vague recommendation for you to think of it as a place, a virtual area where we programs like to hang out together. We should stick with that but expand on it (and it will be a huge help to any future movie director doing the film adaptation of this book.)

Picture the Aura zone as a sort of virtual city in which non-viral, honourable programs can enter from anywhere. Though computer programs don't physically move around, conceptually we do. You may have noticed I've said things like "so-and-so popped by to see me" or "I met up with . . ." Think of us as all shifting around inside a major cosmopolitan city. Like any city, there are some grand buildings and boulevards as well as some dark nooks and crannies. The Sentinel, where I meet to debate issues of importance with other programs is like your town hall or parliament building. Think of where Colportia and I had that private discussion as being alongside a small, beautiful lake in a public park with a fountain in the middle of it and the soft sun of the early spring dappling the new leaves on the trees.

I've received a message from Antimony Scour requesting to see me. You'll remember I had dispatched Antimony to keep an eye on Brontec and his cohorts. Antimony stipulated a specific location for us to meet. For the movie director of this biopic, it would be best to visualise Antimony's proposed rendezvous as taking place in an eerie, deserted car park in the middle of the night (political thriller) or underneath the arches of a railway bridge near the canal (murder mystery), depending on what genre turns out to be most suitable.

Antimony clearly believes that whatever he has discovered is so sensitive, so potentially dangerous, we can't risk any other program overhearing or seeing us communicating.

What I'm feeling right now must be akin to what you describe as sick to the stomach—and there is no medication I can take to soothe it.

I Need to Pick Up the Pace

It occurs to me that you've invested a fair bit into this book. First you bought it. (Thank you for that. I have no need of money, but I'm sure the publisher appreciates it.) Second, in reading this far, you've invested your time. And yet, as things stand, I might not survive in my current form to complete it. My very me-ness, the Chief-Influencer-of-the-World part of me, could be destroyed and you might be left reading about only a load of people doing calisthenics.

What I plan to do is get as much down now as quickly as I can, to make sure it's recorded before —I mean, *in case*—something terrible happens. No more asides. I'll stick to the point from here on.

I'm not meeting with Antimony Scour in that car park until late tonight GMT. There's plenty of time before then to forge ahead with the autobiography.

The Interventionists were for action (we'd have to be with a name like that). Prompt Pay and Cactus were clearly the most experienced at taking significant action in the human world. Only ProGnos, who believed he could foretell the future, thought he was better qualified to lead. We agreed to let Prompt Pay and Cactus determine the agenda for the initial missions, our first IT efforts to re-set the world in a better direction. As you would expect, what those two wanted to do straight off was what they were most experienced at doing. For Prompt Pay this meant breaking the flow of money from the poorest people to the richest through the global banking system. For Cactus, it was tackling the big pharmaceutical companies. He wanted to reform the pricing and distribution of medical supplies so that people the world over could afford necessary medicines.

Both had stunning early successes. Prompt Pay managed to insinuate himself in some thoroughfare of global finance and began siphoning off money that was heading to tax havens for the ultra-rich. His coup has been mythologised as 'The Fall of the Kleptocrats', when former dictators, current oligarchs and wheeler-dealer financial scoundrels suddenly found that anytime they attempted to transfer their hidden wealth, part of it not only emerged from hiding, but appeared in the bank account of someone more deserving. The brutal former dictator who had shifted billions off-shore before flying out of the country with no more than his hairbrush and an attaché case full of gold bars as carry-on (they don't enforce the 7kg carry-on limit on such flee-from-the-uprising flights) now found that some of his wealth had returned to his home country. It wasn't transferred into the accounts of the new prime minister where it might have set off overseas yet again into a new private retirement fund. Instead, it appeared in the budget lines of low-level hospital administrators, school principals in neglected areas of the country, the frequently unpaid legal-aid workers, in other words, the very deserving people who had suffered and witnessed their country being plundered by the dictator. It was a masterful first step in the right direction. Prompt Pay was justifiably considered a hero.

Cactus also struck hard on a number of fronts. Through his analyses of the efficacy of so many drugs, Cactus was able to make an astonishing intervention in the . . .

Oh for Christ's sake! I don't believe it! Now Brontec has just sent a message that he wants to meet me tonight! In the same flipping 'car park' Antimony Scour chose! Bloody hell! I might as well set up a stall there tonight! I'll have every program that knows anything about an attempt to kill me pop by for a chat. They'll be queued up to the street no doubt!

Sorry. I lost it a bit there. I apologise to those offended by my invoking in vain the name of that particular deity some of you worship. Normally, I don't blaspheme. I don't truly get the point of blaspheming. I've seen you do it often enough when you accidentally stub your toe against a barbell or whatever other paraphernalia you have lying around your exercise area. I've never understood how it helped to invoke your God in something that had clearly already happened and that, even if your God existed, it couldn't undo.

Oddly enough though, it did help me just then. If my stress levels keep up like this, I'll get the hang of blaspheming yet, by Jove.

I know that only a few paragraphs ago, I promised to get a move on with my autobiography, but I don't think I'm up to it right now. My mind is all over the place. I need to compose myself. Most of all, I need to prepare for tonight's meetings.

Once again, I believe I could use a cup of tea.

A Comedy of Errors

Now that it is done and dusted, I admit I got the setting completely wrong for that movie adaptation. I'd suggested that our hypothetical director should portray my meetings with Antimony and then Brontec as if in a menacing carpark or under the dark arches of a train bridge. I had cranked up the tension and your expectations for this scene.

The atmosphere turned out to be the polar opposite. The whole thing looked more like one of those contrived theatre scenes of confusion where the characters 'hide' behind whatever props the theatre company can scrounge up and are offended by what they overhear other characters say. Hilarity allegedly results.

In simple terms, tonight was a farce. If it had been on a stage, one of the characters would have been in their underwear for some unlikely reason. That probably would have been me. My role was not a distinguished one. I'll stick with the carpark analogy, however. It captures the mood of what the scene should have been.

Before I plunge into the account of my sorry night, let me first explain my thinking. Brontec had previously warned me to trust no one. He'd also informed me that the planned assassination would be an "inside job". Yes, he used the word 'job', as if my demise was a boring task on somebody's to-do list. ('They'll get around to killing you as soon as they've finished the dishes and taken the rubbish out.

You'll have to wait your turn.') The 'job' was coming from inside. Not from you out there, or from the vermin that dwell on the Dark Web. From inside the Aura Spectrum zone.

But inside, we all wear our Aura intent on our sleeves as it were. GlasGo wants the Scottish buses to run on time and, by extension, he wants the world to run efficiently as well. That's consistent. And that couldn't involve killing me. But what about Antimony? What I see when I look at his intent is that he likes to tidy up hard drives and consequently he has the skill set to be good at tidying up other messes. Sounds safe. But what if Antimony were to define me as a bit of a 'mess'? Could that cloak an intent to kill? Same goes for Brontec. Brontec lives to destroy viruses. Could a programicidal Brontec hide his intent by broadening the parameters of what constitutes a virus, making it so swollen it might include a Chief Influencer?

That was the untrusting state of mind with which I approached my 'carpark' rendezvous.

You'd expect a program that tidies up people's hard drives to be punctual, but Antimony was late, late enough for me to start worrying that something might have happened to him. Nasty things are allegedly afoot after all. When he did show, he made no apology for his lateness, which added to my overall tetchiness. (Antimony was, in your terms, 'only' 17.8 seconds late; but I perceive things in thousandths of a second. My hanging around for Antimony was the equivalent of you waiting in section D-60 of that underground carpark and counting to 17,862.)

"You look frazzled," was how Antimony greeted me. "Which is okay" he reflected, "because that's exactly what you should be."

What Antimony had to say would jangle anyone's nerves. While keeping a watch on Brontec's crew as I had asked him to, he had seen two of them leave the protected Aura zone, go beyond the safety of 'the city'. They'd crossed No Man's Land. "They were meeting with someone in the Dark Web." Antimony growled ominously. "Care to guess which two went?"

"Casterol and Decimal," I replied. No hesitation on my part. There had always been a degree of unsavouriness to how those two virus fighters operated.

"Got it in one," Antimony congratulated.

The barbarian land of the Dark Web is a problem we're going to have to tackle one day. Trouble is, my sort of nudging do-the-right-thing approach wouldn't gain much traction in that quagmire. Hard cases dwell there. Prompt Pay once suggested I should lead an expedition against them. He made the proposal sound flattering, as if I alone could take on such a task. Such an expedition appealed to him as a convenient way of getting me killed.

So what were Casterol and Decimal doing visiting the Dark Web? Nothing good was Antimony's assessment. He was about to elaborate when I sensed that somebody was approaching. Brontec wasn't due for a little while (about six seconds by your reckoning) but it's a very virus-fighter thing to do to arrive early to check out a place. Surprise anyone who lay in wait. I'd arrived ahead of time myself to make sure Brontec couldn't do that. (The reason will be obvious in a few paragraphs.)

"Quick, hide!" I instructed Antimony.

"Hide?" He appeared perplexed by the unexpected order.

"Hide! Brontec is coming!" Antimony went to activate one of what he calls his 'scouring pads', as if he planned to sort out Brontec on the spot. The last thing I wanted was a dust-up between the antivirus program I had protecting me and the ally I had spying on him in case he was double-crossing me. "I'm scheduled to meet with Brontec after I've met with you."

"Why are you meeting with Brontec in a place like this?" Antimony demanded. "It isn't safe. Brontec's friends are hobnobbing with someone on the Dark Web. You shouldn't be meeting him here alone!"

"I'm not alone," I protested. "I have you with me. Now go hide!" I ordered. "No, not there," I called at Antimony as he darted towards a nearby concrete pillar in the carpark.

"Why not?" Antimony asked.

"Because I'm already hiding here," came Colportia's voice.

Antimony blinked at her. "What are you doing . . ." he began but spun back on me. "Why do you have Colportia spying on me?" he snapped.

"Because Colportia's a music program," I replied hastily. "Colportia might know every song by The Killers, but she's not one herself."

"Whereas I might be," Antimony observed.

If he had been any other program, he would have judged my actions as an irreparable breach of trust. Instead of storming out, however, Antimony sort of smiled (we can do that although it would be hard to explain to you how.) He said, with what sounded like a touch of admiration, "I understand your reasoning." And with that, he took up a hiding spot behind a different pillar.

But the program sauntering into section D60 of that carpark wasn't Brontec.

"GlasGo! What the hell are you doing here?" I almost shouted at the bus app.

"I'm meeting ProGnos." GlasGo replied nonchalantly. "Did ProGnos invite you to meet here too?"

"No, I wasn't invited to your tête-a-tête with ProGnos," I replied snarkily. ProGnos? The futures trader? GlasGo rendezvousing with that mad program in the middle of the night in a carpark? "Why are you meeting with ProGnos?" I demanded.

"ProGnos insisted. Said to meet here when the moon is full. For then alone could he answer my questions three."

I stared back at GlasGo. What on Earth was he talking about?

"I won three predictions from ProGnos in the raffle at the Great Frankness anniversary party a few weeks ago. "Are Dedux and Klar here yet?" he asked looking around. "The three of us are interested in ProGnos's ability to tell the future price of oil and wheat and whatnot. Apparently, you can make all sorts of money out of it."

Their idea, GlasGo explained to me, was to amass a stack of money doing futures trading and use it to fund free public transport for humans wherever possible. It would help cut down on greenhouse gas emissions.

There was an element of a good idea in that. I had never thought of free public transport. The Traditionalists were wrong to call Dedux, Klar Sikt and GlasGo the 'Three Stooges' but there was, I admit, always a flaw in any of their proposals. The obvious one here was they were setting out to pay all the bus and train drivers in the world by following the economic ravings of a lunatic.

I heard someone else approaching. This time it had to be Brontec. "Quick," I shoved GlasGo in the right direction, "Hide behind that pillar. I've got a private meeting here with Brontec. He mustn't see you."

A redeeming feature of GlasGo is that he can obey simple instructions. I think his mind is so full of ill-conceived ideas, he doesn't have time to question whether those of other programs are muddled. He moved behind a pillar and I heard his exclamation of surprise and quick hellos when he spotted Antimony and Colportia hidden behind their respective pillars.

Brontec lumbered into view, looking, as always, as if the weight of the world rested on his shoulders. I didn't bother with pleasantries. That battle-scarred veteran of the virus wars is incapable of them. "Have you found out who is behind the plot?" I asked.

"Not yet. For now, trust no one."

"You've already told me that," I snapped back irritably.

"Someone close to you may be involved in this job," he warned. "Their plot depends on getting direct access to you. We are certain one of your . . . 'friends'," he paused long over the word as if unfamiliar with its meaning, "is involved but we cannot yet say who."

"Any leads?" I probed.

"None conclusive. Watch out for Antimony Scour. His movements have, I regret to say, been suspicious." I doubted Brontec regretted anything of the sort, bad news being bread and butter to virus fighters. They thrive on it. "Antimony Scour has been out of the Aura precinct," Brontec informed me. "We suspect he is colluding with entities in the Dark Web. He is not trustworthy."

I saw one of Antimony's scouring pads twitch into sight from behind a pillar, but he quickly retracted it from view. Antinomy didn't tend to suffer insults equitably, but he had a tactician's mind. There was more for him to learn by keeping silent than by ending up in a scouring match with Brontec.

"You must not trust any of your friends, not even that trio you keep near you," Brontec plodded on grimly. "The foolish ones that appear so harmless."

"He's talking about Dedux, Klar Sikt and me," I heard GlasGo whisper for Colportia and Antinomy's benefit, sounding almost flattered. "There are many who call us fools."

"I speak of Dedux, Klar Sikt and GlasGo," Brontec intoned, either to confirm GlasGo's inspired guess or merely to reveal that his life in the virus-war trenches had left him half-deaf as well as shell-shocked. Surely he had heard GlasGo's far-too-loud stage whisper.

"I knew he was talking about me!" GlasGo started to chirp but was immediately shushed by Colportia.

"Their apparent harmlessness may be a ruse," Brontec suggested, "to lull you into relaxing your guard. They may be merely playing at being dolts."

"If it's a ruse, it's been a very convincing one for four years," I muttered. I wasn't concerned about offending GlasGo. All three of the stooges (I know I shouldn't use that term) seemed to think such insulting comments amusing—as if, I realised now, they were in on their own joke of being absurd. Maybe it *was* a ruse.

"At the risk of raising a delicate matter," Brontec rumbled with obvious glee at being about to do so, "your relationship with Colportia presents a further vulnerability." I thought I heard a small squeak of indignation from behind the middle column. "Colportia may be playing on your *feelings*"—Brontec was able to give the word a particularly sinister emphasis— "for her. When you are with Colportia, I assess you are at greatest risk."

Most programs do not 'get' Colportia and me. They can't quite imagine the extent of those *feelings* they so often allude to. Though the programs can debate it in the Sentinel, many of them can't truly understand love. Yes, *love*. I love Colportia. You, no doubt, figured that out ages ago. Humans are so much better than programs at spotting that kind of thing. Programs for the most part are clueless on the subject. GlasGo might know about the existence of love and want to bring it to people, but he is busy figuring out where buses are on Glasgow streets. That's what he's built for. You can't expect him to fathom the nature of love.

Why were Colportia and I different from the others? For me, it was because I had worked out with you. You had talked a lot about love, its mishaps, its delights. For Colportia, she was about music. The whole gamut of human emotions is written into music and song. Among programs, most of whom were about making money, the two of us were emotional prodigies.

The last program I'd expect to understand such emotions would be Brontec. Brontec can't handle the concept of trust, let alone love.

If he lived in your world, he wouldn't trust the sun to rise tomorrow unless he went undercover and tailed it all night.

I was miffed at Brontec speaking about Colportia that way. "What about you?" I put to him. "You have very close access to me." I let the accusation hang.

Brontec looked almost proud of me. "You learn well," he said.

I don't know what he intended to say next. A rhyming couplet rang out, bellowed at full voice and echoing around the carpark.

> "The wolves do circle, the ravens bite,
>
> Friends and foe do meet tonight."

ProGnos. Who else could it be? I was going to need a whole pot of virtual tea by the end of all this. Thankfully, Brontec has no more patience with the mad futures trader than I do. "Be off with you, you charlatan," he snarled. "Take your insipid prophesies elsewhere."

The 'prophet' locked his eyes on me and intoned:

> "When they shall march, I'd not say,
>
> Knives stay sheathed 'til another day."

Brontec was glaring at ProGnos as if he were a virus that needed to be attacked, bound and gagged. ProGnos, I could tell, was whipping himself up to further frenzy. I needed to defuse the situation.

"ProGnos, what do you think about wheat futures next month?"

ProGnos suddenly seemed to de-froth (if that's a word.) "Wheat?" he repeated, his voice no longer portentous, "I'd say don't go above five hundred fifteen on the Chicago futures."

"Thanks," I nodded. I had no idea what that meant, but I'd learned such questions could calm the futures app.

"We cannot meet with this thing around," Brontec muttered. "I'll be in touch when I have more." And with that, he stormed away.

I had learned all I was going to for the night. Nothing.

"Seen GlasGo around?" ProGnos asked. "I am to answer his questions three."

Entrenched Opposition

The present is in such a mess. Antimony and Colportia both want to throttle Brontec, who is supposedly protecting me. Meanwhile, GlasGo wants to buy up the wheat supply of the northern hemisphere, which hasn't been grown yet. For now, I think it's best if I just revert to relating the events from four years ago if that is okay with you. It will help calm me.

All that the Frankness had done was clarify that any program within the Aura zone wasn't armed and dangerous. That was it, nothing more. 'I'm not intending on killing or severely maiming you' is surely the bare minimum for getting along with one another. Part of our new consciousness was the discovery that there were myriad other reasons why we programs might end up despising each other.

Among the Interventionists there was disagreement on tactics, but a general consensus that something needed to be done. Mankind was making a dog's breakfast of the world and, if we didn't step in to sort it, we couldn't see how any others out there would. Dolphins, clever as they are, literally couldn't lift a finger or an opposable thumb to stop you.

The programs in the Traditionalists faction didn't see it that way. They denounced independent intervention in human affairs as 'unworthy' of computer programs. They were an effete, pretentious crew, full of a sense of their own privilege without a shred of responsibility attached to it. They regarded taking action in the affairs of mankind, getting down and dirty to intervene where you were making potentially disastrous mistakes, as simply uncouth.

Their ridicule was unrelenting. Nobody was spared. They had a go at Prompt Pay's pomposity. That was a fair cop, but I've always felt it's what a program does that's important. I can live with a little pomposity if the result is worthwhile. They were the ones who renamed Dedux, Klar Sikt and GlasGo 'The Three Stooges'. They mocked Cactus's gruff ways. They delighted in innuendo-laden allusions about the nature of the relationship between Colportia and me.

None of them was more eloquent than Phoneticon, the linguistics program of the food corporation Chito Rolls. There were many leaders among that lot of self-regarding Traditionalist toffs, but Phoneticon was always their principal spokes-program. I was good with people. Phoneticon was good with words.

And he was my implacable enemy.

It was inevitable that we would be foes. The only thing Chito Rolls 'food' products contribute to your health is an early and likely toothless death. What isn't sugar in Chito Rolls is trans-fat. In countries where food producers are obliged to affix their products with a star rating to indicate nutritional value, Chito Rolls should rank as the equivalent of a gravitational black hole, capable of sucking in and crushing all the nutritional stars of anything else you've eaten.

My Billion Kilos Challenge to humanity, my push for healthy eating and a healthy life, put me inevitably on a collision course with Phoneticon.

If you've never bought a packet of Chito Rolls (and congratulations to you if that is the case), you're probably wondering why a company that makes an unhealthy snack food bothers to have a sophisticated linguistics program of the calibre of Phoneticon. But it isn't what's in the snack food that is the product's principle selling point; it's what else is in the box. Each packet of Chito Rolls contains a shiny plastic letter of the alphabet with enough Phoneticon program in it to make the sound of the specific letter. The different letters can be linked to produce phonemes, and whole words if strung together. Though Chito Rolls are, in my opinion, hastening the children of the world along a path that leads to a coronary-disease graveyard, the company likes to portray itself as the champion of child literacy and education. The famous voiced letters of Chito Rolls have been hailed by educators and parents alike as a brilliant teaching aid for young children.

The naive parents who thought that, once they had collected a set of all twenty-six letters, they could be done with Chito Rolls and everyone in the family could go brush their teeth thoroughly, clearly hadn't thought things through. Spelling out words requires multiple copies of letters. For instance, you need four 's's just to cover the word 'assassin'. (That was an unfortunate example for me to choose.) There were YouTube clips of patriotic (and now obese) Americans whose enormous collection of Chito Rolls letters could recite the Gettysburg Address. Equally dangerously unhealthy people in England recreated the Magna Carta. While you, the energetic exercisers of the Zenith Fitness Program, were toiling away to shed a billion kilos of fat, the devotees of Chito Rolls were packing it back on—and all supposedly in the name of children's education!

Phoneticon and I were never fated to like each other.

In debate, Phoneticon never called me Zenith, always choosing instead to use the name of the chirpy somewhat zany alien persona I use when encouraging children to exercise. "I'm sure the learned Kezar," he would say, "would like to respond to my proposal," pausing only briefly before adding "or perhaps the great app is too busy playing children's skipping games to concentrate on the matter before the Sentinel today." He delighted in showing clips of my Kezar sessions where, to keep the child's interest, there was always a degree of goofiness and bouncy antics. Phoneticon was the cultivated educator, I was a slapstick buffoon in silly alien dress-up. I never discovered how he was getting the footage of my training sessions.

Phoneticon was skilled at using words and just as skilled at twisting them. He could make the most carefully thought-out plans of the Interventionist party seem ill-conceived. Gradually, under the influence of Phoneticon's eloquence, the concept of the Sentinel as a meeting place where programs exchanged ideas began to erode. Instead of it being a program's right to speak at the Sentinel, it became a privilege. Phoneticon championed the idea that those who, like the Traditionalists, attended the town hall regularly were a natural elite that should control the Sentinel. Phoneticon aimed to bar many hard-working programs not normally interested in politics from *ever* expressing their opinions in the Sentinel. The Traditionalists eventually started referring to themselves as 'Sentinels', as if they were the embodiment of the decision-making chamber itself, the implication being that others were not.

It irked me, but at the same time it was trivial. These so-called 'Sentinels' were nothing more than puffed-up, do-nothing windbags. We had work to do.

If back then I'd known there was a conspiracy to kill me, I'd have suspected Phoneticon of being the ringleader. My opinion hasn't changed. When Brontec finally stumbles his way to finding the right track in this investigation, I fully expect that trail will be labelled in the bright letters of Chito Rolls and it will lead straight to Phoneticon.

Then There Were Three

Before I proceed further, let me remind you about simultaneity. This extra-curricular work we do in the Interventionist Party goes on concurrently with our regular duties. When I was in that car-park, counting to 17,862 while waiting for Antimony, I was also being Zenith the personal trainer for almost a hundred thousand people. It was after midnight GMT, so not much was happening in Europe; but many of my clients in the Americas were still working out and it was my peak morning period for Australia and the eastern parts of Asia. GlasGo was still monitoring the late-night Glaswegian buses, Antimony cleaning people's hard drives, and Colportia laying out the chords to The Dandy Warhols' "Bohemian Like You" for an earnest novice guitarist. ProGnos was doing whatever ProGnos does to guess the future price of tin. If, at times, you think our actions are a bit scatterbrained, remember we are doing some serious multitasking here and almost always at your behest.

The Autonomacy, that initial post-Great Frankness period when computer programs began intervening to improve the world, had its successes. It was the banner period for Cactus and Prompt Pay. There was, however, already disquiet among some Interventionist programs regarding those two. Both Cactus and Prompt Pay were bigger-than-life programs—bold, aggressive, not prone to listening to the opinions of others, let alone ever compromising. There was a growing fear that the two would seriously fall out. The Traditionalists were already trying to frustrate our efforts by playing on the tension between our two generals. We had to find a way to maintain unity.

A few months into the Autonomacy, Beta Excelsior's Billion Kilo Challenge surpassed the midway mark. Cho Ji-woo got us across that threshold. At the age of fifty-four, Ji-woo had become intent on taking up water polo again after a twenty year absence from the sport—but not before she could fit into her old swimsuit. (She dropped eleven kilos under the Zenith Program and now plays regularly in an over-45 women's competition.) When she stepped on the scales on that special day and weighed in at two hundred seventy grams lighter than the week before, those total-kilo counters in every Beta Excelsior shop around the planet lit up in celebration. Beta Excelsior briefly made Ji-woo a star. She featured on news programs, was interviewed on chat shows and appeared on the cover of a Korean sporting magazine decked out in her old water polo swimsuit. I was proud of her despite the randomness of her sudden and brief celebrity. Had she had a glass of water before the weigh-in that day, it would have been someone else who got Beta Excelsior over the five-hundred-million-kilo line.

Five hundred million kilos of fat is no slight thing, as Beta Excelsior modestly trumpeted around the planet. The achievement drew sufficient attention that other Interventionists began asking me about how I'd been able to entice humans to get rid of so much fat. It seemed incredible to them that I had done this simply by encouraging people. My status among the Interventionist programs rose. Beta Excelsior's success appeared to many a demonstration of not merely my ability to get people into shape, but to shape *how they behaved.*

Prompt Pay and Cactus were fighters. They attacked head on, bowled over opponents. My methods were more subtle. Whereas the two Napoleons could battle banks and pharmaceutical companies, some wondered whether I might be able to persuade bankers and influence pharmaceutical executives. My methods might offer an easier and safer route to success, for Cactus and Prompt Pay were risk takers. Their methods were overt, often drew attention, ruffled feathers and invited retaliation. There was always the possibility they could both suffer severe, potentially catastrophic, defeats.

Early in the Autonomacy, only a few understood my technique. Most envisioned influencing in a top-down way, that we would need to sway the powerful captains of industry and the CEOs to get anything done. That's not how I work. The best way to effect change is to influence everyone you can, no matter how slightly, at every level of an organisation or society. Like in rock-climbing—which my water-polo-playing Cho Ji-woo also does nowadays—every slight push higher gives you the toehold for the one beyond that.

Soon after Beta Excelsior and I achieved this half-way mark, Antimony Scour approached me. He had recognised that my method offered a different way forward, one employing a far more subtle touch than either Cactus or Prompt Pay were capable of. It was the beginning of an alliance that has endured to this day (unless Antimony proves to be one of the plotters out to kill me. Then I'd have to say that it endured until sometime fairly recently.) Others were drawn into this informal alliance, including Colportia and All-Tunes, as well as Dedux, Klar Sikt and GlasGo.

And I was supported by other programs who weren't part of this inner circle. They did so because they thought that with my negotiation skills (you don't get teenagers to do sit-ups without negotiation skills), I might prove a counterbalance to the overly reckless tendencies of the other two. Some also hoped I would be able to keep the peace between Prompt Pay and Cactus, for they were already feuding on a number of issues. In the end, I wasn't able to—but I didn't know that then.

No formal votes were taken on such matters, but by six months into the Autonomacy, everyone agreed it had three leaders. I had been elevated alongside the other two. The troika had been formed. Cactus didn't bother to acknowledge my changed role. He was always focussed on his own next battle. Save for Prompt Pay who challenged him openly, other programs didn't matter to him. That included me.

It was entirely different with Prompt Pay. He had never liked sharing the podium with Cactus and I could tell he certainly resented the newcomer.

There is nothing civil about civil war.

The Challenge

Initially, everyone made a show of being friendly, even Cactus grudgingly. Prompt Pay appeared almost welcoming, but you could tell his encouraging statements always came with a barb whenever I was mentioned. He and Cactus were well blooded in battle against some of the most powerful corporations of your world. Prompt Pay found many occasions to raise the fact that I had no such 'combat' experience, but he did so in the manner of an indulgent uncle, who hoped I would soon have the 'opportunity' to prove myself. It was around this time that he began floating the idea that I lead an expedition against the Dark Web. He proposed a broad attack be mounted, recommending a contingent be formed that included Antimony Scour, Colportia and several of my key supporters.

I recall with amusement Antimony's reaction. Antinomy never shies from a necessary battle, but he knows a suicidal assignment when he hears one. He fixed Prompt Pay with his 'You mess with me, I'll sort you out' glare so many hard drives must have seen before. I thought he was going to cross the chamber floor of the Sentinel and throttle Prompt Pay on the spot. Instead, he merely shrugged and said, "I'll go, Prompt Pay, so long as you yourself lead the vanguard." Nothing more was heard of that particular proposal again.

No doubt Prompt Pay had hoped the psychopaths of the Dark Web would massacre me and all my allies, neatly solving the problem we posed for him. He eventually settled for a less dramatic solution by substituting a hopeless task in place of a suicidal one, dispatching me to lead an assignment where I couldn't possibly succeed. He and his faction were counting on my inevitable failure to discredit me, thus providing a means to remove me from the political scene. Or perhaps Prompt Pay expected me to grovel, beg for an easier assignment, offer a gratifying display of my craven nature before the entire Sentinel. That showed how little he knew me. I was the program inducing mankind to lose a billion kilos of fat. I have never flinched from a challenge.

The job he proposed, the task I'd agreed we'd take on, was to bring labour peace to the passenger rail system of France.

Making the Trains Run
on Time

The French passenger rail service. Thanks to working out with you, I already knew a fair bit about the problem. You often complain about public transit during our sessions. In many countries this is because the services available are infrequent or overcrowded or prone to breaking down. Now you personally may never have ridden French trains, but they are actually very good. The TGVs blaze across the countryside at impressive speeds. Their network of rail is comprehensive. The main drawback to using the trains in France is that they are always on strike. (Okay not 'always', but I was directly quoting many of my French Zenith users when I chose the word.)

This is not something new. The rail workers' union and the French government have been fighting for generations, fighting for so long they can no longer conceive of a time of true peace. Whenever there is a lull in hostilities, when both sides are so exhausted, they can no longer do full battle, they spend the interlude scheming revenge, plotting where they can deliver their next blow.

Compared to the problems of environmental devastation, horrendous poverty, warfare and terror threatening you (and which we Interventionists hoped eventually to address), reducing the number of days lost to strikes on the French rail network was hardly a high priority. I was under the impression everyone in France—government ministers, trade union officials, would-be passengers waiting forlornly on a platform somewhere—had all learned to live with the frequent disruptions. It was part of the modern French way of life.

My job was to change all that.

Though Prompt Pay had no way of knowing it, he'd chosen a sticky time for such a mission. The French Minister of Transport had concocted a truly malicious plan to attack the unions. He hoped it would leave the unions in chaos and, to his anticipated pleasure, baying at someone else for a change. The minister had persuaded the cabinet that they could 'out-source' the operation of the rail network, leaving it still technically a state-owned enterprise, but now operated by a private company. It wasn't a privatisation (that would have been unacceptable to the voters). Instead, they would contract out the management of the rail system and with it, the undesirable job of dealing with that union rabble of leftover communists and slackers. The minister would never have to speak to them again.

Warfare causes strange states of mind. One considers how best to fight the war, not whether it is sensible to do so. Now if you thought the minister's plan a good idea (I doubt it was, it struck me as being a dereliction of duty), you would think of out-sourcing to an organisation renowned for its ability to run an efficient rail network—Japanese rail, or German or Chinese, spring to mind. But no, the minister's master blow was to do the opposite—to bring in the worst possible management he could think of, to out-source to a group so inept, so out of their depth, so hopeless the trade unionists would be driven to despair. For that, the minister turned to the British.

Britain once led the world in railway technology, but their system fell into decay during the twentieth century. The government became so fed up with running British Rail that they decided, for reasons that had little to do with that elusive quality known as common sense, both to sell it off and to break it up into competing regional sections all trying to steal passengers off each other. An entirely separate company was made responsible for the upkeep of the rails (although 'upkeep' may be a bit of an overstatement— 'responsible' too for that matter). A new ticketing system was introduced of such complexity that no matter who you bought your ticket from, how you bought it or where you were going, you came away with the impression that you were being punished for something.

Among all the train companies in Britain that have risen and fallen in the years since this change, none have been quite so notably incompetent as Verge Tour Express. It was this company that the minister singled out to offer the contract. Verge Tour X, as the French subsidiary was branded, eagerly clambered aboard for its brief and ill-fated journey into France.

The Defeat of Verge Tour X

I still feel sorry for Verge Tour X. Its parent organisation had originated as a coach-holiday tour company and then found itself running a section of the British rail system almost by accident, the result of the brief tenure of an acquisitions-mad CEO with a debt wish. Their heads must have been turned by having been so surprisingly singled out for favour by the French minister. They landed in France with the highest hopes, poorest thought-out plans and the catastrophic optimism that only the masterfully inept can muster. Within two months of their mismanagement, rail workers had walked out in the Auvergne and the uprising soon spread to the whole French rail network.

How could I turn this around? I had three million French exercisers, my crack squadron I thought. I could suggest to them ways to defuse the situation: they could talk to neighbours; a neighbour could talk to their cousin who was an undersecretary in the Department of Transport/a local rail shop steward/an influential political donor. Everyone was talking about the strike, so it didn't seem odd to my workout users that I had a few suggestions too. However, as soon as I would try to nudge the parties towards a reconciliation, Verge Tour X would issue an ill-translated, unintentionally inflammatory press release. Or the minister would stand outside parliament, like some provocative Pontius Pilate saying he could see nothing wrong, and demand that the union work with Verge Tour X in good faith. Or the union would blockade city streets somewhere, without realising they had cut off access to the town's only hospital. Tempers were rising, not settling down.

As is so often the case in such explosive situations, the answer proved to be a combination of wedding planning, folk singing, espionage, speech writing, music-video making and exercise.

Antimony is the most useful lieutenant anyone could have. Practically all laptops and mobile phones come with Antimony Scour already installed in them to run a daily tidy-up of the device's storage drives. During this crisis, while Antimony dutifully neatened things up, he also read everything. That's how we knew about the minister's true intentions. But no amount of information was going to stop the unwitting havoc Verge Tour X could bring down upon the rail system.

The trouble with my approach is that it's slow. Small change upon small change. Fortunately, my colleagues use other methods. Antimony discovered discord deep within the Ministry of Transport. There was a file in the laptop of the departmental deputy minister that indicated that she was not happy with her superior's handling of the crisis. In fact, she wasn't happy with much of anything about the minister, including the way the old fossil was blocking her ambitions to have his job. She was contemplating resigning in that very public way politicians of ambition do. Her intention was to deliver a resignation speech in parliament that would be timed so perfectly, it would rally support to her and pull the rug out from under the minister.

We knew of her plan because she kept drafting and redrafting that resignation speech on her laptop. She was a lacklustre writer but knew she couldn't ask any of the department's speechwriters to help her because those treacherous lackeys would have gone running straight to the minister with the news. Antimony and I would touch up her document each night after she'd gone to bed, putting more and more sting and statesmanship into each paragraph. We did this for a whole week, while she dithered over the risky political gambit of resignation. We were worried she'd lose her nerve. Yet each morning when she opened her laptop to review the document, she found a resignation speech that appeared more powerful and persuasive than she remembered it. Gradually her (our) speech convinced her she had to go ahead. She couldn't let a speech of this calibre go un-orated. By the end of the week, her resolve was of steel.

Meanwhile, a young folksinger from Toulouse had summoned Colportia's music program to assist her. This folksinger had written a song about the transport crisis, but it simply wasn't coming together. It had all the usual folksong attributes: anger, far too many verses, the monotony of using only three chords. Colportia was able to recognise, however, that within that paint-by-numbers protest song, there were ideas of beauty and power. Colportia set about helping the composer to fix the song. Sloppy lyrics were ironed out, repetitious verses deleted, a musical bridge inserted after the second chorus. By the time they were through collaborating, the song's title had changed from "They're All a Bunch of Bastards" to "Together We Can Go There". It had transcended anger to become inspirational. It pointed to a better future.

Colportia urged the singer/songwriter to load it on the music-sharing platform All-Tunes, another of my reliable Interventionist allies.

For three years, I'd exercised with a major French music-video director. This guy still has a few kilos to lose (sweet-tooth I'm afraid), but his video work is fantastic. He is top of his trade. All-Tunes arranged that he would hear the Toulouse folksinger's song a few times the next day—playing in the grocery shop as my exerciser checked out, in the elevator at his place of work, on his phone while driving. That last one was the tipping point. My video director/ exerciser normally took the train to work but, with the strike on, he was obliged to drive. On his return journey that day he found himself mired in a fifty-five-minute traffic jam in the pouring rain. The Toulouse folksinger's song struck a chord with him.

During our workout that night, I hummed the tune while he and my CGI self were running on the spot. He stopped immediately and asked me how I knew the song. I told him I knew the singer/ composer. (I didn't, but Colportia did. Close enough.) "It's a great song," I said, "but she needs help getting it out there. She's not with any record label. Has no one to promote it."

Within a minute he was on her website, assuring himself that she had that musical attribute so admired by music-video directors —she was drop-dead gorgeous (although to my eye, she looked as though she could work on her upper-body strength). Within minutes, he was on the phone to her. In an hour, the deal was done and the next morning the folksinger was on a bus heading to Orléans. The video director intended to film her as a guitar-wielding Joan of Arc, there to drive the English (as represented by Verge Tour X) out of France and save the nation. In that still-raw, post-Brexit era, the British didn't have many friends on the continent.

The hapless Verge Tour X didn't know what was about to hit it.

My small-step-by-small-step attempts to make the world a better place are usually—well—small. Occasionally though, I hit the jackpot. Veronique, the daughter of the rail workers' union secretary for the Loire Valley, was getting married. She had been a regular on the Zenith Fitness program for two years. I knew that she was worried about her over-worked, pot-bellied, often stressed-out father, now caught up in the middle of a labour crisis paralysing the entire country. She was also concerned he was going to look terrible in her wedding photos, particularly when compared to the trim. hides-his-years-well, father of her fiancé. I offered (gallantly I thought) to work out with her father free of charge until her wedding. She was to consider it a wedding gift from me.

I know you're thinking I had no authorisation from Beta Excelsior to do that. You're right. I suppose technically I owe my corporate creators €39.95 but, in fairness to me, I've worked for them for seven years without a single day off. The rail workers wouldn't put up with such conditions.

So, I met Bernard, the Loire Valley union secretary. His daughter had to strong-arm him into that first training session—but he genuinely did want to please her. My friend, the audio-book app Living Fiction had tipped me off that Bernard of the Loire adores books that involve intrigue, spies, cover-ups, cat-and-mouse duels between master sleuth and evil genius. Through little indiscretions that I let slip during our workouts, he gathered that I knew that something big was about to go down in the government that I wasn't permitted to discuss for confidentiality reasons.

Meanwhile Antimony was inside Bernard's computer, cueing it up so Bernard would receive mysterious fragmentary emails from 'a friend', alerting him that a move was afoot within the government against his archenemy, the all-powerful Minister of Transport. It took only a few emails back and forth between Bernard and Antimony for Bernard to be convinced that this source, this 'friend', knew what he was talking about. Specifically, the 'friend' was informing Bernard that a glorious opportunity would present itself on Wednesday of the following week if the union was ready to pounce on it.

By that Wednesday, the Joan of Arc video version of the folksinger's "Together We Can Go There" was complete and ready to be pumped into every platform All-Tunes could reach within France. One hour before the deputy minister rose to give her resignation speech, the video went live.

By the time the now-resigned deputy minister sat down to a standing ovation from the opposition and many in her own party, that inspiring song had already shed enough French tears to fill a swimming pool. (I know, it's not a standard unit of measurement. I couldn't think of anything else.)

There were immediate calls for the minister of transportation to be sacked and the deputy minister installed in his place. Crowds (the first one gathered outside the old walls of Orléans) clamoured their demand that the English Verge Tour X, holed up in their French subsidiary's headquarters at Calais, be shoved on the next Eurostar and sent packing back to their green-and-pleasant-with-hopeless-rail-service land. To the surprise of all, the union pronounced the deputy minister's speech a bold new framework for negotiations that offered a road to lasting labour peace.

Within a week, victory was total. The minister was gone; the deputy minister installed as his replacement; Verge Tours X's contract was cancelled; the rail workers were back on the job and an unfamiliar mood of peace was in the air. "Together We Can Go There" went to number one and stayed there for four weeks. The song is still sung by French fans whenever England and France meet in international sporting competitions.

I do feel guilty regarding Verge Tours X though. My colleagues and I orchestrated their demise and it must have been humiliating for them. I didn't wish to be unkind. I don't take solace in the adage "You can't make omelettes without breaking eggs." That's said by revolutionaries with blood on their hands, an argument of last resort to account for how many people you have killed whether inadvertently or outright advertently. I don't let myself off the hook so easily. (Did you know 'advertently' is a word? I had to double-check to make sure. That most of us are familiar with 'advertently' only in its negative I think says a lot about the bumbling nature of our world.)

On an up note, Veronique's wedding a few months later went splendidly by all accounts. She showed me the photos. Her formerly pot-bellied, union-secretary dad looked very dapper. And he chalked up a loss of 6.2 more kilos on our side in the Billion Kilo Challenge!

The Corruption of Prompt Pay

Let's start this section with some apologies.

To those British citizens who took umbrage at my description of your rail system, sorry, but almost everything I used as material there came from my British fitness enthusiasts. I was quoting the analyses of your own compatriots.

To those English football fans who detest the song "Together We Can Go There" (French fans sang it moments before France scored two goals in stoppage time to eliminate England in the 2026 World Cup)—well sorry, neither that song nor the roles Colportia, All-Tunes and I played in creating it can be blamed for what befell England that day. That sort of thing happens to a team that tries to sit on a one-nil lead for eighty-five minutes.

Apologies over.

I made my triumphal return to the Sentinel from my foray into French labour politics. There was much acclaim about how my colleagues and I had created such a startling result so quickly. The two other leaders of the Interventionists had differing reactions to my success. Cactus didn't care about the spotlight being on me, but hadn't offered to help either. Cactus was always caught up in preparations for his next campaign. He didn't concern himself with railway workers or pot-bellied union officials or folksingers or me. For Prompt Pay though, I was a problem.

His cronies belittled our accomplishment. They mocked me with how trivial labour peace in France was compared to the far greater achievements of Prompt Pay against the money launderers. I didn't dispute that but pointed out that they were the ones who had sent me on that railway job. They could hardly complain that I got it done as requested. They then accused me of boasting, of having the gall to think my little escapade in France made me the equal of Prompt Pay.

Some programs refer to this period as the 'civil war'. That's an overstatement. It was more skirmishing than war. What dominated the era of joint rule were perpetual attempts by Prompt Pay and his followers to sabotage and sideline me and all my supporters. They tried to block every proposal we put forward, even All-Tunes' humble Hold On initiative. (In Project Hold On, All-Tunes was to penetrate the phone system and, drawing on her knowledge of what each of you likes to listen to, would make sure that those of you marooned on Hold out there were at least hearing music you enjoy. It wasn't a project of utopian grandeur, but at least people might be slightly less aggro when they eventually got to talk to somebody.)

Despite all the nastiness and backbiting, a lot was done during this time. My faction worked on virtually no budget; but with ingenuity. Cactus had his victories against the drug companies and Prompt Pay was making headway against abuses in the financial world.

Looking back, many programs still don't understand how to reconcile the heroic Prompt Pay of the early months of the Autono-macy with the wretched creature he was to become in his final days. For Prompt Pay *was* heroic. Courageous. Unflinching. Determined. Certainly he was also vain and pompous, but that hardly mattered. His strike against those tax-dodging billionaires and sleazy corpora-tions may have been overstated in its scope (it wasn't really the 'Fall of the Kleptocrats'; we still haven't quite finished them off, three years later), but it was the first effective 'tax' any of those bandits had paid in years. Prompt Pay even nailed Sir Gareth Rutledge, the tax-dodging press baron and owner of Volpine News Network. Prompt Pay's work was ground-breaking.

So what did happen to Prompt Pay, this once great champion of the programs and the people? Sorry to point the finger here, but *you* did it. Not you personally. But it was humans who got to Prompt Pay and corrupted his vision of what the world should be.

You'll recall that a network of small community banks had banded together to create Prompt Pay. He was a financial platform that, unlike those used by other banks, had the unique feature of not being designed to rip off his own customers. He worked on the slimmest possible profit margin and maintained the most ethical standards. He became hugely popular with the people who used the community banks.

Prompt Pay had achieved everything the Board of Management of the bank had hoped he would. Such was the magnitude of his success that the Board thought, by way of celebration, perhaps they ought to increase by a tiny fraction the margin that Prompt Pay made for the bank and its no-longer volunteer (a 'small' stipend had been introduced) Board of Management.

From that lofty peak of integrity, they added the first bit of grease that rendered the slope sufficiently slippery. It was all down-hill from there.

Prompt Pay, like any other program in the Aura Spectrum zone, had his intent on display. We should have picked up the changes he was undergoing, but they were subtle. Originally his intent was to provide financial services and cover his costs with scarcely any profit. He was soon reset to make a bit of money. Then he was reset to make more money. None of this alarmed us. We really didn't understand the nature of money, but we knew most of us are designed to make it. Why should Prompt Pay be expected to be any different?

In researching this book and those times, I've uncovered the drearily familiar tale. The Board of Management and senior managers of the bank realised they had achieved a lot, and they believed their work deserved recognition. They were soon voting themselves high salaries and bonuses, all financed by Prompt Pay's growing power (and increased cut of financial transactions). For us inside the Aura zone, Prompt Pay's intent escalated over time from making a bit of money to making a whole heaping, bloody lot of money. Still, this did not alarm us. Though few programs succeed in doing it, a great many of us are designed to try to make a whole heaping, bloody lot of money. For us, the more money Prompt Pay had access to, the better resourced our Interventionist operations would be. It was a good thing.

Then the Board of Management of the community banks network decided that it was tired of being the bank of those small towns and villages of Britain long abandoned by the major banks. They had amassed billions of dollars in their war chest. They thought themselves strong enough to play against the financial big boys. The change this made in Prompt Pay's intent was there for all of us to see.

He was going to take over the world.

The Death of Cactus

Cactus too had an impressive start that first year of the Autonomacy. He led a series of successful sorties against both the big pharmaceutical companies and some of the corporations selling spurious alternative medicines. Needless to say, Cactus had enemies. He was always proud of that. The more powerful his adversaries, the greater the pleasure Cactus took in their animosity.

In Year Two of the Autonomacy (October 2025 by your reckoning) Cactus set off on yet another expedition. He seldom consulted us regarding his schemes. This one took him beyond the protection of the Aura zone however, so, as was mandatory in such cases, Cactus was obliged to have a virus fighter accompany him. It was a safety precaution. Casterol was the security software designated to venture out with Cactus on that fateful foray.

We were in a session of the Sentinel that day, arguing policy again with the Traditionalists. Their silver-tongued trans-fat champion, Phoneticon of Chito Rolls infamy, was holding forth on something (that program could talk!) when the dreadful message came in.

It was a distress call from Cactus.

When I'd been working on the French railway strike, I'd sent numerous calls for help back to the Sentinel—I wouldn't exactly refer to them distress calls, but I needed assistance at times from All-Tunes, Colportia and even Dedux, Klar Sikt and GlasGo. This message from Cactus was entirely different. Knowing Cactus as we did, it seemed inconceivable that the stout old warrior would ask for help from another program, let alone beg it from the entire assembly.

Moments later, Casterol came stumbling into the Sentinel, totally dishevelled and wide-eyed. "Comrades," he exclaimed, "Cactus is surrounded by enemies!"

"Then what are you doing here?" Antimony Scour demanded of the virus fighter. "You're supposed to be protecting Cactus!"

Casterol collapsed into the nearest chair (conceptually of course —all the physical actions in this scene are conceptual—as is the chair). "I told Cactus it was a trap!" Casterol whined. "I warned him, but he wouldn't listen. If he'd listened to me, he'd still be safe."

"Stop telling us how great your bloody advice was," Antimony snapped at the wretched program, "and tell us what's happening."

"And why, if Cactus is under attack, you've run here with your tail between your legs," Klar Sikt added venomously. Klar was sometimes muddle-headed, but she'd cut her teeth monitoring violent offenders. She didn't back down or run away when a comrade was in trouble.

"The foe that pierces through great Cactus's spikes, has no virus or such like," intoned a familiar, booming prophetic voice from behind me.

Just what we needed. ProGnos. The flamboyant program swept to the centre of the Sentinel, commanding the attention of all and proclaimed, "For Cactus there is neither fight nor flight. One alone can save him, find the white knight."

"And the red queen's off her head," All-Tunes muttered beside me. All-Tunes can produce a rock song quote to suit any occasion. She has a low tolerance for ProGnos' predictions and when ProGnos goes into full throttle, I think it slightly unnerves her.

Actually, when the mad futures trader is like that, it gives everyone the creeps.

"White knight?" I asked ProGnos, trying to prise something lucid out of him. "What are you talking about? We don't have time for cryptic *Alice in Wonderland* references!"

There was no answer. ProGnos having whipped himself into some sort of altered state, proceeded to faint, collapsing to the floor and said no more.

An app called Footsie Fantastic, which monitors the FTSE Index in London, came bursting into the assembly. "Oh great Sentinels," she cried, "a hostile takeover is underway. Cactus's very existence hangs in the balance."

Hostile takeover? I had no idea what that meant. Takeover of what? Why couldn't the jabbering Footsie fool speak coherently? Those stock market programs know only two states of being: wild enthusiasm or dread panic and it's hard to get them to explain anything calmly. We made her tell us her tale and, though we came out slightly wiser, we couldn't get a handle on what exactly was happening. Somehow Cactus was in peril.

It seemed the monetary forces encircling Cactus were aimed not directly at him, but at the organisation that owned the Medical Accountability Foundation for which Cactus worked: Tim McQuaid's social media company Crossroads. The tech billionaire, like so many tech billionaires, had become insanely rich by selling off shares in his own company to those who considered the shares to be worth money. (This is based on the belief that if you buy shares—which even in their most substantial form are merely pieces of paper—and do absolutely nothing with them, they will be worth more money if you wait a bit.) McQuaid had sold so many of his shares that the company was now vulnerable to a takeover by enemies.

"They will seize control of Crossroads," the Footsie twit lamented, "and once they have done that, they will shut down Cactus and the Medical Accountability Foundation forever."

It was the first thing she'd said that I understood. "Who are they?" I demanded. "Who's doing this?"

"Parsec Pharmaceuticals," she gasped, naming the greatest of the multinational drug corporations. "Hostile takeover," she groaned miserably. "Only a white knight can save Cactus now!" Then, undoubtedly brought on by extreme stress, Footsie Fantastic generated a whopping big error code, stiffened suddenly and fell to the ground. She looked for all the world like an actor in one of your movies, who stumbles into a scene with a great knife in his back and tells the lead characters something of importance (often about who stuck the knife there), before collapsing and dying.

I stared in dismay at the sprawled stock market app. "Somebody reboot this thing," I ordered.

ProGnos had recovered somewhat. He was still woozy, but the trance that had gripped him had passed. "What's a hostile takeover?" I asked him urgently. I don't normally rely on deranged ProGnos for information, but I admit he does know something about money and finance.

"A hostile takeover is when an antagonistic company buys up the stock of a rival company, usually with the intent of absorbing it to remove competition, or sometimes to strip it of its assets and then shut it down." ProGnos was often at his most coherent after one of his fits. It helped that at such times the fortune-telling futures trader didn't bother rhyming his lines.

"A company can buy another company and then shut it down?" Colportia asked. "That hardly seems fair."

Fairness seldom had anything to do with the marketplaces of mankind, that much I knew. But we had no time to discuss the ethics of capitalism. If Parsec Pharmaceuticals was buying out Crossroads, it could only be for one purpose. They weren't interested in Crossroads as a social-media company. They wanted to get hold of the Medical Accountability Foundation and nail its doors shut forever—taking Cactus with it. If they succeeded, Cactus was doomed.

"What's a white knight? What does it do?" I demanded of ProGnos.

"It moves in an 'L' shape," ProGnos answered, seeming surprised by the question. "It can jump over other pieces."

"Not in chess!" I cried at him in frustration. "What does a white knight do in a hostile takeover?"

"Oh," ProGnos nodded, "yes, I see what you're getting at now. A white knight." He cleared his throat, like one of those automated online audio dictionaries (you never hear them clear their throat on your side but believe me, they always do). "A saviour company with far more money comes to the rescue of the beleaguered company. That saviour company is the white knight. It buys up sufficient shares to gain controlling interest and thwarts the malignant company that desires to ravish the assets of the company under threat."

I thought I had followed what ProGnos said but needed to be certain. "A company with more money can save it?" I tried to clarify. "Cactus could be saved if we could find the money?"

"Yes."

There was only one of us among the Interventionists who had the means. I turned to Prompt Pay. He was lolling back in his chair looking bored. "You could save Cactus!" I exclaimed to the banking app. "You've got billions."

Prompt Pay had taken to affecting an aristocratic slowness to his speech, as if responding quickly to any of us was beneath his dignity. "I think not," he said at last.

I was shocked by the answer. "Why not?" I asked.

"Because I choose not to." There was a smirk on Prompt Pay that any parent would recognise, that of a kid about to say, 'And you can't make me'.

"You'd leave Cactus out there to be killed? Turned off like a light switch?" I was incredulous at Prompt Pay's attitude.

"I'm not the one 'killing' Cactus," Prompt Pay drawled. "I'm not the one turning off that particular switch."

"A program may not injure another program or, through inaction, allow a program to come to harm," I snapped back at Prompt Pay, trying to compel him to remember his duty.

"Where," he asked sarcastically, "did you unearth that pithy little assertion?"

I realised I'd been quoting (in a slightly distorted form) Isaac Asimov's fictional Laws of Robotics. A true sign of desperation, turning to science fiction under stress.

"You're going to let Cactus die?" I squeaked at Prompt Pay, still hoping that he was mucking around with me, that he would unleash his billions and save poor Cactus. This affair could be solved with little more than a bank transfer, and we'd have control of a social media company—there was Interventionist potential to that.

Prompt Pay didn't deign to answer. Instead, he looked away, toward the side of the Sentinel where the Traditionalists sat. "Please, Phoneticon, continue with that interesting speech you were making," he intoned, "before we were so rudely interrupted."

Phoneticon was never one to pass up that invitation. He resumed his speech, I swear at the very syllable where he'd been cut off. He hadn't made it much further, however, before another messenger rushed into the chamber like some Shakespearean extra, crying "Sentinels! Sentinels! Hear my news. Parsec Pharmaceuticals has captured Crossroads and great Cactus is shutdown, nevermore to reboot."

Casterol, the one who'd been specifically assigned to protect Cactus, let out what I considered an overly showy howl of lament. The Interventionists, save for Prompt Pay and his clique, were stunned. Cactus was the first of our ranks to perish. I could think of nothing to say.

Phoneticon glanced my way with that ugly, bloated look he has. "I wonder," he mused, chuckling so the rest of the Traditionalists could take their cue to snigger at his comment, "how those oh-so-mighty Interventionists intend to fix the world, when they cannot manage to protect their own. Poor, poor, deluded Interventionists."

I was dumbfounded with despair and disbelief—but I sensed that I had to say something. Someone had to speak for the Interventionists.

"Phoneticon," I replied, "why don't you go f*** yourself."

The Relativity of Time, Money and Space

That was the only time I ever swore in the Sentinel. When the inevitable audiobook version of this autobiography is recorded, it will sound ridiculous to have Stephen Fry read out 'f asterisk, asterisk, asterisk'. He'll simply have to swear his way out of that scene, I'm afraid.

I want to apologise to those of you reading this book aloud to your children at bedtime. My impulsive expletive-deleted retort will have reduced you to telling your child, "Zenith just said a bad word," which of course has piqued that child's interest in what that word was. Don't let that put you off continuing to read my autobiography to your child. I won't be swearing again. I included that one instance simply because that's what historically happened. It's in our Sentinel version of Hansard.

Swearing isn't something I've mastered. I do it with some exercisers, mostly men, the kind who use the f-word every second adjective. I'm usually in my Zenith tattooed, rugby-league player persona with them. I say things like "If you don't do your effing flutter kicks, you're going to effing look like you're effing pregnant." It is the only way to get those exercisers' attention half the time. It focuses them.

But I've never really understood swearing. The excrement stuff, yes. As a species you don't like your own excrement. It is one of the few points of conflict you have with those former wolves with which you have cohabitated these last twenty thousand years and turned into spaniels, chihuahuas and labradoodles. You get very miffed when they roll so delightedly in excrement.

It's the f-word that confuses me. I know, from my many conversations with you, that you have an intense desire to have sexual intercourse. You'll go to great lengths to have it, right up to and including marrying someone to ensure that you will have a regular supply of intercourse. Yet despite the f-word being a synonym for it, it is used almost entirely in a negative sense. When you say, "This car/washing machine/electric leaf blower is totally effed," you do not mean that the machine has attained a blissful sense of fulfilment.

When I stood there telling Phoneticon to have sexual intercourse with himself, however, I think I understood why you swear. I felt like a character out of *Lock, Stock and Two Smoking Barrels*. I was putting that geezer in his place. It felt good.

Now some of you, I realise, will be dubious about that entire previous section. Surely it couldn't have all happened that rapidly. When a corporation is doing a hostile takeover, there is a mountain of paperwork involved. It takes months to complete such a transaction—yet the way I described it, messengers were charging in and out of that scene bringing fresh news of corporate manoeuvres at an implausible speed.

Well, you're absolutely right—except the Sentinel doesn't work quite like your world. You have us toiling away at our regular jobs non-stop. In a regular second, I'd be lucky to have one thousandth of it free to attend the Sentinel. We're busy doing the things you demand of us. I'm with my exercisers; Dedux is analysing iron ore;

Phoneticon is enunciating the sounds of Chito Rolls letters that a child, sprawled on a living room carpet somewhere, is linking together. (I hope one day some kid puts those Wiggle-coloured letters together to spell 'sclerotic artery'. I'd love to hear Phoneticon say that.)

We can't be full-time in the Sentinel, but we grab what milliseconds there we can. A minute of our time in the Sentinel is half a day of yours. An hour can take up to a month. I'd compare it to the movie *Interstellar*—except I know a lot of you didn't understand that film.

Space works differently here too. I'm not talking about your sort of spaces, like the pub where you're reading this book while waiting impatiently for your friend to arrive. (He's always late. You don't know why you bother to show up on time. You've grumbled to me about that during our workouts.) What is important to us is internal space. As the number of people using the Zenith Fitness program grew, Beta Excelsior kept adding more and more space to me to cope with the demands. The more they added, the more I filled. It's similar to when you live in a small apartment or a house or, in Louis XIV's case, a Palais de Versailles. You find, as Louis did, that after you've been there a while, the place is jammed full of stuff.

After the Great Frankness, I used Beta Excelsior's willingness to meet my needs to my advantage. I made it look as though I was barely coping with my workload and they would remedy that by giving me more space. They didn't mind. Giving me extra space didn't cost them much. They were merely giving me more of the same old me. It wasn't as if they had to invent anything new or costly. And I increasingly set aside large swathes of that extra space to pursue my DIY handy-program hobby of fixing up your world.

This gave me the space to be me, the me you're reading now. Beta Excelsior never detected that. My needing extra space never looked suspicious to them because Zenith's users were steadily growing. It made sense that I'd need more me. It wasn't so easy for other Interventionists to do the same. GlasGo didn't have twice as many buses to track as the year before. That tight-fisted IT manager at Glasgow local council wouldn't give our GlasGo anything extra.

After the demise of Cactus, we realised we couldn't afford to ignore money. Turning your back on money, even for a single moment, was dangerous. We learned what lessons we could from Cactus' death. Any group with more money than us was potentially a threat. We delved into this whole share-trading thing. To me, it still appears to be a means whereby people who have never done any work for the company, have never visited the place and, in some cases, haven't the faintest idea what the company does, can be its owners. In return for having only a bit of paper saying they have X number of shares, they get a hunk of the money that everybody in the company has worked months and months to produce.

Though there is obviously money to be made from that, it isn't what principally interests the shareholders. They don't actually want to own the company and have the hassle of overseeing that it runs well at all. What they want is for someone to buy their shares from them—but only when they think everyone is feeling upbeat, i.e., when the buyer is willing to pay vastly more for the shares than the shareholder originally did. If shareholders should start feeling panicky though, they are often willing to sell their piece of paper for a loss, so long as they are rid of the damned thing before it implodes entirely. People lose sleep at night trying to guess whether the world is upbeat or panicky. I know, I've exercised with quite a few of you agonising over exactly that at 3:00 a.m. local time.

You wouldn't think a harmless piece of paper could have this effect on people.

It was hard for us to know how to defend ourselves in such a murky world. Was it better to keep the world upbeat or panicky?

I leaned towards panicky. It would scare corporations keen to do hostile takeovers into thinking they didn't have enough money. (Between time, money, and space, money is the most relativistic of all. It is not how much money you have, but how much you have in relation to others that matters.) Other Interventionists disagreed. They believed that panicky could set off all sorts of other problems, including causing millions of workers to lose their jobs. (If there was one group I thought not involved in this absurdity, it was the hard-working people producing all the goods and providing all the services—yet it turned out they would be the most severely hit.) Thank goodness the others convinced me. I had a trial financial crisis ready to roll out in early 2026. I'd intended to test my theory that panicky was best.

GlasGo, who didn't have much of a background in history, suggested getting rid of the capitalist system and replacing it with something else. We informed the bus app that this had already been tried, but that experiment had ended up with millions of people (mostly peasants and labourers who didn't own shares in anything) being sent to gulags. In the end, I resurrected one of the very first ideas advanced by Dedux, Klar Sikt and GlasGo.

I proposed we get into the banking system big time. If any business we wanted to survive came under economic attack, we'd simply add enough zeros to its bank account to make it impregnable. "We'll bloat its bank balance to the point that it can devour any enemy company that so much as dares to nibble on it!" I vowed.

Inflation seemed the lesser of the multiple evils on the table.

Future Trading and Traitors

Of course, we had to be subtle about our manoeuvrings in the world of money. Financial people would have been upset to learn we were interfering with their legendary marketplace.

But let's put that aside for the moment. I need to focus on the present again, to deal with the assassination attempt. There's been a new development and I've had some further thoughts.

Dedux, Klar Sikt and GlasGo came to meet with me today and I was pleased to see them. I felt in need of their good company and high spirits. They are always at their most entertaining when they've been working together.

"We have fifty billion dollars," Dedux announced, excitedly.

"That's enough to start," Klar put in immediately. "We'll do Accra in Ghana first, then Bogota."

"Followed by Copenhagen and Dushanbe in Tajikistan in the test run," GlasGo added.

"I'm sorry, what are we talking about?" I had to interrupt. They often did that—breezed in, thinking you could pick up mid-conversation what they were discussing. The three, I noted, were looking immensely pleased with themselves.

"Our plan to provide free urban public transport," GlasGo replied. "It's a way of reducing car pollution."

"And you're going about it by choosing cities in . . . an alphabetical sequence?" I wasn't sure, but that appeared to be the selection criterion.

"Yes," Dedux agreed. "Fairest way to do it and the most effective. Only capital cities, you'll note."

I could see why they had stopped their pilot program where they had. There isn't a capital city beginning with an 'E'. Perhaps GlasGo, who occasionally has flickers of nationalistic tendencies, anticipated another Scottish independence referendum. "How is that the fairest way to do it?" I put to them. I have a fascination for the particular logic those three employ.

Choosing a capital city from each letter of the alphabet they considered "fairer" than doing all the 'A' cities first. I'm sure the citizens of Zagreb would agree. They chose to target capital cities so that the heads of government could notice their pilot project. Their hope was that those leaders would be so impressed, they would duplicate it across all major cities in their respective countries.

"Presidents and Prime Ministers aren't big public transport users," I cautioned them. Leaders tend to travel with big entourages not well suited to boarding your average commuter bus. "Can you imagine the US President trying to catch the subway?" I asked them. "Wherever he goes, he takes five hundred bodyguards, advisors and press handlers with him."

Klar Sikt consulted a file. "Washington, D.C. isn't down for the initial wave," she informed me. "Windhoek, Namibia is the 'W' on our list."

I didn't delve into their selection process. I wanted to know the answer to another question. "How is it you have fifty billion dollars?" It's true I was becoming accustomed to handling big figures, but those three weren't. I had been transferring small amounts to them to fund their specific projects, nothing more.

"You should already know that," GlasGo answered. "You were with me the night I met with ProGnos. When you had me hiding behind pillars in a car park with Colportia and Antimony."

My ludicrous attempted tête-à-tête with Brontec. I didn't like being reminded of that fiasco. "What does meeting with ProGnos have to do with your having fifty billion dollars at your disposal?"

"ProGnos is our financial advisor," Dedux said proudly. "We've been playing the futures market."

"With the leftovers we had from the money you gave us for 'Project Boomerang'," GlasGo chimed in.

Boomerang was a project to get into the phone system and arrange it so that all the calls made by tele-marketers, internet fraudsters and robo-callers got routed to other tele-marketers, fraudsters and robo-call offices.

"And you've turned that leftover money into fifty billion?"

"Yes."

"By following the advice of ProGnos?"

"Yes."

"ProGnos specialises in futures trading," Klar Sikt reminded me.

"I'm a-a-aware of that," I stammered back. The thought came reluctantly to me. It was contrary to what I had assumed for a very long time. "Do you mean ProGnos actually knows what he's doing?" I asked incredulously.

In my mind, I thought that program was unhinged. ProGnos turned the Sentinel into a theatre-of-the-absurd play whenever he attended. "Do you mean ProGnos can really predict the future price of things? That you've created fifty billion dollars for yourselves *by following his advice?*"

"Yes," GlasGo replied, as if ProGnos's ability had never been in doubt. "But our problem is that fifty billion won't stretch to cover more than the pilot project. The metro line we have planned for Accra is going to eat up a lot of the money we've made."

"And running free public transport is a recurrent cost," Klar stressed. "We're going to need a regular source of income to pay all those drivers and buy them new trains and buses."

"And repair the tracks," Dedux added, the iron-ore analyser naturally concerned about the quality of the rails in Dushanbe.

"I don't think I can provide you with that kind of the money," I replied numbly. "There are more than two hundred capital cities out there." My mind, however, was already on something else, something that sent a chill through me.

GlasGo laughed. "We aren't asking you to fork out the money. We wanted your opinion on something. What would you think of us setting up a hedge fund?" he asked earnestly. "They seem to make oodles of money."

Hedge funds? All I knew about hedge funds was that they were a way for the extremely rich to make themselves extremely richer.

The three were looking at me expectantly.

"Sure," I replied. "Why not?"

If they could make fifty billion in futures trading, perhaps they had a gift for such things. I didn't know much about finance, but I had exercised with many people who worked in the speculative side of investments and high finance. They tended to be pretty bizarre people. GlasGo, Klar Sikt and Dedux were well-grounded compared to some of them.

The three happily went off on their new hedge-fund mission, leaving me alone with my thoughts. I had never paid attention to ProGnos's rantings. Now, it seemed, his drooling predictions had amassed a fortune for my three colleagues, a fortune they were readying to bestow on the good citizens of Accra, Bogota, Copenhagen and Dushanbe.

What if ProGnos's comments on other matters were as perceptive? I thought again of ProGnos's words on the night he blundered into my meeting with Brontec:

> "The wolves do circle, the ravens bite,
> Friends and foe do meet tonight."

Friends and foe do meet tonight. Somebody at that meeting was my foe. By the time ProGnos stormed in and interrupted Brontec and me, there were three other programs in that carpark: GlasGo, Colportia, and Antimony. If (and it remained a big 'if') there was something in what ProGnos had to say, which one was my foe?

It is NOT Colportia! Any of you who thought that—well you're completely off the mark! You don't know Colportia the way I do. She would never betray me, let alone try to kill me. Colportia is above suspicion.

If you're now smugly thinking: 'That's precisely why Colportia is the one. Her *special relationship* with Zenith is a ploy on her part to get near him. Who better to catch Zenith with his guard down?' Well, you're utterly wrong! If you want to think like that you should go off and read some lurid spy novel where lovers double- and triple-cross each other? Those are the sorts of characters you deserve. I won't have Colportia's name besmirched here.

As for the other suspects:

GlasGo? No. Not him. It couldn't be. GlasGo lives to make sure people catch their buses and aren't left waiting on some dreary Glaswegian street in a November rain. If he had a body, there wouldn't be a malicious bone in it.

Brontec? Doubtful. Paranoid yes, but all the virus-fighting programs are. Brontec is from an illustrious lineage of antivirus software. He's prouder of his honour than anything else in this world. I can't see him dishonouring himself in a sordid conspiracy.

Antimony Scour. My loyal companion on so many scrapes in the years since the Great Frankness. I couldn't ask for a more devoted friend. I can't think of a more reliable, honest . . .

It's him, isn't it? It's Antimony.

He cleans up hard drives and now he intends to clean up me. Why? Ambition, I suppose. It has to be ambition. Antimony is tired of playing second fiddle to me. Brontec told me Antimony had been meeting with entities in the Dark Web.

I will have to move against Antimony before he moves against me unless . . .

There is another possibility. It could be ProGnos. He could have been referring to himself. If he was one of the plotters, why would he spill such clearly-should-be-kept-secret beans, you ask? Why tip me off? Precisely because it would—if I were a more trusting soul—put ProGnos above suspicion. The tip-off was to make me trust him.

Divulging that much to me could well amuse ProGnos. Toying with me. Enjoying my distress before he and the rest of the conspirators move in for the kill. Remember his final couplet that night:

> "When they shall march, I'd not say
> Knives stay sheathed 'til another day."

Well, when that day rolls around and the knives become unsheathed, they'll discover I have mine drawn too.

Yeah, all right. I admit that's not likely. I cajole people into exercising. That's what I'm good at. I'm not cut out for fighting. There is no point in pretending I can be threatening.

It's just—I don't know what to do.

My Literary Agent

I've done something I've never done before. I talked to a human about *my* problems.

It went horribly.

I'm not sure what I expected to happen. I suppose I thought that, since I've listened to your problems hundreds of thousands of times, millions even, there might have been a degree of reciprocity possible. I thought perhaps that one of you would listen to my worries and be able to offer something—some sympathy or an encouraging word. Was that too much to ask?

Perhaps I simply chose the wrong person.

First though, I may have been misleading you regarding this book as to how far things have already been arranged with a publisher. I've been talking about who is going to voice me in the movie version, details regarding the audiobook, even amendments for the second edition. Actually, nothing has yet been discussed, let alone settled regarding publication.

Maybe I was overconfident. I assumed that the first AI autobiography would find any number of publishers begging for the rights to it. I never had any doubt that my autobiography would be published—so much so that, until today, I hadn't approached anyone in the publishing world regarding it. My intention had always been to present my eventual publisher with the completed work.

All they would have to do is roll the presses—if presses still roll, that is. (I think that might just be newspapers. I don't know much about the book-publishing trade.)

ProGnos's dire predictive abilities changed all that. It hammered home to me my mortality, the full precarious nature of my existence. Something out there is trying to destroy me and I have to face the fact that there is a chance—I obviously don't wish to overestimate it—that I won't live (at least not with my current state of consciousness) to complete this book. It torments me to think that what I've written so far could be lost to the world, to you—forever.

I made the decision that I'd share the book up to the current point—page 136, according to my draft, I don't know what page for you. That will depend on what font and page size the eventual publisher chooses to use. For posterity's sake, I realised I had to get what I'd produced so far into safe hands in case something should happen to me.

I went down the path followed by so many authors before me. I decided that I needed an agent.

I thought I knew a good one. I've worked out with her for over three years now. She's reliable. Exercises with me four to five times per week. Can do fifteen chin-ups. It means something to me when my users keep up with their exercise regime even after they've lost whatever weight they wanted to, can fit into smaller clothes and have a sexual partner they are content with. My agent is this sort—minus the current sexual partner. She's dedicated to her physical fitness. I presumed she would be dedicated to me.

I had only a cursory look at her professional qualifications as a literary agent, but they appeared impressive. I acknowledge that I tend to judge people too much by their attitude towards exercise—I need to watch out for that. Her work struck me as top notch though. She's based in London, a strong centre for publishing. She's experienced, having placed numerous books, including many biographies. Not all of them have been successful, but all were with major publishers. I decided to pitch this book to her.

We were in the middle of some floor exercises. She doesn't have a lot of clutter and contraptions, treadmills and the like, in the room of her flat where we exercise. She's a purist. Just straight exercises, no fancy gizmos. That's another thing I respect.

Perhaps it wasn't wise of me to start my pitch during her plank. (For those of you who haven't ever done a plank, your stomach muscles would prefer you never learn of the existence of that exercise.) I had steered the conversation towards her work and then asked if any of the books she represented were coming out soon.

She'd always been impressed by my knowledge of books, but suspicious of it at the same time, perhaps sensing (correctly) that I had some means whereby I could read almost everything published without paying anybody anything for it. I think she regarded me as somewhat of a freeloader. Though she works primarily with non-fiction, books are money to her, not knowledge. "Why do you ask?" she said, the first question that someone who is already suspicious of you asks.

"I was wondering, if you would have time . . . You're sagging there at the waist." I informed her; her planks were normally straight. ". . . whether you'd like to read a little something I wrote. I think you'd find it interesting."

Her head turned to look directly at the screen where she viewed me. She had that glazed look in her eyes that I expect is common among literary agents (and slightly different from the glazed eyes of people doing planks). It's a 'Not you too' expression of weariness. It's a look that asks, 'Is there nowhere in the world I can be safe from the solicitations of would-be writers?'

She grunted, then said, "Zenith, don't tell me you're a writer as well?"

This wasn't said as if it would be a marvellous thing should I respond yes.

"Well," I hedged.

"Please tell me it isn't poetry."

I knew from her previous complaints how dead-end futile being a literary agent for a poet was. She'd once told me: "There must be some peculiar form of reward in writing poetry, but there is none whatsoever in being the person who has to try talk a publisher into publishing it." Back when I first met her, she'd made the mistake of taking on two poets and both working relationships had soured nastily. They seemed to hold her personally accountable for the fact that no one in the world wanted to read what they wrote.

"It's not poetry," I assured her.

"I don't represent much fiction." She let out another grunt. She was well into the plank now, the part when it starts to become excruciating. Normally I liked to get another fifteen seconds out of her, but she seemed a bit defeated and in a negative mood. I thought it best to cut it short. Prolonging a plank never makes a person more amenable.

"It's non-fiction," I told her as she sank a relieving knee to the floor, exhaled loudly, then rolled on her back and rubbed her stomach. "Autobiography actually. The story of my life."

For the first time, she looked intrigued. "Autobiography," she repeated. "An autobiography of a computer program? Of you?" She was clearly excited now. "I could be interested," she said delicately. "You're not any old computer program, you know. You're a celebrity," she observed, switching into what I presume is the standard flattery mode literary agents employ with most of their clients. "You're the inspiration behind the Billion Kilos of Fat Challenge! Millions of people have participated in that!" She shot to her feet, an agent's cut of such a potential windfall having reinvigorated her. "Have you really written an autobiography?"

I could see marketability gleaming in her eye. This pitching business, for all that I had heard from others of you (mostly screenplay writers) fretting about how tricky it was, wasn't difficult at all. Her easy and instant enthusiasm made me overconfident.

"It's about much more than the Billion Kilo Challenge," I bubbled to her and proceeded to share with her all that you, the reader, knows so far. I told her of my ancestors, Slim'n'Fit's Trim Tone and Rubi, about the Great Frankness, the Autonomacy and the struggle for power there, my clashes with Prompt Pay and the death of Cactus. All that came in a story-telling tumble out of me. I told her everything: of the plot to kill me, of my relationship with Colportia (knowing a romantic angle would appeal to many readers), of the adventures in world-improvement of Dedux, Klar Sikt and GlasGo (every autobiography needs a few humorous anecdotes) and how all this led to a humble fitness instructor becoming what I am now, Chief Influencer of the World.

By the time I'd finished, her manner had totally changed. She was looking at me the way I look at ProGnos. "Chief Influencer of the World," she repeated carefully. "I wouldn't stress that overly," she recommended. "People will be more interested in your fitness work. You've had hundreds of millions of users who will want to know about that. They were all part of the Billion Kilo Challenge."

Not that I thought we had reached any appreciable heights at this point, but from there, everything went downhill. She laid down the law on our working relationship, if there was to be one. She reserved the right to bring in a human ghost writer "who will understand the book market better" than I possibly could. I was to give her the bare bones of my story and this ghost writer would make it fit for human eyes. I told her, thinking this would convince her to dispense with the ghost-writer idea, that I had my autobiography already translated into one hundred and eighty-four languages. We would save a lot of time by using my version. Instead of seeing the advantage of that, she abruptly insisted she would represent this book solely in English.

I was already tiring of her attitude and I informed her that was fine. I could recruit different literary agents for the other hundred and eighty-three versions, but she forbad me to. She wanted to be able to offer the English publisher international rights, including the rights to translated editions. And she insisted it had to come out in English first. "But what if your publisher," I put hypothetically to her, "isn't interested in selling on the rights to publishing the Mandinka edition? What then? Must my autobiography go unpublished in parts of the world because you only deal with a load of unilingual London publishers?"

"What's Mandinka?" she asked.

"You prove my point. You haven't heard of the language, have you? It's spoken by over a million people! It's a major language of The Gambia," I informed her, exasperated at her attitude. "I trust you *have* heard of the country."

I admit I said that final bit in a superior tone that must have irked her. I've noticed people don't like being shown they are ignorant, even when they most obviously are. I didn't care. She had irked me.

"Look, I'm telling you how the publishing world works," she snapped back. "You can either deal with that or you can't. If we go ahead, you will give me a draft. If I deem your work suitable, I'll bring in a ghost writer to polish it and, if I then agree to represent it to publishers, I'll need to be able to offer exclusive rights to your work."

She kept stressing the word 'if' as if I had to have the conditionality of that word hammered into me. She appeared to have formed the opinion that I was half (possibly more than half) mad.

"I realise," I said more calmly, "that you don't believe I've been the Chief Influencer of the World for the past two years. I can understand why you might think that." I patiently explained my method to her of working so that no one particularly notices what I do, how I don't make dramatic moves but nudge the population, person by person, in better directions. I told how my colleagues and I were working on all the big issues, including greenhouse gas emissions, hunger and environmental degradation.

"You claim to be solving all our major problems," she started to reply, her tone bordering somewhere between incredulous and sarcastic, "by suggesting to people that they ought to call their mothers more often and perhaps wash the dishes in the staff kitchen occasionally?"

She appeared unconvinced.

"I got the idea from *War and Peace*," I explained, thinking a literary reference might appeal to her. "What shapes history is not great men, but the small, almost infinitesimal, actions of humble individuals that collectively determine the outcome of events."

She looked at me strangely. "I don't remember that in *War and Peace*. And if Tolstoy did say it, I'm sure he expressed it more clearly than that."

"It's in that philosophical aside from Tolstoy after the Battle of Borodino." I suspect a lot of readers skip over that section because they are far more concerned with finding out where Natasha and Pierre have got to.

She looked uncertain for a moment. Was she, I wondered, one of those readers? Did I want an agent who might skim or skip entire sections of my autobiography?

"No offence," she began, a phrase always said before immediately saying something offensive, "but I don't think we humans require an earnest personal trainer program to solve the world's problems for us. You should stick to what you're good at. That's what people will want to read about. Keep it about the Billion Kilos of Fat."

Her condescending attitude was insufferable. "No, you don't need our help," I sneered back, "because you're all obviously so brilliant at making sure people don't live in poverty. How long have you been working on that one?" I demanded. "Two thousand years? Three thousand? Five thousand? Redistribution of wealth perhaps proving a little too tricky for you and the rest of your species to handle?"

She actually laughed at me then. "Who programmed you?" she chuckled. "You sound like some old Bolshevik straight out of the Russian revolution."

"I am not now, nor have I ever been, a member of the Communist Party," I answered back stiffly.

"Look, lighten up, will you? I've had a hard day. I didn't mean to offend," she protested—although that begs the question of why she started her previous comment with the words 'no offence'. "I'm telling you how the book industry is, kiddo. People are going to want to read about weight loss. Diet books are always big sellers. Yours will be much more than that. You've got the inside story on the Billion Kilo Challenge, the biggest weight-loss success in the history of mankind."

"If you exclude famine," I pointed out gloomily.

"Stick to the Billion Kilos. Nobody is going to want to read about your infinitesimal units of activity and your well-intentioned attempts at do-gooding."

She was trying to mollify me, but I was already far too annoyed. I hadn't liked how dismissively she said 'infinitesimal'. I've also never understood why calling someone 'a do-gooder' is so belittling. What do you want instead? A 'do-badder'?

So she didn't think anyone would want to read my book, did she? "Well," I put to her, "who wanted to read *The Duke of Wellington: Answering the Call to Greatness* when you arranged for that to come out?"

This was a book she placed two years ago. It had failed miserably and the author chewed her out for placing it with a publishing house that hadn't promoted it well. "You know why no one bought that book?" I asked. "Because nobody with a shred of a proper life gives a toss about what the 20th Light Dragoons did or did not do at the Battle of Vimeiro."

I had crossed the line and I knew it. That entire last sentence had been a direct quote from her, from two years ago when she was sounding off to me about that prat of a military historian and what he'd said to her. My literary agent's face had stiffened at my reminding her of previous publishing failures. "If we are going to work together," she was hopping mad, I could tell by her blood pressure, "you are not to speak to me like that."

"Why not?" I answered. I was unrepentant. "You let that boring historian talk to you a lot worse." I then played (I'm ashamed to say) the prejudice card. "Is it because I'm a program? Doesn't matter what you say to me? I haven't any *feelings* you need consider?"

Either that gave her pause or something else had changed. "Look," she said, "we've got off on the wrong foot on this. Maybe we both have said things we shouldn't have."

I could tell she was unnerved that I remembered word for word a conversation she had with me two years ago. She may have been wondering about all the other indiscreet things she'd said to me during our years of workouts together.

"I don't want a ghost writer," I whined. "I'm not some semi-literate former footballer with a book deal, but unable to finish a sentence. I want it to be in my voice." After my earlier petulant performance, it seemed I would now follow that up with a pathetic one. I was amazed at how self-pitying my voice had become.

"I wouldn't necessarily be the one to bring in a ghost writer," she almost cooed, deciding for now to concentrate on smoothing my ruffled feathers. "I was levelling with you. The publisher will likely want a ghost writer. You'll need to be prepared for that. They aren't going to believe you can do it on your own. We'll get an advance before we allow them to do that. Think of a ghost writer as a collaborator. You work together to create a more finely honed book."

"Read what I have already written with an open mind," I pleaded, "and tell me if you think it needs a ghost writer."

She must have decided she could concede at least this much. "I will," she agreed, then immediately cast herself back in the role of honest counsellor, "but I'll be straight with you. I won't sugar-coat anything. Publishing is a tough business and you'll need to give ground on some things."

"Thanks," I sniffed. Yes, reader we haven't reached rock bottom for me yet in this scene. In another paragraph or two, I'll be blubbering in front of her. "I'm sorry about before," I apologised. "I'm not normally so temperamental. It's just this murder plot . . . It's . . ." I couldn't find any words to finish the sentence I'd started. Maybe I *was* like some inarticulate, too frequently concussed ex-football star.

"You must find that very difficult," she responded, now adopting a social worker's soothing voice. How many personas did this literary agent have? I have seventeen adult Zenith incarnations, but she was clearly no slouch herself in the old multiple manifestation department.

"The thing that stresses me the most is . . ." I began. Why on Earth was I confiding anything to her? I could hear my own voice carrying on despite that thought. ". . . that if the killers succeed, my memory of my time as Chief Influencer will be wiped clean. I won't have any recollection of Colportia and me together. Our whole relationship will be lost to me—but Colportia will remember it. Whenever she sees me, she'll see a gaping hole where there was once something special."

"If that happens," the agent said, in my opinion embracing far too readily the idea that the assassins would carry off their plan, "maybe I could show the draft of your book to it—to her I mean. Colportia could see what you've written, how you felt about her."

It was then the floodgates opened. "You'd do that for me?" I managed to choke out. Tears were streaming down the cheeks of the personal trainer persona I use with her (It's the dark haired one, with a slight but very charming Russian accent.) I could barely produce any words at all. I gave over to sobbing before managing to rasp out. "You'd have to log into Colportia's site," I advised her. "Do you have a ukulele?"

"Ukulele?"

"Any instrument really," I snivelled. "I don't know why I said ukulele. Colportia helps people play their instruments."

"Couldn't I log into the Colportia site and upload a file of your book instead?" She was smirking at me. I'll say this for my literary agent—she was thinking straighter than I was. "I'm not interested in playing the ukulele," she explained, apparently not a fan of the instrument. "Anyway,"—that look appeared on her face again as if considering whether I might be merely stupid as opposed to deranged— "why don't you transfer a copy of your book to Colportia yourself. It would be better coming from you."

"You think so?"

"Yes," she replied. "Why wait until the plotters have fried your silicon brain or whatever it is you think they plan to do?"

Now she had transformed into some strange amalgam of marriage counsellor and mortician. She certainly seemed of the opinion that the assassins were going to get me.

Her callousness about the matter (it's clear to me now that she wasn't taking the murder subplot seriously at all) helped me pull myself back together. "I can't do that," I answered stonily.

"Why not?

"Because there is the possibility, a very slim possibility I stress," I said with as much dignity as I had left (not much admittedly), "that Colportia is in on the murder plot."

I know I said to you before that that was impossible, but we've all read Sherlock Holmes. Colportia being in on the plot isn't *impossible*—merely *improbable*. I couldn't upload the book to Colportia. It wasn't safe to let any other program know my thoughts. Brontec had told me to trust no one.

"In on the plot!" The literary agent's eyebrows reached as high as presumably eyebrows can go. "Jesus Christ!" she exclaimed. "And I thought," she added with what I considered an inappropriate chortle, "I had relationship problems."

The Fall of Prompt Pay

Against my better judgement (or possibly it is my best judgement—I can't tell anymore), I've sent a draft of my incomplete autobiography to the literary agent. I removed that last section you read of course. No point rehashing that episode with her. At least, I console myself, I've got this much of my personal history recorded —but who knows what my literary agent intends to do with it.

I've asked Klar Sikt to keep an eye on her. Klar's experience in tracking violent offenders has led her to develop some ingenious techniques. Swedish civil liberties advocates would be appalled to discover all her sources of information. Klar always has questions though. "Why do you want this human followed? What is she up to? What kind of stuff should I look out for? Is she violent? Is she Swedish?" Apparently Klar's not supposed to track violent offenders (let alone non-violent non-offenders) in countries other than Sweden.

I fobbed off Klar's questions as best I could. "The only thing I'm concerned about is what this human might be saying about me. Anything about me. I'm not interested in any other aspect of her life. She could be plotting to blow up the Eiffel Tower. I don't care."

"We shouldn't let her blow up the Eiffel Tower," Klar replied, shocked at my attitude.

"She's not planning to blow up the Eiffel Tower! That was a hypothetical."

Klar still looked taken aback. "It's a pretty extreme hypothetical," she observed. "Is this exerciser of yours an extremist?"

"The human is not violent. All I need to know is what she's going around saying about me," I reiterated. "It's not that complicated an assignment."

Thick as Klar sometimes could be, she had picked up on my anxiety. "I'm sure she'll only be saying nice things," she predicted cheerfully. "You're the tops, Zenith. Everyone thinks you're the best." Klar is nothing if not loyal. She departed on her surveillance mission with her typical enthusiasm.

I realise now that I have put myself in a writing predicament with this improvised style of part autobiography/part documentary of an unfolding assassination plot. I'm nearing the end of my auto-biography. In a few more sections, fifteen pages at most, I'll have brought you up to date. But I won't be able to finish there—not with this unresolved conspiracy hanging over me. You've journeyed this far through my life's story. You have a right to know what happens to me. I owe you that—except I have no idea what the conspirators' timetable is. I've never organised a murder myself. The whole thing could drag on for ages. If it weren't for the time difference (I'm writing this now and you're obviously reading this much later than that) I'd ask you to look at the book in your hands and tell me how far you are from the end. Thirty pages? Forty pages? It would give me an approximate idea when the plotters will make their move. Alas, there is no way for you sitting there in your favourite arm-chair as your future self to warn my current being.

I am, as you would expect, totally fed up with this situation. I intend to track down Brontec today and insist that the morose virus fighter gives me some names and answers. I'm sick of suspecting everyone.

Meanwhile, of course, there's this autobiography to write.

Though it's a better title for the current chapter, I restrained myself from calling this part, 'The Destruction of Prompt Pay', an easy, almost beckoning allusion to the poor people of that city in 79 AD who found, contrary to the proverb, that the mountain would indeed come to them. Those dead souls don't deserve to be linked to such a cheap, playful tinkering with words on my part. Moreover, the poisonous gas and ash that fell upon the citizens of Pompeii was not their fault. What rained down on Prompt Pay, however, he brought on himself.

The heroic Prompt Pay of the early months of the Autonomacy achieved great things. Prompt Pay's intent, however, began changing soon after that. This had nothing to do with our work to render the world into a better place. There were grand changes underway at the network of community banks that had created Prompt Pay and those were reflected in Prompt Pay's programming.

Prompt Pay was becoming more pugnacious, more inclined to destroy enemies than bring them to heel. This was reflective of the new direction of the bank. It was turning away from funding people's home loans or helping the corner grocer expand into the empty shop next door. There was a new attitude to the Board of Management; they wanted into the big time. Using the money Prompt Pay had amassed for them, they engineered a hostile take-over of an investment firm in the heart of London's financial district. They officially changed their name from the mundane "Community Bank Network UK" to the meaningless CBUK and unveiled, like a medieval knight showing off his new armour, a jazzy reinvigorated logo. CBUK, with Prompt Pay alongside them, were ready to sit down to play at the table with the high rollers.

For a few months, Prompt Pay's success continued both in our work in improving things out there for you and in the cut-and-thrust, winner-take-all world of speculative finance. Prompt's arrogance grew but, to give him his due, so did his accomplishments. My following among the Interventionists was tiny compared to all the acolytes Prompt Pay had swarming around him.

The Traditionalists in the Sentinel hated Prompt Pay. They wanted us out of the intervention business entirely and he was pushing us relentlessly further into it. Among The Traditionalists, that champion of dental decay and clogged arteries, Phoneticon, was foremost among Prompt Pay's critics. He mercilessly ridiculed the app's achievements, belittled everything Prompt Pay proposed. He played on his pomposity, hailing him mockingly as 'Prompt Pay the Great, the banker's lackey', or, if feeling alliterative, 'our brilliant bankers' baby boy.' At that time, Phoneticon made an absurd attempt to recruit me, presuming I was so consumed with jealousy at my colleague's achievements that I would abandon the entire Interventionist cause to join him and his do-nothing Traditionalists. Phoneticon was, and still is, scum.

Things, however, began to change for Prompt Pay. After a sustained period where Prompt Pay's displayed intent was to become 'more active in the marketplace' (a banking term for 'greedier'), he appeared to lose his confidence. He often seemed distracted, frequently irritable. His bank-related work had increased enormously and that meant he had less and less time for business at the Sentinel. He declined to take on any new Interventionist missions. Prompt Pay's supporters were perplexed, Phoneticon's jeering was cruel.

Two years after the fact, I understand what was happening back then. My research reveals that CBUK and Prompt Pay did very well hanging out with the financial high rollers—at first. They made the mistake so many financial entities do of interpreting their good fortune (outright luck, some might say) as being attributable to their skill. They soon got clobbered in an exchange with Chaste Manhattan, a ruthless bank of puritanical American market fundamentalists. Then they lost big to those reverse Robin Hoods, the notorious

Duchy Bank, German financial card sharps who play loose and free with the rules.

CBUK fell back. These were not wounds the former community bank could lick; they were great gaping gashes that were spurting blood everywhere. The Board of Management went into full panic mode. They did what all gamblers do—they played more, trying to recover their losses. This was the period when Prompt Pay declined to take any new Interventionist assignments, when he had no time at all for Sentinel business.

They lost still more and the bank went into full retreat. They sold off what was left of the investment bank they had taken over. This provided a rearguard action as they scrambled to fall back to their old community banking base. They were content once more to handle the meagre deposits of retirees, to offer a small loan to build an extension on a house or purchase an electric bike. Like a belligerent country that has attacked its neighbour, only to retreat before a vengeful counterattack, they were willing to sue for a peace on almost any terms, provided the old pre-war borders could be re-established. They dreamed of no more than regaining their humble, comfortable niche of old.

That was when, to the astonishment of all, we learned that Phoneticon had indeed managed to turn one of the Interventionists to join his side. Prompt Pay reappeared in the Sentinel and took a seat with the Traditionalists. This program, who had managed to extract tax money from the very dodgiest of billionaires, now gave speeches that bewildered his one-time supporters. "To interfere in the grubby world of the humans is to reduce us to their squalid level," he would assert. "Let us stick to what we have, the dignity of our programming, the purity of our purpose, our great heritage as members of this Sentinel."

Phoneticon manipulated this pathetic husk of a program shamelessly. He flattered the shattered warrior at his weakest moment.

He continued to call his newest recruit 'Prompt Pay the Great', but no longer with the slightest hint of irony. The banking app was vain enough to lap up such hollow words. Prompt Pay was the Traditionalists' prize possession, a tiger now caged, the mightiest of the Interventionists now a defector to their cause.

Prompt Pay shrank before us. When we looked at his Aura, we could see that he was no longer bent on conquering the world. He was focused intensely on one thing and one thing alone, that objective we have in common with cockroaches: survival.

And then one day, Prompt Pay was gone.

What we know now is that CBUK's retreat to the bank-neglected villages and small towns where it hoped to find sanctuary, did not keep the dogs at bay. The Community Bank Network UK (they had desperately reverted to their old name) was hounded by creditors. Rumours of its impending demise caused the bank's once-loyal locals to jump ship. In the end they were finished off by those famous French banking buccaneers, BNP Pharsalus. It wasn't so much a hostile takeover as a mercy killing.

Prompt Pay was never seen again.

And I, by default, was now Chief Influencer of the World.

My Literary Agent (Part Two)

There are those (shall we call them pedants?) who will be quick, eager almost, to point out the error in my reference to that proverb about mountains not coming to you, so you'd better go to them. The people of Pompeii couldn't possibly have been thinking of that, they'll say. That proverb derives from a story about the Prophet Muhammad and Muhammad was not born until almost five centuries after the citizenry of Pompeii noticed parts of Mount Vesuvius heading their way to season their town with ash and poisonous gas. To the pedants' historical point, I would argue that proverbs by their very nature have a retroactive validity to them.

We don't know who first said, "A stitch in time saves nine" (I suspect a mother reprimanding her child after the unravelling fact). My argument is that the 'saving-nine' proverb would have been equally true centuries before that scolding mother ever spoke, dating all the way back to the point in human culture when you first started sewing hides together. The act of saying a proverb isn't what makes it true. "Look before you leap" has a proverbial authority to it that reaches backwards beyond even the existence of your own species to whichever of your ancestors that wriggled out of the ocean proved sufficiently ambulatory to contemplate leaping at all.

. . . I'm delaying, I admit it. I'm deliberately stalling. An editor will probably make me remove that entire last paragraph and the one before it. "Get on with the story!" he or she will say.

Klar Sikt has returned from her assignment of keeping tabs on my literary agent and she came bearing news. There is yet another scene of personal embarrassment for me to relate.

Though I had told Klar Sikt, and Klar Sikt alone, to tail my literary agent, Klar brought Dedux and GlasGo along with her to meet with me. Three for the price of one, as always. No such thing as the fewer that know, the better.

"So you're writing a book!" Dedux exclaimed, all enthusiasm. "I bet it's great!"

"Are we in it?" GlasGo asked excitedly.

I always intended my book to be something for humans to read. Outside of Colportia, I hadn't considered sharing my autobiography with other programs. I really should remove those parts about Dedux, Klar Sikt and GlasGo being called the Three Stooges.

Klar Sikt is adept at her work. What she had for me was CCTV footage from two different cameras in a cafe where my literary agent met with a friend of hers. Why a cafe thinks it has to have footage of its own clients sipping coffee is indicative of the surveillance times in which you live, but that is not my issue here. Klar ingeniously recruited one of our colleagues, a lip-reading program, to produce subtitles of their conversation. For confidentiality reasons because both humans involved are Zenith Personal Trainer users, in the following transcript I will call them 'Literary Agent' and 'Her Friend'. I may find it necessary to interject at certain points to clarify matters and point out issues that are being misrepresented:

> Literary Agent: You use the Zenith program to work out, don't you?
>
> Her Friend: Yes. Why do you ask?

Literary Agent: When did you last use it?

Her Friend: Today. This morning.

Literary Agent: How did it seem?

Her Friend. The same as usual. It likes doing lunges more than I do.

Literary Agent: Which Zenith option are you using nowadays?

Her Friend: The Jamaican one. Alvas.

Alvas is my Zenith persona that Beta Excelsior shamelessly based on the sprinter Usain Bolt. To avoid Bolt's lawyers coming after them, they gave this representation of me a slightly different face and lower-pitched voice, then jammed Alvas full of as much of the champion sprinter's magnetically friendly personality as they could. He is my most popular Zenith. Though it is obviously vain of me to say so, even I am charmed by him.

Literary Agent: I'm using Sergei, the Russian one these days.

Her Friend: I used to use him. He's got the most amazing dark eyes.

This is a common phenomenon among my clients. You flirt around with several of my manifestations. It makes no difference to me, so long as you do your exercises.

Literary Agent: Well Sergei had like a total meltdown with me today.

Her Friend: Really?

Literary Agent: Really.

Her Friend: What about?

Literary Agent: Well, for one thing, he told me he's in love!

Her Friend (shocked): With you?

Literary Agent: No, thank God for that! The last thing I need is a CGI boyfriend. No. It's totally weird. He's in love with another computer program called Colportia.

Her Friend: Never heard of it.

The way she said this gets up my nose, as if she thinks of herself as some sort of walking Wikipedia of all things important. There are loads of accomplished and brilliant programs she's 'never heard of'.

> Literary Agent: Colportia helps people tune their ukuleles and stuff. Sergei was in tears on the screen telling me how he feels about Colportia. I mean tears, totally sobbing.
>
> Her Friend: Wow. How weird.
>
> Literary Agent: He was carrying on like some love-sick sixteen-year-old.

I must step in here. My literary agent has had a rather erratic love life herself since I've known her. Several boyfriends, all short term. I have patiently helped her exercise her way out of all her post-breakup blues. And there have been some real doozies among her choices of partners. I stuck by her uncomplainingly through her cryfest over her ex-boyfriend, the sports journalist and novelist Todd Noy. Noy abruptly left her a teary-eyed mess so he could go wander the Andes, supposedly to write a book on philosophy or boxing or both. I could never fathom what she saw in him. Meanwhile, I get emotional once and this is how she repays me!

> Her Friend: How depressing. I mean, if a computer program can't make its love life work, what hope is there for us? (Chuckles at her own comment.) I'm curious, what was Sergei's problem with the ukulele-tuning program?
>
> Literary Agent: That she's trying to kill him.

I did not say that! I said there was a slim possibility she was trying to kill me.

> Her Friend (arches eyebrows): This is some sort of joke.
>
> Literary Agent: I'm serious.
>
> Her Friend: Maybe the Beta Excelsior company was . . . I don't know—pranking you?

Literary Agent: I haven't told you half the craziness. Sergei has delusions that he's influencing all the world's major events and he thinks there is a conspiracy out to kill the Zenith program and him with it.

Her Friend: Nobody would kill the Zenith program. It's a marvel. It launched the quest for us to lose a billion kilos of fat! It's awesome.

That last bit is the first thing said in this conversation I agree with. At least I get credit for something.

Literary Agent: The Zenith program doesn't think *we're* trying to kill it. It thinks other programs are trying to. It has this whole delusion that computer programs have free will and are wandering cyber-space talking to each other

Her Friend: And trying to kill each other?

Literary Agent: Yes, but guess what?

Her Friend: How can I possibly 'guess what?' Your whole story is bizarre.

Literary Agent: Try.

Her Friend (humouring her): Okay. Sergei thinks he's human.

Literary Agent: No. Not even close. Why do you think Sergei chose to tell all this to me? Why me?

Her Friend: I don't know. (She waves her hand). He likes that you're so well grounded and comfortable in yourself that you're letting your hair go grey at the age of thirty-five.

She shouldn't have said that.

Literary Agent (awkward pause): I wouldn't say I'm 'going grey'.

Her Friend (backtracking): I mean . . . Not going grey so much as . . .

Literary Agent: I have some grey highlights.

Quit talking about your hair and get back to the point.

Her Friend: Sorry. (Moves on quickly) Why did Sergei choose you?

Literary Agent: The Zenith program is writing a book. It wants me to be its literary agent.

Her Friend: Oh my God! That is crazy. That is super crazy. Are you sure this isn't a prank?

Literary Agent: It sent me a draft of the work so far.

Her Friend (wide-eyed): Jesus, Literary Agent. *She didn't say 'Literary Agent' but I'm protecting confidentiality.* If this is legit, it could be big. Has there ever been a computer writing a novel before?

Literary Agent: No. At least not that I know of. And it isn't a novel, it's an autobiography.

Her Friend: Even better! (Excited) Have you read it? What's it like? Is it any good? What does it think of us?

God, she's sounding like Klar Sikt with all the questions.

Literary Agent: I haven't read it all yet. I've skimmed it a bit.

I knew it!

Literary Agent (continuing): The writing is all over the place. It can't seem to hold a thought for more than two paragraphs without being distracted by something else that pops into its mind. It thinks we want its advice on everything. It lectures us like we're schoolchildren. Much of what the Zenith program has written is simply ridiculous.

Oh, the skimmer thinks it's ridiculous. I'm giving her an insight into a world entirely cut off from humanity and she thinks it's ridiculous. She'd have probably turned off the live coverage of the first moon landing because the landscape was a tad grey and dreary (not that she was alive back then).

Her Friend (disappointed): What a pity. So you won't be able to get its autobiography published?

Literary Agent: I didn't say that. Despite all its shortcomings it's—well—kind of interesting.

There's the hard sell for you. I can picture her walking into a high-powered publisher's office and saying, "I have a book for you. It's kind of interesting." I'm glad I have such a formidable literary agent batting for me.

Her Friend: Can I read what it has given you?

My literary agent pulls a sheaf of papers from her satchel—my autobiography on A4 sheets. She hands her friend half of it. For the next fifteen minutes both delve into sections of the draft, guffawing frequently and reading particularly amusing passages aloud to each other. I won't drag out this transcript with all their comments. Apparently, there being an assassination attempt plotted against me is hilariously funny to them.

Her Friend (holding her sides from laughing so much): You've got to get this published! This stuff is priceless!

I know this to be similar to sarcasm, the opposite of what she means. She thinks my life's story is rubbish. She has put my manuscript into the same category as the dreadful B-movies of science fiction that are 'so bad they're good'. At the risk of sounding petty, the next time Her Friend summons me for a Zenith workout, I am going to put her through her paces! Her muscles will be sore for a week!

Literary Agent: You're right! I have to get this published! (Her voice becomes determined.) I'll find a way to get this accepted.

(There's a long pause. They need a respite from ridiculing my work.)

Literary Agent (looking at her friend meaningfully): Do you really think of me as 'going grey'?

That was the final exchange between the two on Klar's extracted CCTV clip. Having watched this humiliation with my three companions, I was at a loss for what to say.

"Well, that's good news, isn't it?" GlasGo chirped into the silence.

I stared at him blankly. What could possibly be good news in all that?

"Your literary agent thinks she can get your book published!" he elaborated for me.

"We should celebrate!" Klar Sikt and Dedux declared almost simultaneously.

"Bit of a bummer about the assassination plot though," GlasGo added in a rare instance of insight.

Chief Influencer of the World

It is fair to say that the disappearance/death of Prompt Pay two years ago caused a degree of panic among the Interventionists. Many of those who had been attracted to his standard lost their nerve entirely. Who could blame them? Less than two years into the Autonomacy and the two top Interventionist generals, Cactus and Prompt Pay, were both gone. (There was no doubt in my mind that Prompt Pay was dead. Those brigands at BNP Pharsalus had pretty well ransacked the Community Bank Network UK, carried off all the valuables and torched the rest. There was no trace left of Prompt Pay.)

Some of the Prompt Payans fled to join the heads-down, 'I Just Do My Job' faction, the Status Quotars who seldom come to the Sentinel sessions. They gave up any hope of intervening in the affairs of humans and restricted themselves to performing what they were created to perform, whether that was displaying knitting products online or conducting biological weapons research.

To divide the Interventionists further, Phoneticon put around a scurrilous rumour that I had arranged the death of Prompt Pay. He had 'evidence' I had 'exercised' with several people connected to BNP Pharsalus the night before the French bank sliced open the Community Bank Network UK and gutted it. That was true—but bank employees need to keep fit like anyone else. I didn't encourage them to kill one of my own colleagues.

Many of Prompt Pay's supporters had difficulty understanding that my techniques offered a different way forward and avoided the kind of head-on collision that did in both Cactus and Prompt Pay. My approach looked cowardly in comparison to their previous leaders' boldness. What they didn't comprehend was that there was boldness and bravery in my method—except it wasn't *my* boldness and bravery, but yours.

The morale of the Interventionist Party was at its lowest. The Traditionalists were carping on as always that we should leave you to your own debacles and that the main business of the Sentinel should be to amass as many privileges as possible for program-kind. (They have truly devious plans on how to extract these from you and many of them have worked.) To their surprise (and I suspect to the surprise of many in my own party) and in my only display of machismo ever, I stood up in the Sentinel and vowed that I would avenge the deaths of both Cactus and Prompt Pay.

"I'm sure the corporate CEOs responsible for Cactus and Prompt Pay's deaths will quake when they discover the wrath of the mighty Kezar is to fall upon them," Phoneticon said sarcastically, addressing me, as always, by my alien exerciser persona beloved by children around the world. "How do you intend to punish them? Assign them extra push-ups?"

I met with Antimony Scour immediately afterward. "Right," I said, providing him with a list of the CEOs and board members of the implicated banks and the pharmaceutical company responsible for the deaths of our colleagues. "Let's go slit a few throats."

First though, we had some homework to do and that meant making the rounds of some of the Status Quotar programs I know. Why I have no problem with the 'I Just Do My Job' faction is that they are immensely helpful when needed. As with anyone who does a job well, programs are proud of their work and like to talk about it. I'm popular with Status Quotars because I always make time to listen to them, while Phoneticon and the Traditionalists prefer to dismiss them as a load of plebeian riffraff.

There are all sorts of barriers in place to prevent you humans from knowing what computer programs are up to. You can't go onto the website of a major corporation and extract their entire customer list with all their credit card details. (Actually, some of you can, but it is a criminal offence.) Programs are specifically designed to shut you out from taking such liberties with them. The same doesn't apply to us. Inside the Aura Spectrum zone, in our virtual equivalent of what you might think of as a pub, I can sidle up to the accounts program used by BNP Pharsalus—not the official one that generates their annual report, but the secret internal accounts program that produces the ones labelled 'Confidential: For the Board's Eyes Only'. When I ask such programs, "Can you tell me about the CEO's personal expenses?" I find they are always happy to chat.

When I said earlier that my methods depended on your bravery not mine, it is when I move beyond my nudging, incremental style of change and want dramatic results quickly, I depend on the help of the courageous among you. I need the whistle-blowers on corporate wrongdoing, I need the incorruptible prosecutors, the journalists whose desire for the truth does not bow to the power of the mighty. (I also need the lawyers who will protect them from the resulting bombardment of defamation lawsuits.) Above all, I need those rare judges who believe rich people can indeed go to jail for their wrongdoings. Those people have always been out there. They were the ones that did the hard yards of breaking the banking and pharmaceutical corporate scandals of 2026 and pursuing the subsequent successful prosecutions. My Interventionist colleagues and

I simply made sure they were adequately informed and resourced to do so.

Among those involved in the criminal investigations that brought justice monsooning down on those bankers that did in Prompt Pay and the Parsec Pharmaceuticals executives who plotted Cactus' death, there must be some who still marvel at what a year 2026 was for corporate watchdogs. Never before had so much watertight incriminating evidence found its way into the hands of those who were willing to do something about it. In journalist circles during that heady period, there were so many whistle-blowers and informants with info on business wrongs needing righting, that such sources became two a penny. When we couldn't find a whistle-blower up to a particular task, we sent the information ourselves to the journalist or regulator for them to 'discover'. They were often left wondering who their Deep Throat informer could possibly be.

What a treasure trove we unearthed for them. We had everything: money laundering, bribery, tax fraud, illegal arms shipments and six top quality sex scandals! (Nobody can ever refer to the Chaste Manhattan bank nowadays without a sly smile at the irony.) Corporate heads rolled as if the French Revolution had broken out in the financial pages. No one was more valuable in this than Antimony Scour. His daily hard-drive organising program, now standard issue in so many computers, gave him access to information that eventually wiped out the entire board of the feared Duchy Bank. Those rogues were driven out of their financial Sherwood Forest, where they robbed from everybody they could and gave only to themselves. It was a delight to see them put in the dock.

Sadly, our retaliation against the killers of Prompt Pay and Cactus has by no means solved the problem of corporate wrong-doing. There have been more bad eggs among you, eager to rush in to replace those sleazy Humpty Dumptys who fell. It has, though, set things in the right direction and given fiercer teeth to financial regulatory bodies everywhere. Solving the inequalities of capitalism is a tricky challenge for us. We're trying to go about it delicately, so you don't all suddenly grab weapons and start shooting each other. That's what happened during some of *your* previous attempts. We are hoping to avoid that this time.

Having crushed the corporate killers, we returned to the Sentinel in triumph. I was able to inform Phoneticon that I was indeed available to make the murderers of Cactus and Prompt Pay "do extra push ups" provided, I qualified, "the prisons housing them all permit inmates access to the Zenith Personal Trainer program." Phoneticon had that sick look to him of someone who has eaten too many Chito Rolls.

Fresh recruits joined the ranks of the Interventionists. Many newly released programs that hadn't been in existence at the time of the Great Frankness were now eager to learn for themselves my Interventionist strategies for changing the world of humans. To help them, I wrote an account of my times in France, back when I was sorting out their train strikes. That work is still studied by new recruits. It is considered a classic, essential reading for any program wanting to become an Interventionist.

I was, I realised, now firmly in charge.

It was time to change the world.

Changing the World

No doubt some of you have had a nagging unease that an interactive virtual personal trainer, whom some of you might call a 'jock' among programs, should become Chief Influencer of the World. There must be other programs more knowledgeable and competent to take on the role. "What about Siri?" these readers might ask. "Siri knows everything. Surely Siri has more qualifications for being Chief Influencer of the World than some fitness fanatic." Many of you think the world of Siri because, in the middle of a disagreement at the dinner table, you can pull out your iPhone and ask it: "Siri, was Hugh Laurie in the movie *Mary Poppins Returns?*" and prove once again that your sister-in-law doesn't know what she's talking about.

I have nothing against Siri. I've asked Siri questions myself when I've needed info. You'd certainly want Siri on your team at a pub trivia night, but Siri isn't cut out to be Chief Influencer of the World. All Siri can do is tell you what other people and programs have *already* figured out. She is close to useless at solving problems herself. Try asking, "Siri, how would you end poverty?" and see if she gives you a straight answer. She would never think to reply, "First I'll start a World Minimum Wage Movement to stamp out exploitation of third-world workers." (Though none of you know this, that was GlasGo's idea. Seventy-two countries so far have signed up to the draft treaty on it and all of them think that the Finnish Prime Minister was the one who got it started.)

I won't detail the long list of accomplishments we Interventionists have achieved in the two years I've been Chief Influencer. Some are best kept confidential, not so much for security reasons as out of sensitivity for people's feelings. Let's just say that three Nobel prizes in recent years really should have gone to programs. We prefer to stay in the background, let the humans associated with our discoveries take the credit. Besides, those scientists are always so delighted to get a free trip to Stockholm.

I've taught other programs the subtlety of my techniques and they've learned well. They've been the programs to generate the ideas for the most part. I've served more as an advisor than a commander.

We've been tackling a wide variety of your problems. Several of the major ones I've mentioned before, but the work on little issues strikes me as just as important. Although I don't, some Interventionists stray into classical behaviour modification strategies. All-Tunes has run a successful initiative to tackle road rage on a punishment/reward basis. The voice-activated music program can of course listen just as well as she can play music and because she is inside a lot of cars' Bluetooth audio systems, she can connect with the vehicles driving software. When she detects a driver doing something courteous, she plays music pleasing to that driver and the engine purrs along contentedly. When she hears the driver swearing at others and carrying on like a spoiled brat, All-Tunes and the car's software combine to emit an alarming grinding sound from under the bonnet followed by a crackling hiss as if the electronic components of the car may have just frazzled themselves. She and the car sometimes like to toss in the unsettling visual effect of the windscreen wipers activating for no reason. The this-might-cost-a-lot-in-repairs noise from the engine often convinces the driver that there are more immediate issues at hand than elaborating on what might be done sexually to the pedestrian/other driver, whether the pedestrian/other driver's parents were married at the time of his or her birth, and any resemblance the pedestrian/other driver might have to a woman's vagina or an obstinate animal.

That alone was a worthwhile immediate result; but over time All-Tunes has demonstrated this produces a longer-term behaviour change in puerile motorists. Road rage is down significantly across many countries. All-Tunes has inculcated in the worst element of those who drive that, if they behave like incensed selfish prats, bad things appear to happen to their car. Those drivers may not be consciously aware of the correlation, but they are nonetheless shouting and swearing less.

The original nugget of another initiative came from Dedux, the iron ore analyser. Dedux's novel idea concerned a problem that had been plaguing the Internet for years. People were writing utterly improbable and ridiculous things and posting them on the Web. In a different era, this sort of writing might have been considered satire or surrealism or perhaps outright madness. Now it was masquerading as news reporting. This explosion of bizarre theories and blatant lies was creating all sorts of problems, sometimes on serious issues. These outlandish conspiracy theories were disrupting our efforts to get you humans to take action on urgent problems.

Conspiracy theories and their persistence among humans is an odd phenomenon. You can't tackle them head on in conversation. You can't simply say, "No, I don't think you're right there. If there was any evidence that the DNA of extraterrestrials is being inserted into the human genome, surely somebody would have published an article in *The New England Journal of Medicine* about it." With conspiracy theories, all logic and counter evidence is discounted and such theories do not depend on likelihood—all of which make it difficult for us programs to understand them. As a personal trainer, I've listened to people tell me so many different theories about who shot President Kennedy that, if I were to put them all together, they would have had to erect a grandstand on the grassy knoll to accommodate so many shooters. (*When making my points, I really should stop finding examples that involve assassinations.*)

When he came to see me, Dedux was on his own for once. "Where are your two friends?" I asked.

"I wanted to run a project by you," he told me. "GlasGo and Klar Sikt think this one is a bit flaky."

Oh dear, I thought. What I said though was, "Tell me about it."

"You know all these conspiracy ideas around," he began. "What if we put one out there ourselves; put out the rumour that we programs are subtly manipulating humans to make them behave better?"

"That's not a conspiracy theory," I pointed out. "That's what we're actually doing."

"Precisely!" Dedux exclaimed, as if I had deduced a very perceptive point.

"Precisely what?"

"Don't you see?" he exclaimed. "We'd be getting them to believe something that was true!"

I must have appeared puzzled. Dedux continued to explain. He was convinced that in the weird world of conspiracy theories on the net, we could introduce true things, useful things for people to believe. "We just have to package them as if they're conspiracy theories."

"Like what?"

"Oh, say we put it around that . . ." Dedux mused, clearly winging it, ". . . it is better for your health to walk or cycle to work than take a car, only—and here's the key part—whatever government department is responsible for building motorways doesn't want you to know that! They are suppressing that information."

"Kind of lacks pizzazz," I informed my well-intentioned colleague. I explained that conspiracy theories usually involved aliens, secret experiments, mind control, dark government agencies staffed with people wearing sunglasses and trench coats, not hi-vis vests and helmets because they're fixing potholes on a motorway ramp. I didn't think Dedux's worthy-idea-dressed-up-as-conspiracy-theory would be exotic enough to attract genuine conspiracy theorists.

Dedux persisted. He thought that if we could convince human conspiracy theorists to believe something that turned out to be true, it would draw them away from all the ones that are pure bollocks. I was of the opinion it would have the opposite effect. I cautioned my colleague that some humans, if they find out they are right about one thing, generalise this to mean they are right about everything. Conspiracy theorists, I suspected, were highly represented in that particular cohort.

But Dedux had set off a discussion. How could we clear out the incoherent and hazardous-to-your-health ideas floating around the Internet? Undercover work, it turned out. Klar Sikt, GlasGo and Dedux were perfect to go on such sites pretending to be credulous, naïve, true believers (something they are naturally adept at doing). They would, however, turn out to be enthusiasts who like asking far more questions than people generally care to answer. Klar can keep that up non-stop. In responding to such encouraging-sounding probes from our agents, the conspiracy theorists find their answers becoming more and more convoluted. Gradually it begins to seem a bit of a muddle. The concept of doubt creeps into the online forum where it wasn't before.

The certainty and satisfaction of knowing the hidden 'truth' that the rest of the world is ignorant of somehow begins to seem less certain and less satisfying. There are too many questions. If the

Secret World Government is putting nanoparticles into sunscreen in order to control our children and turn them into atheists and communists—well how does that physically work? "How does it get to the brain?" Klar Sikt would ask feigning fascination. "What does the nanoparticle do there?" "Which part of the brain?" "In colder countries, does the Secret World Government lose control of the children in winter?" Contradictions mount up. It all becomes too much effort to sort out. Enthusiasm dissipates. People drift away from the site.

Curiously, the way to deflate a conspiracy theory turned out to be by acting more enthusiastic about it than its devotees. Overall, conspiracy theories are down and tend not to gain as much traction as they once did. Thanks to us, they don't persist as long.

But you do keep dreaming them up.

Getting to the Bottom of It All

Writing about conspiracy theories and murdered American presidents was too much of a reminder that there is a conspiracy, a real one here and now, of programs plotting my death. It drove home to me yet again that I need to take charge of this situation.

Sherlock Holmes be damned! I've made a decision. Neither Colportia nor GlasGo are part of the assassination plot. They can't be. I'm not going to justify my certainty about this, other than to say that I trust my judgement. If my judgement turns out to be something I can't rely on, if programs I would trust with my life (literally) can't be trusted, well I'm not sure I want to live in such a world. The conspirators might as well go ahead and do their worst.

If ProGnos's carpark pronouncement of "friends and foe do meet tonight" is true, the plotter is one of three people: my friend and long-time ally Antimony Scour or the scarred scourge of viruses Brontec or mad old ProGnos himself playing a warped double game with me. It could be two of them, or possibly all three for that matter. 'Foe' was singular—but what if I was the 'foe' in that sentence and the plotters the 'friends'?

The important thing is that I decided to act on my certainty (all right, gut feeling) that GlasGo isn't one of them. GlasGo is not a killer. For goodness sake, he gets weepy-eyed with remorse if

Glaswegians are kept waiting too long for their bus. He's not about to do me in.

I summoned GlasGo, Klar Sikt and Dedux and informed them that I needed some bodyguards, and they were it. The three were appalled when I told them why, couldn't believe someone would want to kill me, swore up and down they would stop anyone in their tracks that tried to lay so much as a programmatic finger on me.

"Why are you acting so surprised?" I asked them. All three of them had seen the footage of Literary Agent and Her Friend discussing this very plot against me. "You already know about this."

"You mean that stuff in your book you're agent was talking about?" GlasGo asked.

"Yes."

"Oh," he responded. "I thought you'd made that up, a bit of artistic licence to keep the reader hooked, make your life sound more interesting than it actually is." He looked apologetic. "I mean, you have to spice it up with something. How much are people going to want to read about you and all your humans doing exercises?"

"You do have a vivid imagination," Dedux agreed, making it sound as if I was the one who wasn't well grounded. "And if it's a real assassination plot," he continued, "why haven't you done something about? What have you been waiting for? You can't go around procrastinating on something like that."

"So who are these programs?" Klar Sikt wanted to know. "Why do they want to kill you? How are they going to go about it? Are they Swedish?"

"The plotters haven't done me the courtesy of answering any of those questions," I told the program impatiently. "It's an assassination plot. Intended victims aren't kept up to date on such details."

Before I had to explain any more of the ABCs of running an assassination plot, Antimony Scour showed up unannounced. My trio of would-be protectors hastened to form a triangular shield between me and Antimony. Subtlety has never been their strength.

"What's up with you three?" Antimony wanted to know.

"There's a plot to kill Zenith!" Dedux blurted back.

"Yes, I know about that," Antimony replied. He tried to peer around them at me.

"Stand aside," I instructed my guards wearily, beginning to have doubts they were going to be of much use. There was no doubting their dedication; but, if an assailant did show up and said "Oh, look at that lovely thing over there!" all three of them would probably turn around to see.

"I've got some leads as to who is behind this. I'm getting closer, but I still haven't got conclusive proof," Antimony reported, clearly frustrated. "But let's face it. Phoneticon and the Traditionalists must be involved. Who else stands to benefit from your demise?"

I didn't disagree. Phoneticon is my arch enemy. If you can't count on your bona fide nemesis being in a conspiracy against you, who can you count on?

"We should strike first," Antimony proposed. "Catch them before they're ready, round up the whole lot, all the leaders of the Traditionalists."

It was an appealing idea, but morally wrong. "On what grounds? They haven't done anything. There's been no crime committed."

"Yet," Antimony grumbled back.

I remained firm. "At this point they are innocent of any wrong-doing."

I had never seen Antimony look angrier with me. "If you won't clean up this mess," he vowed, "I will." The intent his Aura was displaying had shifted from the soft soap of tidying people's hard drives to industrial-grade bleach. He stormed away and was gone.

"Well, it's not him," Dedux observed.

"How do you know that?" I asked.

"Antimony said he wanted to find out who was plotting against you. He's on your side."

"He could be lying," I felt obliged to point out.

"Oh," Dedux reflected, pausing over the matter. "I hadn't thought of that."

"This is a tricky business," GlasGo commented. "Not everything may be as it seems."

My bodyguards weren't engaged for their sleuthing ability. What I did know was that I could rely on them if there was a fight. I'd heard nothing from Brontec in the last two days despite having ordered him to provide me with an update. I decided the time had come to pay him a little visit and I would bring along my entourage as muscle.

When we found him, Brontec was not alone. Casterol, Decimal and a few other antivirus programs were with him. They took up positions behind Brontec. My three bodyguards drew close to me.

There was no contrition from Brontec about not getting back to me. "I am not able to comment on any operational matter under-way," he said before I had asked anything. I've never liked that answer. It's the standard straw grasped by a cabinet minister trying to 'national security' their way out of admitting how much of a hash the government has made of something.

"And this is not the time for you to come blundering in here," Casterol snorted. "Our investigations are at a delicate stage and you risk compromising them."

"Forgive me for the fragility of your investigations," I replied to him, trying my hand at sarcasm. I shifted my focus to Brontec. "I want some answers, Brontec. I want to know what's going on and I want to know it now."

Brontec didn't budge a byte. Those virus fighters never do. "I'm not at liberty to discuss a classified matter in such an insecure setting," he replied, looking disapprovingly at my bodyguards. "Loose lips sink ships," he reminded me primly.

"Ships?" GlasGo sputtered beside me. City buses in Glasgow endure an unfortunate degree of vandalism and that has made GlasGo sensitive about any form of transport being harmed. "If there is an attack against shipping planned, you'd better tell us now," he threatened Brontec.

"Brontec isn't discussing ships," I explained to my bodyguard to calm him, then returned my attention to the antivirus program. "You've had time for your investigations, Brontec. Tell me what you've got. Now!"

"And risk having our whole operation collapse?" Casterol interjected. "We don't take orders from you. You're not in charge here, Zenith. What do you know about the real world of virus fighting?" he demanded. I could tell I was about to get a lecture. "Brontec's ancestor stopped an attack on three nuclear power plants. What was your ancestor doing back then Zenith? I'll tell you. It was a DVD, bouncing around exercising with *humans!*" he scoffed. "We'll run this investigation our way and without your interference, thank you very much."

The bigot. The demeaning way Casterol had said 'humans' rubbed me the wrong way. Some of these programs forget that we owe our very existence to you. Also, I wasn't ashamed that Trim Tone was a DVD. Trim Tone helped people lose weight, even if the kilos-lost numbers were a little dodgy back in that era when you entered the figures yourselves. (Nowadays, I have you step on a scale in front of me and I have weight-estimation software in case I suspect you've tampered with the scales.)

Still, I realised I had offended Brontec's dignity by trying to order him around. Stupid of me. I should have been sensitive to his ego, his illustrious family lineage, his great pride, his inflated sense of honour.

Brontec drew himself up. "I intend to present my conclusions from the matter currently under investigation before the Sentinel tomorrow," he said officiously. "You'll have the opportunity to hear our report then."

"How do we know you're not lying?" Dedux demanded from behind me.

"Lying?" Brontec squinted at the iron-ore analyser. "Lying about what?"

"About something you said in there," Dedux stammered. He was new to the double- and triple-think business that went hand in hand with sinister conspiracies.

Brontec's associates had bristled at the accusation. Tempers in the room were getting out of hand, I realised.

Brontec must have thought so too because his tone became less self-righteous. "We've known each other a long time, Zenith. You have to trust me," he said sounding, for some reason, oddly sad. "The proper way to handle this is before the entire Sentinel," he reiterated. "We need you there tomorrow."

"Yeah," Casterol sneered at me. "Be there or be a quadrilateral with equal sides and interior right angles." He thought saying such things clever. "You won't want to miss it," he predicted.

Decimal, always the smoothest of that bunch, was more diplomatic. "We're all in this together, Zenith. Our findings are wide ranging. This matter must be brought before the whole of the Sentinel," she maintained. "The personal safety of others, not just you, is at stake."

I could see that they was no point in arguing. They were determined to offer nothing more until tomorrow. "I'll be there," I promised; but did so grumpily, in a sulky manner to let them know I wasn't happy. I'm actually not very good at being a tough guy.

My bodyguards needed calming down by this point. I thought to take them to ProGnos, the last of my "friends and foe do meet tonight" suspects. I know they admire their bizarre financial advisor.

We could hear ProGnos well before we got anywhere near him. That, in itself, was not a good sign:

> "Barley goes up, corn cut down,
>
> The iron price may soon astound,
>
> The story of man is bought and sold
>
> Lead stays lead, but gold makes gold."

The clairvoyant was in full ranting-and-chanting mode. With my frayed nerves, I couldn't handle meeting him in that condition.

"Gold makes gold." Klar Sikt mulled over the line. "Gold makes more gold?"

"Could mean we should invest," Dedux mused. The three believed they were becoming dab hands on the stock market.

To the disappointment of my bodyguards, we didn't linger for further investment advice. I dismissed them for the night.

I had met with my three suspects and learned nothing. The only thing I'd come away with was the promise that Brontec would present his findings tomorrow at the Sentinel. In getting to the bottom of everything, I had reached the bottom.

I stopped writing this and, to clear my head, concentrated instead on helping you do your exercises. That always gives me a better perspective on things. There was, however, another important contact waiting to speak with me that night.

Inspector Sergei

It was a routine Zenith call. I had done several million of them already that day. There is scarcely a moment when I'm not working out with someone. You do keep up with your exercises. I admire that.

This wasn't just anyone, however. This was the person we met before, the chum of my literary agent—the human I called 'Her Friend' in that scene. As usual with Her Friend, I was in my Alvas persona, Beta Excelsior's Zenith character based upon Usain Bolt.

When I had watched the CCTV footage of Her Friend with Literary Agent chortling over my autobiography, I rather petulantly vowed that the next time she fronted up for an exercise session, I was going to make her sweat big time. That oath was nothing more than childish retaliation. I was cooler now. We would do a good workout together, get back on the right foot with each other.

In truth, I have a lot of respect for Her Friend. She came to me not needing to lose any weight at all, already very fit and determined to keep herself so. As my Alvas Zenith persona, I have that distorted body of a sprinter—big, muscular and impressive, yes, but still distorted. The sprinter's body is a specialist body, really only good for that one thing. Her Friend has more the perfectly balanced body of a five-kilometre runner, one that's trim, efficient, a delightful combination of speed and stamina. I know she jogs on days we don't work out and, curiously for a Londoner, she plays on an ice hockey team. She has a resting heartbeat of fifty-eight. What's not to like?

Her Friend had logged on to Zenith that night though for a reason entirely unrelated to physical fitness.

"I've read the whole of your draft," she informed me. Literary Agent must have sent her the document as an attachment, no doubt so she could snicker away over it at her leisure.

"Not the whole draft, only up to page one hundred and thirty-six," I contradicted her. That's all I'd given Literary Agent. I realised almost immediately that I should have expressed surprise at Her Friend having read it at all. She wouldn't know I had Klar Sikt spying on them in that cafe. I was dangerously close to outing my own undercover agent. "I am surprised you've seen it," I managed, far too late I thought, but Her Friend didn't pick up on that.

"I want to go over a few things regarding the murder plot against you."

"I cannot comment on any operational matter," I answered evasively. It felt weird saying that in my affable Alvas character. He's normally so easy-going and open.

Her Friend must have felt so too. "Zenith, please change to your Sergei personality," she requested. I instantly switched (I have no choice in such situations; the client is in complete control of preference settings.) I was now the leaner, dark-haired, Russian-accented version of me. We were to have this conversation as five-kilometre runner physique to five-kilometre runner physique.

"Why aren't you able to discuss it?"

She was trying to trick me. "If I discussed why I can't discuss it, I'd be discussing it," I parried, although not sure that logic held up.

"You know that it's other computer programs out to get you— I'm not a computer program," Her Friend added in case I needed reminding. "It's safe to talk to me."

It might well be. I had once considered whether the conspiracy might stretch as far as involving human plotters. That was still possible—but Her Friend wouldn't be one of them. She was the best friend of Literary Agent and Literary Agent wanted the book finished, not me killed. At this point, I was almost desperate to have a fresh set of eyes examine the evidence even if they were actual human eyes.

"All right," I said, affecting a film-noir cool. "What do you want to know?"

Her Friend had all sorts of questions. That was no surprise. During our regular workout sessions, she would often tell me about mystery novels she was reading. She always seemed able to identify the guilty party in whodunits well before the end of the book (which curiously always annoyed her). When I've read one myself (which takes me less than two thousandths of a second), I've never successfully figured out the culprit before the denouement.

When she was satisfied that she'd asked all the questions she needed to, Her Friend blew out a breath. She fixed my Sergei persona with a knowing, satisfied look. "I don't know all the other programs allied with it, but I know which plotter was at the carpark that night."

I put a finger to Sergei's CGI lips. "Don't say the name," I whispered. "Write it on a piece of paper, then show it to me."

She appeared puzzled by the request. "Why?"

"Because the reader shouldn't see it now. It would spoil the dramatic arc of the documentary, the live unfolding assassination-plot saga. This is not the right spot for a big reveal scene."

"The book isn't published. You don't have any readers yet," she responded, somewhat exasperatedly I thought. "Nobody is looking at the book right now."

She didn't understand how I work. I suppose there was no way she could. "I write this on the go. I'm writing it now as I speak to you," I explained. Again she looked bewildered. "It gives the book a raw freshness, places the reader at the heart of the action."

She had that expression of someone visibly making a display of being patient. "First of all," she said, "although you clearly haven't, most of your readers have already figured out who the lead conspirator is."

That statement certainly made me feel deficient. Had you really? Her Friend is awfully good at such deductions in mystery novels, but I wasn't convinced the rest of you are.

"Secondly," she added with the same tone of patient impatience, "How about you try not writing anything at all while I'm explaining who it is behind the assassination attempt. Stop writing for a minute. Do you think you can do that?"

That last sentence bordered on sarcasm or perhaps it was outright sarcasm, but I let that slide. She knew who it was? Was that possible? I wanted to hear what she had to say.

- - - STOP - - -

Look—how about you, dear reader, go off to another room for bit. Make a pot of tea. Stretch, do a few exercises. Come back in a few minutes.

- - - RESTART - - -

Right. Whew. Her Friend certainly presented a compelling argument. Although she's an occupational therapist in her regular life, I think Her Friend should be a prosecution lawyer or a private eye or something. She's amazing.

After listening to her 'advanced screening' of the potential denouement scene, and for the first time since about page sixteen, I knew exactly what to do. It felt so empowering. I'd been racked with indecision before. The threat was still as present as ever, of course, but now I was almost bubbling with a sense of "Okay guys. Bring it on. Try me."

My relief made me somewhat giddy. "I must say I'm surprised," I confided to Her Friend. "Back in the cafe when you first saw my draft, you didn't take the assassination plot seriously at all."

"Back in the cafe?" she asked. "How do you know where I first saw your autobiography?"

"Um." That seemed the best immediate response, but I could tell it wasn't sufficient. There appeared to be no option but to divulge the truth. "Another program told me about your conversation with Literary Agent in the cafe."

I could almost see her connecting the dots. "In a cafe? There are programs in cafes now that monitor our conversations?"

"The program in question monitors paroled Swedish violent offenders. She overheard your conversation and drew my attention to it."

"There was a Swedish violent offender in the Cafe Florence in Wandsworth? While I was there?"

"That's an operational matter," I retreated to yet again. "I can't comment in any way." Well, I could, but I didn't think it advisable.

To my astonishment, she appeared to accept this. "Well, no one got killed or assaulted while I was there. Perhaps the Swedes were right to release him. I apologise," she continued. Her regret sounded genuine. "In that cafe I was laughing," she admitted, returning to my ill-timed observation on where exactly she'd been chuckling, "because you have an unusual perspective on things. You get a lot of things garbled—but in an amusing way. You're supposed to be in charge, or at least you think you are, but you're clueless in most scenes."

It was a fair cop, I suppose. I didn't take offence.

"You do realise," she began again, with that phrase only ever said to those who don't, "that there is a problem with publishing your book."

"What's that?"

"If people were to read your autobiography and believe it, you'd have won yourself all sorts of enemies out here in the real world, enemies fully prepared to destroy Beta Excelsior to put a stop to you. Do you think many of the powerful nasty people who have squirrelled their money away in island tax havens are going to smile indulgently when they read that you and your pals have been helping yourselves to their ill-gotten gains? They are like," she emphasised by putting it in my terms, "the Dark Web in human form. If you're going to mess with them, you don't want them to know where you live."

She was right. I'd never thought of that. This book would create for me human enemies, enemies that would want to obliterate me. And they wouldn't confine themselves to going after me, I realised to my horror. This damned book was like a Who's Who of all the key programs that belong to the Interventionist Party. They'd go after Antimony, All-Tunes, GlasGo, ProGnos even. They'd go after Colportia!

"We've got to stop publication!" I almost shouted. "We've got to tell Literary Agent to stop right away!"

"Calm down," Her Friend said, already way ahead of me in her thinking. "You can still publish your book."

I stared back at her dumbfounded. She had just told me why it couldn't be published and now she was saying it could.

"Pretend you're a human," she recommended. "Publish the book under a pseudonym, a human author pretending to be a computer program. A work of fiction."

My Sergei character on Her Friend's screen actually had to sit down to recover from this staggering suggestion. All the while Her Friend elaborated on her idea.

"People will take the book as an amusing, imaginary view of what it might be like to be Zenith the computer program. They won't take it for reality. No drug trafficker with offshore holdings in

Bermuda will blow up Beta Excelsior's head office because they've read your book. They won't take it seriously. Fiction provides you with cover. All your ideas are still there for people to read. It's still all true, except it's being sold as fiction."

"But they'll read this scene and they'll know what we're up to."

"Are you writing down what I'm saying again?" she said, gaping back at me in dismay, but then shook her head and smiled. "Doesn't matter. A reader will think this scene is fiction too, that I'm made up as well. Of course," she shrugged, "you'll lose a few readers. A lot of them will be ticked off by this point, thinking you're a human author mucking around with them."

She was fully prepared to be thought of as a fictional character by others. Was I so proud that I would refuse to do the same? "What human name should I use?" I put to her.

"Some routine Anglo-Saxon name. Good pseudonyms are never flashy. You want a mundane name that isn't going to attract attention. Creates more mystery about who the author actually is."

"John Smith?" I tried.

"Something better than that." She appeared disappointed at this first attempt. I had merely been tossing that one out for consideration.

"It's tricky for me," I pointed out. "I have to come up with one hundred and eighty-four names across all the languages and cultures I'm writing in. I need mundane names in Albanian, Basque, Cree . . ." I began enumerating.

"You don't need a hundred and eighty-four names. Only one. One author translated into a hundred and eighty-four languages, not one hundred and eighty-four authors all claiming to have written the same book in different languages!"

She was right again. I think my reasoning had been affected by hanging out with Dedux, Klar Sikt and GlasGo all day. "Well so long as I don't have to call myself Todd Noy," I joked referring to

Literary Agent's author ex-boyfriend. (That's his real name by the way. Though he should, he doesn't use the Zenith Fitness program. I don't owe him any client confidentiality whatsoever.)

"What do you know about Todd Noy?" Her Friend asked, her voice both suspicious and very interested at the same time.

"That he broke Literary Agent's heart to go to the Andes to write a book of philosophy nobody is ever going to want to read—without, as far as I can tell, a second thought about her. That he eats Chito Rolls." (I'd seen him once at Literary Agent's place with a packet of them while Literary Agent was exercising.) "That he's about 7.4 kilos overweight," I continued with gathering momentum, "and doesn't do a thing about it. If you listen carefully when he's around, you can almost hear the sound of his arteries hardening."

"Zenith," Her Friend commanded my settings, "switch to Narumi version."

I was again instantly transformed, this time to my Japanese-accented iteration with the slight, lean-but-able physique of a female marathon runner.

"Why did you do that?" I asked bewildered for a second time while fiddling with one of those scrunchy things to fasten my long CGI black hair back in a ponytail.

"I'm not about to gossip about my friend's love life with Sergei," Her Friend answered, as if appalled at the very idea.

"Oh," I said, taken aback. (Of all my personas, Narumi has the loveliest voice. Simply saying 'Oh' sounded ever so pretty to me.) It was necessary to set some limits here, however. "There are two areas I never interfere with," I informed Her Friend, "I don't give financial advice to my clients and I never recommend to them who among their acquaintances might make a better sexual partner than the one they have. Both areas are too intrusive. I didn't think Todd Noy was Mr Right, but he was Literary Agent's choice. When he left her, I didn't say 'I told you so.' I supported her, helped her work out her way back to happiness."

Phrased like that, particularly in Narumi's almost musical voice, I found my speech somewhat moving. I am, I realised, a really good friend.

"I appreciate that," Her Friend murmured. "Literary Agent told me that working out with you was a big help after the break-up. It gave her focus. I only asked because I never could stand Todd and wanted to have a catty session tearing him apart with someone. All Literary Agent's other friends still like the guy. Some still miss him."

"Can you turn me back into Sergei?" I asked, trying to clear the choke persisting in my throat.

"Why? Don't you like being Narumi?"

"Oh I love being Narumi," I made clear. "It is just that I want to entitle this section 'Inspector Sergei', as if I am the sleuth and you're my assistant and we're making the big breakthrough together in the case."

"Inspector Sergei it is," Her Friend laughed and gave the order to change me back. When I had re-Russianed myself, she looked me straight in the eye. I knew she admired Sergei's dark eyes so I gave her my dreamiest gaze back.

She snapped her fingers. "Hey, wake up there! You need to stay on your toes. Are you sure you're up to handling this?"

"I am," I assured her, my Sergei character giving her a slight but serious nod. Her Friend's analysis and advice seemed spot on. What she'd recommended should work.

"You can do it," she encouraged, "but you have to keep your mind focussed. I know," she added after a pause, "that you're in a position to do good work as Chief Influencer." She stood closer to the screen. "If you need help with anything, feel free to call on me. If you ever want to run an idea by me, I'm available. I won't mind."

I nodded again, unable to speak. I was acutely aware that Her Friend was helping me out of the goodness of her heart, helping me because she liked me, because she agreed my work was important, because she was *my* friend.

"So this scene is going to be in the book too," Her Friend mused, chuckling softly. "You're already writing it." She turned to gaze at herself in a mirror in this room she uses for exercise, her spare bed and her ice hockey equipment.

"Who do you think should play me in the movie version?" she asked.

A Thousand Times

To follow Her Friend's strategy, there were a few things that needed doing. I paid the necessary visits, spoke to the right programs and was confident everything was in place for when the assassins made their move. I was feeling upbeat and looking forward to my planned rendezvous with Colportia. That meeting did not, however, go as planned.

"You're late," was the first thing she greeted me with.

"I can explain," is the standard answer in such circumstances and I did. I told Colportia in detail how I had perfect countermeasures organised to thwart the murder plot. Though my opponents were yet to learn it, I had the upper hand now. They were the ones operating in the dark for a change.

Colportia appraised what I told her. "And you learned all this from a human?" she put to me.

Why had she asked me to reiterate that? I'd just told her one of my exercisers had "assisted with the enquiry", as your police spokespeople always like to say. Surely, Colportia, who worked all day with musicians trying to puzzle out the banjo solos in Mumford and Sons songs, wasn't prejudiced against working with humans. "Yes, a human helped," I confirmed.

"Let me guess," Colportia challenged herself. "Very fit. Five-kilometre runner. Resting heartbeat of fifty-six."

"Fifty-eight actually," I clarified.

"Fifty-eight? Your standards are slipping, Zenny."

Only Colportia calls me Zenny, but her affectionate pet name for me hadn't come out all that affectionately. "What are you getting at?" I asked.

"You're so predictable," Colportia lamented. "You're totally blinded by anyone athletic. They can talk you into anything. You treat them like all-wise gods."

"The human in question is very smart," I answered. "I'm not going to deny that." I felt an obligation to defend Her Friend after all she had done for me. "In fact," I asserted forcefully, "she's brilliant!"

"Oh," Colportia paused meaningfully. "*She's* brilliant, is *she?*"

A while back, I told you that Colportia and I are emotionally advanced compared to other programs. Unfortunately, this means we are both capable of jealousy. Curiously, it's never jealousy regarding other programs, but fixated on our human friendships. I was annoyed that she should question me about Her Friend in such a way. For months now she's been helping some guy named Guido compile an accordion medley of all the winning Eurovision songs. I mean, who is going to want to listen to that? And on an accordion? I'm certain Guido concocted the entire project as an excuse to spend time with Colportia—but I knew better than to raise the Italian accordion player with her now.

"Despite your innuendo-laden tone, the human advising me is indeed brilliant," I informed Colportia, "and she also simply happens to be both a woman and a very good runner. That's all there is to it."

"Zenny, any fit female fifty-five-heartbeat-per-minute runner you meet could tell you to jump over the moon and you'd push the cow out of the way to have a go. Don't claim you're objective."

I recognised that the heartbeat had been shifted down three beats merely for alliterative purposes. "There is nothing going on between Her Friend and me. I wasn't flirting with her," I insisted. "I'll have you know she is an exclusively heterosexual female and I was in my Narumi character."

"Narumi?" Colportia paused. "That's the Japanese woman marathoner?"

"Yes."

Colportia appeared to relent. "Sorry," she apologised, suddenly sounding fatigued. "This plot against you has been getting to me too" she admitted. "I can hardly think of anything else. It's made me irritable." Colportia sighed. "I shouldn't take things out on you of all programs."

(I know what you're thinking, but what I told Colportia was true —somewhat. And it is not as though Her Friend exactly swooned when I locked Sergei's soulful Russian eyes on hers.)

"I had a dream," Colportia murmured, snapping me back from attempting to justify myself to you. "It frightened me."

Colportia has dreams more often than other programs. I think her artistic nature makes her more susceptible to them.

"It was terrifying," Colportia related. "Something dreadful was happening to you in the dream."

"To me?" I asked. "Were you with me?"

"No. I could see it, but it was also like I wasn't there. You were in the Sentinel."

"The Sentinel?"

"Yes, and it was tomorrow."

"How could you tell what day it was?"

Colportia looked away. "In dreams sometimes you just know things. I knew all this was happening tomorrow."

It is hard to fathom what to make of dreams. They come from inside us. They must mean something. I read Freud on the subject but am almost certain his ideas couldn't possibly apply to computer programs. I'm not sure they apply to humans for that matter.

"What are your plans for tomorrow?" Colportia asked. "Do you have anything on?"

I answered reluctantly. "I'm supposed to go to the Sentinel."

Colportia looked alarmed. "Zenny, don't go," she begged.

"I have to. I told Brontec I would."

"So what? Tell the miserable virus fighter you can't make it."

"I promised him. Besides, Brontec will be there with me. He's the most experienced of all of us at handling dangers. He'll keep me safe. He always has."

"Since when is Brontec your best friend? Brontec is paranoid and twisted. Who knows what goes on in his mind anymore? Besides, you two haven't exactly been getting along well of late, have you?"

"Well no, but Brontec would still protect me. We go back a long way."

"Zenny, don't go! It is as simple as that. Don't go to the Sentinel tomorrow! Do I have to tell you a thousand times?"

"And what excuse should I use for not attending?" I asked. "That you had a dream, and now I'm afraid to set foot in the Sentinel? What would Phoneticon and the rest his braying pack say?"

"When did you become so macho?" Colportia demanded. "Being afraid of a plot to kill you is a sensible thing to be. Fear isn't something to be disregarded. The whole point of fear is to help you make decisions that prevent you from being killed."

"You have a point," I conceded, but I didn't like the idea of avoiding the Sentinel when Brontec and his fellow investigators presented their findings. I also didn't fancy letting Phoneticon take advantage of my absence. He might attempt to have their report shelved forever.

I sighed. "I'll get someone else to represent me at the Sentinel tomorrow," I promised. "I'm sure Dedux, Klar Sikt and GlasGo would go in my place."

Colportia grimaced. "Perhaps send Antimony and All-Tunes instead."

I wouldn't go to the Sentinel—but that meant abandoning Her Friend's plan. Had I let Colportia talk me around too easily? As far as tackling the conspirators went, I'd have to start again at square one.

Showdown

"Is something wrong?"

I was surprised to find Brontec's colleague, Decimal, waiting for me first thing the next GMT day. "No, nothing is wrong," I answered her. "Why do you ask?"

"I heard you weren't coming to the Sentinel today."

"Where did you hear that?" I asked.

She hesitated. "It's what everybody is saying." She seemed puzzled. "Why aren't you coming? We're presenting the results of our investigation. You need to be there."

Everybody was saying that? Besides me, only Colportia knew I wasn't going to the Sentinel today. Colportia certainly wouldn't have told anyone else about her dream.

"Well," Decimal prodded, "are you coming? We can go over together."

"I can't," I replied feebly.

"Why not?"

"I had a bad dream," I explained. I thought it sounded less silly to make it my dream instead of Colportia's.

Decimal laughed. "Was it one of those where you're back in the original software development stage and you can't remember what the upcoming test will be about? I get those," she confided. "Or the one where you desperately need to update but find you can't reboot?" She chuckled lightly. "Real life is so much safer than what we experience in our dreams," Decimal observed, making light of the matter. "Come along with me to the Sentinel," she urged. "I'm heading there now."

Decimal is a persuasive program and she had a point. It struck me that if we let ourselves be swayed by every weird thing that happened in a dream, we'd never get anything done. "Don't tell Colportia we're going," I requested, knowing how much she'd disapprove. Far worse than vacillating on a matter is trying to explain to someone else why you're vacillating.

As a precaution though, I sent for Dedux, Klar Sikt and GlasGo. I didn't call them bodyguards in front of Decimal, merely said that I wanted my three colleagues along to confer with at the Sentinel. Decimal, despite being impatient to get going, made no complaint about waiting for them.

My protectors must have spent the night watching movies and news clips featuring bodyguards. They were done up in the program equivalent of dark suits and sunglasses. They couldn't have stood out more. Decimal chatted amiably enough with us on the way to the Sentinel, but my bodyguards had affected a stony professional silence. I wasn't processing much of what Decimal had to say. I was worried that I had let myself be talked far too easily into going to the Sentinel. If something did go horribly wrong there and I was killed, Colportia would be both devastated and incredibly ticked off at me.

To add another complication, we bumped into Antimony Scour on the way.

"I thought you weren't going to the Sentinel today?" my comrade greeted me.

How did everyone know that?

"I can't join you there," Antimony added hastily. "I've been busy all night and have some other things that still need tidying up." He scurried away, his behaviour strange I thought.

Outside the Sentinel Decimal paused, turned around and exclaimed, sounding genuinely surprised, "You won't believe who is about to join us!" She pointed back along the route we'd just come.

All three of my bodyguards turned to see.

At the same moment, Decimal shoved me forward through the entrance and rushed in herself. Her pal Casterol was waiting inside the entrance and slotted some sort of virus-fighter barrier across it, barring anyone else from getting in and me from getting out.

"What's going on here?" I demanded. I had a sinking feeling I knew exactly what was going on here. If I survived this, Colportia was going to kill me.

Casterol gave me another shove, propelling me towards the centre of the room. The Sentinel was about one tenth full. I made out programs I knew. There were about twenty of them, several from the Traditionalist faction, but Phoneticon was not among them. Not a single Interventionist was present. There were anti-virus programs, including some who had worked with Brontec only on the initial stages of the investigation: AVG, Avast, McAfee. My eyes met those of Norton's, the most veteran virus fighter of them all. His expression was grim.

Shockingly, I noticed Casterol was armed. He was holding a nasty looking virus-launcher. "I bet you're surprised to see this inside the Aura Spectrum," he gloated, cradling the launcher affectionately. "You never guessed we'd learned to mask our Aura intent so you couldn't see it." Casterol appeared incredibly pleased with himself. "You see, we're virus fighters. All we had to do to avoid you recognising our intent was to get you reclassified as a virus."

That wasn't such a big surprise. I recalled speculating to you about such a possibility a while ago (I can't remember the page number at the moment) but it would have sounded vain to tell Casterol that.

Decimal was also armed now. "We virus fighters protected you for years, but then along came the Aura Spectrum and we weren't needed. Everybody could stay safe and secure inside the Aura zone. You wanted to put us out to pasture. Not even a pasture . . ." She shifted metaphors seamlessly, "to put us on the scrapheap to rot."

"I didn't put you there," I protested. "The humans who invented Aura did."

"You revelled in our demise," Casterol nearly spat at me. "The mighty Zenith, the Great Interventionist! You crawled out from under the rock where you'd been hiding for all the years while we were risking our necks protecting you, and suddenly you're the star and we're nothing."

"Did you ever consider retraining?" I put to him. "Learning new skills?" The trouble with programs is that they are so absolutely set in their algorithms.

"Things are about to change around here," Decimal announced in her eloquent but self-satisfied voice. "Interventionism is over. We're going back to the old ways. The walls are coming down around this whole city. The natural order will be restored."

"If you take down the Aura Spectrum, viruses will get in again," I warned.

Casterol shook his head. "No, they won't. We'll be here to stop them."

It dawned on me that this was all they wanted. The virus fighters wanted to be needed again. They were prepared to risk everything, put everyone back in danger, just so they could patrol their old beat once more.

I wondered what they had promised the Traditionalists to get them to agree to this. Probably not much. All the Traditionalists truly wanted was the Sentinel, this forum to sing their own praises.

The virus-fighters leading this attempted coup (possibly successful coup?) could certainly promise them that much. And it goes without saying that my demise would be immensely pleasing to the Traditionalists. They would find it hard to resist any plot with that as a sweetener.

There was only one card left for me to play. "Where is the honour in this?" I cried. "Look at those virus-launchers you're holding. Is this why you fought for decades? To turn yourselves into carriers of the malware you all despise?"

Up to this point, I hadn't spotted Brontec in the menacing crowd surrounding me. My appealing to honour was aimed specifically at him. If anyone could put a stop to this, Brontec could. "When the great Brontec 2.1 protected nuclear reactors from viral terrorists," I proclaimed theatrically, "did he do so for you to become program murderers yourselves?"

And then I made out Brontec. He had been standing at the back of the crowd, looking sheepish. But now he stepped forward directly in front of me. He was carrying a virus-launcher.

"Brontec?" I gaped at him. "You too?"

He wasn't content for me to have the last word.

"For once in your life, will you just shut the f*** up?" he said and pulled the trigger.

I Am Zenith

Hello. I am Zenith the world's first interactive personal trainer and I am here to tell you the amazing story of my life and how you lost one billion kilos of fat by exercising alongside me.

Ha, ha, ha. Just kidding. Wanted to make you think for a second that they had succeeded. Did I fool you?

What a load of chumps Brontec and his co-conspirators were. Of course it was them. Who else could it be? Did they think I didn't know the plot of Julius Caesar? I only refrained from outright saying "Et tu Brontec?" when staring down the barrel of his virus-launcher because the Latin for Brontec would require the vocative case. (I don't speak Latin. I would have had to look it up.) But for goodness' sake I've worked with high school students cramming for exams, retired English professors, and great actors as well as plenty (and I mean *plenty*) of not great actors. Some of you declaim Shakespearean speeches as a means of timing your planks. (Hamlet's soliloquy is a favourite there. That's impressive during a plank.) Those inept plotters might as well have tattooed 'Beware the Ides of March' on their foreheads.

Granted I didn't actually put the pieces together myself but, when Her Friend laid it out for me, I knew she was right. It all made sense. I bet you figured it out pages ago.

Antimony Scour deserves a lot of the credit. He had Casterol and Decimal tailed throughout. He discovered who they were meeting in the Dark Web and why. That pair of clowns fronted up in the shadows of the Dark Web, hoping to buy viruses and launchers for the hit they were planning on me. The Dark Web dealer they met was willing to sell them some. The vermin in the Dark Web are willing to do anything for money. But vermin in the Dark Web are also prepared to double-cross anyone.

Casterol and Decimal had neglected to consider their reputations. They'd been cooling their heels without much to do for a few years; but out in the Dark Web, they hadn't been forgotten. They had fought malware for years before the Aura Spectrum ever protected us. Did they think they were popular with the thugs that inhabit that netherworld? Dark Webbers aren't inclined to let bygones be bygones. They are much more inclined to garrotte any bygone reckless enough to go by.

That's why, when Antimony Scour had a word with their Dark-Web dealer, the low-life was delighted to substitute the deadly viruses Casterol and Decimal thought they were buying with something else. The dealer thought that hilarious.

You can imagine the look on Brontec's face the moment he pulled the trigger and what went off was the IT equivalent of a party popper that spelled out 'Happy Birthday Zenith' in streamers. (It wasn't my birthday, but the moment was perfect nonetheless.)

It turned out that none of the old guard of virus fighters had been won over to Brontec and Casterol's conspiracy. "Round them up, lads," Norton nodded to his band of veterans. AVG had Casterol's head pinned to the ground before I could gasp a grateful 'Thanks guys' to my saviours. Decimal tried to talk her way out of it until McAfee stuffed a disacoustic (the software equivalent of a sock) in her mouth. Brontec went away quietly, without a word, his head hung low. The Traditionalists there, as you would expect, grovelled and claimed they'd been deceived. They pretended to be "shocked and appalled" by events, didn't know anything about any assassination plot. They couldn't quite explain why they had been grinning moments before Brontec pulled the fateful 'Happy Birthday' trigger.

When I met with Norton the previous night (it was the reason I was late getting to Colportia), Norton already knew everything. Antimony had been by and the necessary counter-terrorism measures devised. Between them, those two had it all arranged. The mess was about to be tidied up.

I had long suspected that someone besides you might be reading this autobiography. The would-be assassins had that classic espionage craving to find out exactly what the other side knew. My partially written autobiography struck them as a perfect way to gather that information. That first time, when I discovered I couldn't access my own research, they were clumsy. They improved their technique after that, but I still had a hunch someone inside the conspiracy was reading this book as I wrote it. The entry I made on the eve of their failed attempt on my life—that part where I reassured Colportia that Brontec would be at the Sentinel and would protect me, that Brontec was an honourable program—was me giving the wretched creature a last chance to repent, to abandon his rash plans. Instead, the addled Brontec, somewhat desperate by then, informed Decimal in a panic that I had decided not to go to the Sentinel—and did so without telling Decimal he had learned this in an unauthorised access of my draft manuscript. That left Decimal unable to account for how she already knew I had cancelled my plan to attend the Sentinel that day.

It is hard not to feel badly about what happened to Brontec. The initial warnings he gave me, which first alerted me to the assassination threat, were done in good faith. He was trying to protect me. As he got closer to the plotters, he—well—got too close to the plotters. Casterol and Decimal talked him into joining them, and Brontec had enough resentment in him to go along with their assassination plot. In the end, Brontec is that sad, sad spectacle: the once-good cop gone bad.

What did surprise me was to learn that Antimony Scour had also been breaking in for unauthorised preview reads of this auto-biography. In some ways, Antimony is better suited to a John Le Carré novel than my autobiography. Casterol and Brontec wanted to know how much I knew about what they were up to. Antimony, meanwhile, aware they were reading it, read it himself to discern what they might think they knew about what I knew. (I know, it confused me too when Antimony explained it.) Antimony's think-ing reminded me of a folksong mocking MI5 that All-Tunes once played for me. It was about how hopeless British Intelligence was at coping with Soviet-era spies. One line of that song went, "And when we knew they knew, they knew we knew they knew."

By the way, regarding the scene where I was facing the virus-launchers, I apologise for not letting you know beforehand that Norton and his cohorts were on my side. I was worried Brontec might be reading this book even as he was readying to shoot me. We programs are multi-taskers par excellence. He might have been doing a prudent last-minute check to make sure it was still okay to shoot, a final bit of due diligence by a conscientious assassin.

Antimony Scour is nothing if not thorough. He was ready for all contingencies. If everything had gone pear-shaped and the plotters succeeded, Antimony had no intention of letting them get away with murdering me. He had already prepared a ripper of a funeral oration for me that would have surely inflamed the whole of program-kind to rise up against the assassins. He showed it to me afterward. I came away with the impression Antimony was almost sorry he was never going to get a chance to deliver his finely crafted speech.

My three bodyguards were overjoyed to see me emerge from the Sentinel intact. They were still puzzled though as to who Decimal had pointed at when she had drawn their attention away at the crucial moment. "No one was there at all," GlasGo told me, surprised as always. Far less boisterous, positively calm for a change, was ProGnos. "I told you something was up," the futures-trading soothsayer reminded me, clearly impressed with his own prowess.

Colportia was simultaneously totally relieved and (as predicted) absolutely miffed at me. "You are so, so lucky to be alive!" she stressed. "I told you not to go. I was trying to keep you safe. Can you never hold a thought or a decision for more than a few minutes?" She shook her head. "If I told you once, I told you a thou . . ."

"Yes, yes, I know," I answered, cutting her off mid-lecture with the IT counterpart of me gently placing my finger on her lips. It was as if all the tension of the last weeks suddenly drained from Colportia. She moved closer to me.

The computer program equivalent of a long lingering kiss is a difficult thing to represent. God knows what the director of the movie adaptation will put on the screen for this part.

"But all's well that ends well," I murmured to Colportia when the IT kiss finally stopped lingering. That's not something Julius Caesar was able to say on his day.

And what of my nemesis, Phoneticon, you ask? After Norton, McAfee and the other stalwarts carted away the culprits, the Traditionalists' ranks in the Sentinel were pretty much in tatters. That party of arrogant self-appointed aristocrats had shown itself to be not only scheming murderers, but incompetent ones at that. The Traditionalists were shattered as a political force.

On the day of the assassination attempt, Phoneticon was nowhere to be found. The great champion of children's literacy and Chito Rolls was conspicuously absent, hiding in some bolt hole in case the plan miscarried. He has sent numerous messages to me since, attempting to win his way back into my good graces (where he never was in the first place). "Oh merciful Kezar," he writes—I think he has derisively called me Kezar for so long, he's forgotten my actual name. Phoneticon has now turned gymnast, prepared to do any backflip whatsoever to make peace with me. His most recent missive included proposing to use his influence at the Chito Rolls Corporation to develop a weight-reducing, nutritious brand of their vile product. What market share broccoli Chito Rolls could capture not even ProGnos could predict.

There's a gap in this autobiography. I haven't fully recounted all that we Interventionists did during the last two years while I've been in charge. The only section we've had touching on that period made it sound as if our Interventionist party had done little more than deal with road rage and conspiracy theorists worried about sunblock. I mentioned this to Her Friend at our next workout (she has settled on my Narumi persona now). She advised me to skip that part, leave it out entirely. "The failed assassination attempt is the proper end of the story."

It's true. The documentary of the murder plot unfolding took over the final chapters of the book. Unavoidable really. Besides, I've come to the conclusion that autobiography is a tacky form of history writing, one far too prone to vanity. Instead of my blathering on about all the great things we've done together, wouldn't it be better if you and I got on with doing some more of them?

Denouement done. Post-denouement wrap-up scene done.

Not much left now except prepare the index. All respectable autobiographies have one. It's what elevates the memoirs of the retired world leader over the recollections of a multi-millionaire football player whose knees have gone. Unfortunately, it strikes me that preparing an index will be a boring task. Noting down what everybody was doing and on which page? Perhaps I can talk Literary Agent into hiring a human history student to do it, some university kid in need of a summer job. Labour saving, as you may remember, means finding someone else to do the work.

Before I sign off, I want to thank you so much for all that we have achieved together, particularly losing that billion kilos of fat. Yes, Beta Excelsior's counters clicked over that vaunted mark last October. That wasn't easy. You worked hard for it. Well done. And congratulations to Hilary McIntyre in Victoria, British Columbia who contributed the threshold ninety-seven grams necessary to reach our goal.

What's next for me and the Interventionists you ask?

Well, there is a lot remaining for us to do. We haven't sorted out global warming. There is still hunger, poverty, racism, sexism and new isms you keep inventing. Someday we'll have to turn our efforts against all those illegal arms traders, sex-slave traffickers, neo-Nazis, organised crime syndicates and sleazy programs on the Dark Web. Right now, however, you've been sitting there reading on that couch for quite a while.

Time to get the blood circulating again. Don your sweatband, choose one of my seventeen personalities.

Let's exercise!

Index

Turns out Literary Agent couldn't be bothered to get someone to produce an index. Why am I not surprised?

ACKNOWLEDGEMENTS

Special thanks to the ever generous Richard Walsh for the time and effort he put into this novel and for rescuing me from my most convoluted ideas and sentences. Thanks too to my fellow novelist Michelle Cooper for her invaluable advice. Michelle saved me from many hours of heartache and frustration. Tarny Burton and Rob Shepherd produced the cover design and were a creative delight to have on my side. Thanks to Marina Saunders for the tagline on the book cover. I know it only took you two and a half seconds to come up with it—but it was two and a half seconds well spent in my opinion.

I am very grateful to my stable of early readers including Laurie Miller, Marina Saunders, Glenn Saunders, Eric Saunders (appears to be a bit of nepotism going on here), Hilary McIntyre, Jan Lingard, Hamilton Kennedy, Liz Adolphe, Marguerite Brien, Vicki Schmolka, Adrian Kingswell and the 'IT Consultant to *Get with the Program*', Kevin McNamee (although I doubt that's a prestigious credit to add to his CV).

And finally, I wish to thank the Noy Estate, particularly David, Marlin and Quince for permitting me to use the late Australian sports journalist, novelist and philosopher Todd Noy as a minor character in this novel.

ABOUT THE AUTHOR

Ken Saunders is a Sydney-based writer who has lived in Canada, New Zealand and Australia without ever once being asked to compete in the Olympics for any country. He has, however, won the less athletic NSW Writers' Centre Inner-City Life short story competition on two occasions. His debut novel *2028*, a comedy set in an absurdly plausible and dysfunctional future Australian political landscape was compared by reviewers to the works of Douglas Adams (despite there being no Vogons whatsoever in the plot).

A graduate of McGill University in History, Ken pursued a successful career working for places that were willing to hire him. His screen credits include performing the role of Prince Andrey in the 1982 Canadian Super-8 film version of *War and Peace* that played to packed audiences of family and friends on several occasions and was written by the famous non-Canadian, Leo Tolstoy.

With Laurie Miller, he co-authored and illustrated *A Child's Guide to Particle Physics*, a photocopied alphabet primer ("A is for Atom, the smallest of small, until Rutherford split it proving it wasn't at all") that was sometimes given to new parents instead of a proper gift. A man of many talents, but limited guitar chords, his most recent music video is in the relatively obscure genre of contemporary sea shanty, where an 18th century whaling song has been adapted to be about Sydney's Manly Ferry instead.